"You do *not* have to earn your way, Virginia. You're my wife. It's my duty to take care of you. As for Millie, she had entered an additional agreement with me to act as a maid and cook for a wage. I do not expect you to do the same."

You're my wife. Her heart pounded. If only she *were* his wife. His loved wife. Instead of a duty. She lowered her head lest he discern the turmoil of emotions reflected on her face. Emotions that unsettled and confused her.

"Do you understand?"

"Yes. I understand." *What you are saying. Not what is in your eyes.*

"We'd better go in now. Before you get cold."

She wasn't at all cold. She was warm from his touch and the look in his eyes. She nodded and they started forward side by side. She looked at the road ahead and fought back tears. It was both too long and too short. Nothing was simple anymore.

Award-winning author **Dorothy Clark** lives in rural New York. Dorothy enjoys traveling with her husband throughout the United States doing research and gaining inspiration for future books. Dorothy believes in God, love, family and happy endings, which explains why she feels so at home writing stories for Love Inspired Books. Dorothy enjoys hearing from her readers and may be contacted at dorothyjclark@hotmail.com.

Books by Dorothy Clark

Love Inspired Historical

Stand-In Brides

His Substitute Wife
Wedded for the Baby
Mail-Order Bride Switch

Pinewood Weddings

Wooing the Schoolmarm
Courting Miss Callie
Falling for the Teacher
A Season of the Heart

An Unlikely Love
His Precious Inheritance

Visit the Author Profile page at Harlequin.com for more titles.

DOROTHY CLARK

Mail-Order Bride Switch

HARLEQUIN® LOVE INSPIRED® HISTORICAL

Recycling programs for this product may not exist in your area.

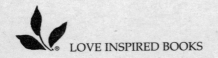

LOVE INSPIRED BOOKS

ISBN-13: 978-1-335-36964-2

Mail-Order Bride Switch

Copyright © 2018 by Dorothy Clark

www.Harlequin.com

Printed in U.S.A.

Who can find a virtuous woman?
for her price is far above rubies.
The heart of her husband doth safely trust in her...
—*Proverbs* 31:10–11

To my readers. Thank you for your years of faithfulness. I am so very grateful.

To my editor, Shana Asaro—
I so appreciate your wonderful editing talent, your kindness and patience, your willingness to answer my questions and much, much more. I will miss working with you.

To the art department—thank you for the beautiful covers you have designed for my books over the years. I truly appreciate your talent and hard work.

And to Sam, my critique partner and friend. Once again, thank you. I don't know what's ahead—but I sure hope you'll be with me.

"Commit thy works unto the Lord, and thy thoughts shall be established."
—*Proverbs* 16:3

Your Word is truth. Thank You, Jesus.

To God be the glory.

Chapter One

Medicine Bow Mountains, Wyoming Territory
January 1869

Garret Stevenson kicked the snow off his boots, climbed the steps to the roofed platform of the Union Pacific Railroad station and stopped. Light from the train's lamp pierced the deepening twilight. Snowflakes shimmered in its gleam, were swallowed by the smoke the wind wrenched from the stack. He slid his gaze over the few passengers whose business had driven them from the train to brave the winter cold. There was only one woman among them. She had to be the one. His chest tightened. The flames in the oil lamps flickered and snow swirled through the frigid air, making vision difficult. He clenched his jaw, yanked the brim of his hat lower and started forward, noted the woman's fur-trimmed hat and coat and stopped. The woman couldn't be Millie Rourk. No maid would wear such a costly coat and hat. Or carry a fur muff. He frowned and swerved toward the passenger car.

A gust of wind swept across the platform, and he caught a flash of white from the corner of his eye and glanced back. The woman had stepped behind the partial protection of one of the platform posts and was struggling to hold down her long skirts. Why didn't she go back aboard the train, out of the weather? A stronger gust of wind hit, whipping her skirts into a frenzy. He stiffened, stared down at the two black leather valises revealed by her flapping skirts. Was he wrong? Was she Millie Rourk?

He skimmed his gaze back up the opulent dark red velvet of her fur-trimmed coat. No, his first instinct had to be right. The woman was obviously rich and pampered.

The train whistle blasted its signal of imminent departure. A few soldiers hurried by him, leaped down the steps and trotted to the passenger car. The conductor glanced his way. He leaned over the railing and cupped his hands around his mouth. "Is there a woman yet to detrain?"

The conductor shook his head, grabbed the metal railing and leaped onto the passenger car's small boarding porch.

His stomach churned. He raised his voice over the moan of the wind. "Was there another woman passenger aboard for Whisper Creek who missed—"

The conductor jabbed a gloved finger toward the station platform. "Only her."

He turned, looked at the woman being buffeted by

the gale. She was staring at the train, a lost expression on her face.

"All aboard!"

The wind carried the words over his shoulders. A door slammed behind him. The train lurched, rolled forward and picked up speed. His stomach soured. His hands clenched. *Where was Millie Rourk?* She must have missed an earlier switch of trains. And that meant the earliest she could arrive was tomorrow morning. And that was too close to his contract deadline for comfort. What if she didn't make it on time? He stiffened, his pulse throbbing. Or—what was most likely— she could have never intended to come in the first place and had simply taken his money. He should have known better than to trust a woman! Not that he should be surprised. If your own mother deserted you, why should you expect decent behavior from any woman!

Well, there was nothing he could do about it now. He would know for certain tomorrow morning when the train arrived. Maybe John Ferndale would give him a little more time when he explained.

He slapped the snow from his hat and collar and looked across the empty platform toward the woman. She was tugging one of her valises toward the station door. He shot a quick glance down the road toward town. There was no one in sight. The woman would need help getting to wherever she was going. Perhaps he had found a client for his hotel. He crossed the platform, his boots thudding against the snowy planks. "Pardon me..."

She lifted her head and blinked, her bright blue eyes fastened on him.

"Are you expecting someone to come for you, or—"

"Y-yes. Are you, M-M—" Her teeth chattered. She frowned, tried again. "Mr. Steven-s-son?"

He stared. *"Miss Rourk?"* He'd found his *bride*—unless she froze to death.

"I—I'm—" A shudder shook her.

His manners overcame his shock. "I'm Garret Stevenson, but that can wait. You need to get inside where it's warm before we talk, Miss Rourk." He grabbed her valises, carried them to the top of the steps and returned. "This way." He placed his hand at the small of her back to steady her against the driving wind, gripped her elbow with his other hand and helped her down the steps. He turned back and grabbed a valise in each gloved hand, crooked his elbow her direction. "Take my arm and hang on. My hotel is not far, but you're so slight, the wind will blow you away."

"We're here."

Virginia shivered and lifted her head, but the snowfall was too thick to see the building. Garret Stevenson helped her up three snow-covered steps, across a plank porch and through a door—painted dark plum, from the little she saw of it in the flickering light of the side lamps. He stomped his boots on a braided rug, then led her straight across the large room toward the end of a stairway climbing the back wall. She caught a glimpse of a long desk standing parallel to the stairs, and an open cupboard of small cubbyholes hanging on the wall behind it. Warmth from the fire in a stone fireplace caressed her cold face as they walked by. She cast a longing look at the seductive flames and shivered her way after him.

The room they entered was small, well furnished. *His private quarters?* Her heart lurched. He put the two valises on the floor at the end of a short hallway on their left and motioned toward a settee and two chairs facing a fire on a stone hearth on the right side of the room. "You can warm yourself by the fire while I get some coffee. Then we'll talk." He strode toward a door in the wall beyond the fireplace and disappeared.

Another shiver shook her. She glanced at a rough wool jacket hanging from one of the pegs beneath a shelf on the wall beside her, then turned and hurried toward the fire. Her long skirts whispered against an oval, fringe-trimmed Oriental rug as she crossed the room. She shook the snow from her fur muff into the fire, laid it on the arm of a chair and did the same with her hat.

Then we'll talk.

Her heart thudded. He thought she was Millie—however would she explain? This whole situation was ludicrous. And it would never have come to be if only her father believed her instead of Emory Gladen. But Emory always had a charming excuse for his small cruelties. She brushed the snow from her shoulders and removed her gloves, reminded herself she was doing Garret Stevenson a good turn by coming to Whisper Creek to marry him. To *marry* him! Her cold fingers fumbled at the buttons in the fur placket that ran down the front of her coat to its hem. She shrugged out of the heavy velvet garment, gave it a brisk shake, then hurried back across the room to hang her things on the pegs. She placed her hat beside a man's wool hat already on the shelf.

The warmth of the fire wooed her back to the hearth, coaxed the chill from her flesh. Snow melted off her long curls and made cold damp spots on the back of her dark brown wool gown. She leaned her head back and shook her hair, tried to rub away the dull throbbing in her temples and remember the story she had rehearsed.

Footsteps drew her attention. She opened her eyes. Garret Stevenson came into the room still wearing his coat and hat. He was carrying two large cups, the steam from them rising to hover like clouds over his hands.

"This should help."

He glanced her way, slid his gaze downward. His face tightened.

She glanced down, saw nothing amiss. "Is something wrong?"

"That's a stylish dress for a maid."

His words were curt, brusque. Her shaking increased. But it wasn't from the cold. It was from the heat of anger in Garret Stevenson's eyes. He seemed to have taken an immediate disliking to her. What would happen when he learned she wasn't Millie?

He handed her one of the cups. "Do you use milk or sugar?"

"Black will be fine." She'd rather chance the bitter taste than anger him further.

He set his cup down on the candle stand at the end of the settee, walked over to the shelf with the pegs and took off his coat and hat. He was a tall man, broad of shoulder and efficient in his movements. She slid her gaze over his suit. Expensive fabric and well fitted—

"All right, Miss…"

He turned and his eyes fastened on hers, sent another shiver up her spine. The coffee she held danced. She stilled her shaking cup with her free hand. "Yes?"

"Who are you? And don't say Millie Rourk. Make it the truth. I can't abide liars."

She squared her shoulders and met the blaze of anger in his dark blue eyes. "And I find people who leap to conclusions about others trying. I do not lie, sir."

He snorted, walked back to the candle stand and picked up his coffee. "And what do you call your presence here in my home if not a lie, Miss—"

"Winterman. My name is Virginia Winterman. And I consider my presence here a kindness to you, and a blessing to me. I believe you will agree, if you will give me a moment to explain, Mr. Stevenson."

"I don't want to listen to some concocted story. I want answers! Why did you say I was going to meet you at the train depot? How did you know my name?"

She reached into her pocket, withdrew a folded letter and held it out to him.

He glanced at the writing, frowned and looked back up at her. "How did you get my letter to Millie?"

"She gave it to me."

"And why would she do that?"

"Millie is…was…my maid. I am in trouble and—"

"You're not *with child*!" The words exploded from him.

"Certainly not!" She lifted her chin, glared up into

his eyes. "And I will thank you not to impugn my character in such a cavalier fashion, sir!"

He stared at her, scowled and nodded. "All right. I apologize for again leaping to a conclusion. But I have troubles of my own, Miss Winterman, and—"

"I know of your trouble, Mr. Stevenson. But, if you will pardon my honesty, it does not excuse your rude treatment of me."

He took a swallow of coffee, studied her over the top of his cup. "Spunky, aren't you? And that, Miss Winterman, is an observation, *not* a baseless conclusion."

Heat flooded her cold cheeks. She put the vanquished chill from her face into her voice. "I suppose I can be—when the situation warrants it." She took a sip of the coffee, fought not to shudder at the strong, bitter taste and put her cup down.

His mouth lifted into a crooked grin. A *charming* grin. She stared, transfixed by the transformation it brought to his face.

"All right, I deserved that. But let's get back to your story. I have a problem to solve and I'm running out of time, hence my 'rude' behavior." He lifted his cup to his lips.

"I know of your time constraint, Mr. Stevenson." She turned slightly to warm her other side. "That's why I came here to marry you."

Coffee spewed from his mouth, shot by her in a violent spray. He grabbed a handkerchief from his pocket with his free hand and wiped his mouth and chin, swiped it over his vest and suit coat. "You came to *marry* me?" He stopped swiping at the coffee and looked at her. "What sort of trouble are you *in*? And what happened to Millie Rourk? Where is she? Did I get coffee on you?"

"No, it missed me." She took a deep breath and plunged into her explanation. "My father is a wealthy man and I am his only child. He wants what is best for me—for my future. To that end, he has given his blessing to a man who wishes to marry me. The man is wealthy, and to all appearances an honorable gentleman. I cannot abide the man's presence. There is something about him…" She shuddered, took another breath, thankful there was no need to say more. "I refused the man's proposal. My father ordered me to accept it that evening." She turned to the fire, shaken by the memory. "When Millie found me…distraught, I blurted out my fear."

She turned back, her eyes imploring Garret Stevenson to believe her. "You see, my father had threatened to throw me out of the house without a penny of support from him until I came to my senses and agreed to the marriage. I had no money…save a few coins of my allowance, and no place to go. I have a cousin, but he stands to inherit all that my father possesses unless I acquiesce. That's when Millie said perhaps she could help me."

He stiffened, stared at her.

"Millie told me she had answered a posting for a woman who would be willing to enter into an in-name-only marriage with a young man in Wyoming Territory in exchange for a comfortable home and living. She said there was to be no…*intimacy* involved in the relationship." Warmth returned to her cheeks. "She told me time was pressing, that the man had to be married by a certain date or lose his business, and so the man had sent her money and a ticket to make the journey. But Thomas—our butler—had proposed to Millie in the meantime, and she had decided to marry him and stay in New York."

He sucked in air, shoved his fingers through his hair. "So, as a resolution to your problem, you came to Whisper Creek to marry me in her stead."

"Yes." He looked furious. And she didn't blame him. A tremble shot through her. Garret Stevenson wanted nothing to do with her. What would she do now? Her mind raced, but there was only one answer. She needed time to make him agree to accept her offer.

She squared her shoulders and rubbed her palms down the sides of her long skirt. "Please forgive me, Mr. Stevenson. I did not mean to…to take advantage of your precarious position. I was desperate and not thinking clearly. I certainly do not expect you to enter into a sham marriage with me when it was Millie to whom you made the offer." She took a breath. "I will wire my father to send me funds to repay you for the ticket and money I used to make the journey. And to pay you for a room if you will be so kind as to allow me to stay here in your hotel until the money arrives and I can purchase a ticket home." *Please, Lord, let him agree. And, meantime, help me to convince him to—*

"I'm afraid not, Miss Winterman."

"But—"

"When you used the ticket and the money I sent, you

bound yourself to fulfill my proposal for an in-name-only marriage. The details of the agreement are in this letter that was in your possession."

What was he saying? "But, Mr. Stevenson, that letter was written to Millie. You expected her to—"

"Come and marry me. That is true. But she chose to betray my trust." He set down his cup. "Let me make my position perfectly clear, Miss Winterman. *I—do—not—want—to—be—married.* But if I am *not* married by midnight tomorrow, I will lose this hotel and all that I have invested in it to the town's founder." His gaze fastened on hers, held it captive. "The marriage I proposed to Millie Rourk was an in-name-only one with no intimacy involved because I *do not care* who I marry. What I *care* about is this hotel. That is why I chose Millie Rourk out of the many respondents to my postings. As a maid, she would know how to cook and clean."

Her stomach sank. "I'm sorry to disappoint you, Mr. Stevenson."

"You won't, Miss Winterman. I'm not going to lose all I possess because you have changed your mind about obeying your father's wishes and returning to marry this man you said you detest." He stepped to the shelf by the door, lifted his coat off the peg and shrugged into it. "The only man you are going to marry, Miss Winterman, is *me*. And you are going to do so right now. You are sufficiently warmed to walk to the church. It's not far. We will discuss the details of our arrangement when we return." He put his hat on his head, lifted her coat off its peg and held it out to her. "Shall we go?"

She could stay! The strength garnered from her

fear of being forced to return home drained away. She made her wobbling legs move, walked over to him and turned her back. His hand brushed against her neck as he helped her into her coat. She jerked away. The spot spread warmth into her back and shoulder. He waited patiently while she fastened the coat and pulled on her gloves, then he extended her hat and opened the door.

"There's one thing more."

What else could there be? And what did it matter? Emory would not find her here. She was safe from his threats. She lifted her muff from its peg and looked up at him.

"John Ferndale knows I was...*am*...reluctant to marry. Therefore, it's important that he believes this marriage is a normal, lasting one. And, as small as this town is, that means that whenever we are in public we will behave like loving newlyweds. In private, there will be no personal contact, as we have discussed. Do you understand?"

"Yes."

"Good. I hope you can put on a good act, because right now you look scared to death."

She lifted her chin. "It is acceptable, even expected, for brides to look a little frightened on their wedding day, Mr. Stevenson. I will play my part well."

"You'd better let me do all the talking until we have a chance to work out a story about our courtship." He ushered her through the hotel lobby to the outside door. The wind howled, rattling the windowpanes. He frowned, tugged his hat more firmly on his head. "I'm sorry to make you go out in this weather, but if you're to stay here, our wedding can't be delayed until tomorrow. There's no chaperone."

She stiffened, fixed her gaze on him. "There's no need for one."

"True. But that knowledge is ours alone. To everyone else, we are a loving bride and groom. You'd best leave that muff here so you can hold on to me." He pulled the door open.

Snow blew into the room, plastered against their coats. She staggered backward. He slipped his arm around her and steadied her, stepped to her side. His body blocked the main force of the wind. She tossed her muff onto a nearby chair, grabbed hold of his arm and walked with him into the storm.

"We're almost there."

Virginia kept her head ducked low and braved a glance around Garret. Faint spots of light glowed dimly ahead. A gust of wind swept swirling snow toward them. She jerked her head back behind the protection of Garret Stevenson's broad shoulders and tightened her grip on the gloved hand he held out behind him.

"The snow's drifted across the walk. Stay in my tracks."

His pace slowed. His booted feet swept side to side with each step, creating a path for her. She added his thoughtfulness to the few facts she had learned about this man she was about to marry, and hurried her own steps to stay close. Her head butted his back. "Oh!"

"Sorry." He turned and looked down at her. "I should

have warned you I was stopping. Hold on to the railing while I clear a path up the steps."

He stepped forward and the wind hit her, whipped her long skirts to the side and drove her against the railing. "Oof!" She grabbed for a handhold, fought to stand. Hands grasped her arm, pulled her upright. Garret's strong arms slipped around her waist and beneath her knees, lifted her. Snow crunched beneath his boots as he carried her up the steps and across the stoop. The buffeting wind stopped. She blinked to clear her vision, looked at a red, snow-spattered door and blinked again as it was opened slightly.

"I thought I heard footsteps." A slender man in a black suit pulled the door wide. Garret stepped into the church, and the man closed the door behind him.

"You're supposed to carry your bride over *your* threshold, Garret."

Heat flowed into her cheeks at the man's smile. *Bride.* Her stomach churned.

"In this weather, we're fortunate to have made it here at all. It's blowing up a blizzard out there!" Garret lowered her until her feet touched the floor, stood behind her with his hands resting on her shoulders. "Pastor Karl, may I present my bride, Virginia Winterman. Virginia dearest, this is Pastor Karl."

Dearest. She made note of the endearment, straightened and drew in a breath. She coughed and took another. Snow fell from the fur brim of her hat and melted on her cheek.

"A pleasure, Miss Winterman. Welcome to Whisper Creek. I promise this is not our typical weather.

At least I hope it isn't. None of us have been here long enough to know." The pastor smiled, dipped his head in a small bow.

She shivered, tried to keep her teeth from chattering, and to return his friendly smile. "Th-thank you…"

"Hold still." Garret brushed the snow from her hat onto his gloved hand and dropped it onto the rug they stood on, removed his gloves, slid his hands beneath the long curls dangling down the back of her head onto her shoulders, and shook them. His action kept the snow from melting on her neck and sliding down her back. Cold as it was outside, his hands were still warm. She resisted the urge to lean back against them.

"You and your bride must be freezing, Garret. Come stand by the stove and warm yourselves. Ivy will be along in a minute. She went to the house to check on the children."

They followed him to the stove. The wind howled. The windowpanes on the side of the church rattled.

A door slammed somewhere in the recesses of the back of the church. Quick footsteps sounded. A short woman hurried into the sanctuary, ducked out from under a heavy wool blanket thrown over her head and shoulders, and gave it a brisk shake. Snow flew every direction. "Konrad, I don't know if they—oh. You're here." The woman tossed the blanket over a pew and hurried toward them. "I wasn't sure you could make it through the storm, Mr. Stevenson. This weather is the worst I've ever seen. The parsonage blocks the wind from the path or I'd never have made it back. I wouldn't have tried if I weren't needed…" The woman stopped beside the pastor, held her hands out to the stove and smiled.

"Miss Winterman, this is my wife. Ivy will be your witness. Ivy, Miss Winterman."

She looked down into Mrs. Karl's warm, blue eyes and some of the tension in her shoulders eased.

"Not for long." Garret's deep voice flowed over her. "I'm sorry to rush this, Pastor Karl, but it sounds as if the storm is getting worse. And Virginia is so slight, she had a hard time staying on her feet on the way here. I'd like to get back to the hotel."

"Yes, of course. You're right, Garret. I'll get right to the ceremony. Step up beside your bride." The pastor looked at his wife and smiled. "We'll dispense with the song, Ivy." He cleared his throat. "And I'll just get to the important part. Oh, did you bring a ring, Garret?"

"No." He looked down at her. "I'm sorry, dearest, I didn't know the correct size. I'll send for a ring after the storm passes."

She stared up at him, taken aback by the look in his eyes, the warmth in his voice. Garret Stevenson was a good actor. Or a practiced lothario. The thought was discomforting. So was the silence. Her answer was expected. What would she say if this wedding were real? She pulled in a breath, spoke softly. "I don't need a ring, dearest. It's your love that is important."

"Well said, Miss Winterman." The pastor smiled at her, then shifted his gaze to her groom. "Garret Stevenson, wilt thou have this woman for thy wedded wife, to live together after God's holy ordinance—"

She stared at the pastor, listened to his words. This

ceremony was *real. Garret Stevenson would be her husband!*

"—forsaking all other, keep thee only unto her, so long as ye both shall live?"

"I will."

She glanced up at Garret. How could he say that so calmly and surely? This was *real.*

"Virginia Winterman, wilt thou have this man to thy wedded husband—"

She jerked her gaze back to the man in front of her. He was a pastor…this was his church…she was making a vow before God! Her breath froze in her lungs. A tremble started in her knees, spread through her. How could she do this? If she said yes, she would be married to Garret Stevenson. Her chance for love and happiness would be over. But she had given him her word. If she didn't keep it, he would lose all he possessed. And she would go home to a forced marriage to Emory Gladen.

"—love, honor and keep him, in sickness—"

God knew she had given Garret Stevenson her word! And God honored those who kept their word. *He that sweareth to his own hurt, and changeth not.*

"—and, forsaking all others, keep thee only unto him, so long as ye both shall live?"

Changeth not… She had to keep her word. She buried her shaking hands in the folds of her damp coat and lifted her chin. "I will."

"Garret, you may kiss your bride."

No! Garret's hands clasped her upper arms, turned her toward him. Panic surged. He lowered his head. She closed her eyes. His lips were hot, soft, gentle on hers, and then they were gone. She opened her eyes, stared down at the floor and resisted the urge to press her fingers to her mouth.

Mrs. Karl stepped into view, held her hand out. "Congratulations, Garret. You have a beautiful bride. I wish you every happiness." The woman leaned forward, gave her a brief hug. "And for you, my dear." The woman stepped back. "I made a cake to celebrate your wedding. It's at the parsonage…"

"How kind of you." She smiled at the pastor's wife, then looked up at Garret to take her cue from him.

"Thank you, Mrs. Karl, but I think we'd better get home. I'll need to borrow a lantern, Pastor."

"Of course. There's one on the shelf by the front door for just such a purpose. No hurry about returning it. You can bring it back on Sunday."

Pastor Karl walked with them to the door, placed a hand on each of them. "May the Lord bless you both with ever increasing love, happiness and healthy children."

Guilt rose, settled in her heart. She had kept her word, but all the same, she would be living a lie. There would be no such blessing from the Lord for her. Or for Garret Stevenson. Not now. Not even God could bless a pretend, in-name-only marriage.

Chapter Two

Garret set the oil lamp on the shelf by his hat, slapped the snow from his leather gloves and shoved them in his coat pockets. "If I may, before you take off your coat…" He lifted her dangling curls and once again shook the snow off them. "No sense in letting this snow melt and wet your gown…"

"Th-thank you." *Lord, please let him think my stuttering is from the cold, not nerves.*

He nodded, helped her from her coat and hung it on a peg. "Give me your hat and gloves. I'll take care of them. You go warm yourself by the fire."

"All right." She handed them over to him and hurried toward the warmth of the blazing logs as fast as her trembling legs would carry her.

There's no chaperone…

The words he'd spoken earlier had echoed through her mind all the way back from the church. Theirs was to be an in-name-only marriage. Why would he even mention needing a chaperone? She lifted her hand, touched her cold fingertips to her mouth. The kiss had surprised her. She'd thought he'd make some excuse. But at least it hadn't been cruel. A shudder shook her.

"There must be at least twelve to fifteen inches of snow out there, and it's still coming. There's no telling how deep it will be before morning."

She pounced on the subject. If she kept him talking about the weather, she could delay any discussion about their sleeping arrangements. *Please, Lord...* "You sound worried."

"I'm a little concerned." He sat on a chair by the door and tugged off his boots, put them on the small rag rug under the shelf. "I'm wondering if this is normal for this area. If it is, it could be a problem."

"I don't understand."

"If it's this deep here in the valley, I can't imagine how much snow there must be up in the high elevations. It might be enough to shut down the trains. And that means no guests for the hotel or dining room. And no supplies coming through. No coal…"

"Oh." She turned to warm her back at the fire. "I didn't realize how dependent Whisper Creek is on the railroad."

"It's completely so." He shoved his fingers through his hair and came to stand beside her on the hearth. "Mr. Ferndale has declared there will be no ranches in this valley. And he owns all of the land. The problem is, until there are some farms and ranches in the area, we have no source for food other than what is shipped in. If we get snowbound, that could be a real problem. Especially if I had a hotel full of guests to be fed."

"What can you do about that possibility?"

"Not much. Order in enough food supplies to fill the icehouse and storage pantry in case of emergency. But even that wouldn't last long if the hotel was full of people."

She lifted her hems enough to allow the heat of the fire to reach her shoes. The loops over the buttons were too stiff with the cold to unfasten. "It sounds as if you need to buy a ranch."

"Spoken like the daughter of a wealthy man."

Her cheeks warmed. "I'm sorry. I'm not accustomed to discussing business problems. Father believes women need to be protected from such things."

"No need to apologize. It's a good idea. If things go as well as I hope with the hotel, I might just do it. There have been rumors of some cowboys from Texas buying land for a ranch in the next valley. They may not be adverse to an investor." He lifted his foot and wiggled his stocking-clad toes close to the fire. "Ah, that feels good." He repeated it with his other foot. "Sit down and I'll take off your boots, so you can warm your feet."

"No!"

His eyebrows shot skyward.

She swallowed hard. "That is…no thank you. My feet are fine."

"Miss—er—Virginia, if this arrangement we have entered into is to work, we're going to need some rules. The first is honesty." His gaze fastened on hers. "I told you earlier I did not care who I married, that what I care about is saving my hotel. Let me explain further. I do not care to have any *personal* relationship with any

woman, now or ever. You have no reason to fear me.
There was no motive other than normal politeness in
my offering to remove your boots. I'd do the same for
a sister. Now, sit down and let me remove your boots.
You might as well be comfortable while we discuss the
rules for our arrangement."

His voice was polite, businesslike and a touch bitter. She had misjudged him. "Very well." She moved
to one of the chairs, sat, arranged her long skirts and
straightened her leg.

He went down on one knee, propped her foot on his
other knee, pushed her hem above the fur trim at the top
of her boot and rubbed the heel of his hand quickly up
and down over the buttons. Warmth from the friction
loosened the loops. Obviously, he had done this before.
He unfastened the buttons and pulled her boot off, set
it aside and cupped her cold, stinging foot in his hands.
She could have purred, it felt so good.

"Your feet are fine, huh? Your toes feel like ice." He
rubbed her foot a minute, then lowered it to the floor
and lifted her other foot to his knee.

"What is your sister's name, Garret?"

He chuckled, slipped her skirt hem over the top of
her boot. "I don't have a sister."

She jerked her foot back. "You said honesty was the
first rule of our arrangement!"

"I was honest. I said I *would* do the same for a sister—not that I *had* a sister." He grabbed her foot by the
boot heel and put it back on his knee. "That is something we should know about one another. We might be
asked questions." All trace of warmth left his face and

voice. "I have no family. And, if I remember correctly, you said you are an only child—with a father, a cousin and an unwelcome, determined suitor."

"Yes." She tamped down the urge to ask what had happened to his family.

"Well, you don't have to be concerned about the suitor any longer." He released her foot, rose and held his hands out to the fire.

Her breath came easier. "And you don't have to be concerned about losing your hotel." She stepped onto the hearth, let the warmth of the stones seep into her cold feet. "It seems we both owe a debt of thanks to Millie."

"To *Millie*?" He snorted. "I think not."

She stared at him, shocked by the anger in his voice. "But Millie saved your hotel for you."

"No, *you* saved my hotel by coming to marry me. *Millie* decided to stay in New York and marry your butler. She would have let me lose everything in spite of her promise. But then betrayal comes easily to women." He strode across the room from the hearth to the short hallway and picked up her two valises he had set there. "We will continue our discussion about our arrangement in the morning. It's getting late, and I've got fires to tend and work to do. I'll show you to your room."

She looked at his taut face, nodded and picked up her boots.

"This way."

They entered the hall, the hems of her long skirts whispering against the polished wood floor. She took a quick inventory. There were four doors, no windows.

Three oil lamp sconces lit the area, two of them on either side of a tall, double-door cupboard. One would have given dim but sufficient light for the space. Garret Stevenson did not skimp with his comforts. That was good to know.

"The room on the left is my office."

She glanced at the closed door and followed him to another a few steps down the hall on the right.

"This first room is my bedroom." His socks brushed against an oval rug that covered the floor from his bedroom door to the end of the hallway. "The door straight ahead at the end of the hall leads to the dressing room. We will share that." He glanced over his shoulder at her. "The dressing room has hot and cold running water at the washbasin and the bathing tub. And a modern flush-down commode. And, of course, a heating stove. I think you will find everything you need in the cupboard." He took a couple more steps and opened the second door in the wall on the right, then walked into the dimly lit room. "This will be your bedroom."

A separate room. *Thank You, Lord!* She stopped in the splash of light from the hall sconce and waited for him to leave.

He set her valises down on the floor at the end of the bed, turned up the wick on the oil lamp on the nightstand and moved to a small, cast-iron heating stove. "I use coal in the stoves. You'll find it in here." He opened a red painted box with a slanted top. "It probably needs some now. I started the fire before I went to the station to meet Millie." He opened a door on the stove, scooped coal on top of the burning embers, closed the door and tugged the handle down again.

She watched him carefully, memorizing his actions. She'd never tended to a fire in her life, but it didn't look too difficult.

"You'll want to turn the draft down a bit more when that coal catches fire. It should last you all night on a slow burn."

The draft? Her breath caught. How much was "a bit"?

He started toward the door, and she stepped back.

His face tightened. He moved close, looked down at her. She stiffened, judged the distance to the bedroom door and wondered if she could run through, slam and lock it before he reached it.

"You can put down your boots, Virginia. There's no need for you to run."

He reached out and took them from her hand. Her heart lurched.

"I don't know what your intended betrothed was like, but I am a man of my word. And I will tell you once again, you have nothing to fear from me. I married because I was *forced* to do so. Women are fickle and untrustworthy."

Her chin jutted. "And men are cruel liars!"

His eyes narrowed at her response. "So we are agreed. We are not interested in any romantic relationship. Our agreement is a *business* arrangement for our mutual benefit, not a *marriage*. Is that clear?"

She studied his face, tried to read what was in his dark blue eyes and found nothing to cause her to doubt him. "Yes. But it may take me a little time to get over being...nervous."

A frown drew his eyebrows down. "In the meantime, don't act this way in public. In public, we are in love with each other. No one will believe that if they see you backing away every time I come near you." He glanced down at her boots in his hand. "I'll put these in the sitting room with your coat and hat." He strode down the hall and disappeared.

She listened to the door to the hotel lobby open and close, then turned and hurried into the bedroom she was to have for her own. A chill chased through her. She stepped onto the Aubusson rug that covered most of the polished wood floor, grabbed the smaller valise and lifted it onto the bed nestled in the far corner. She would get her nightclothes, wash up in the dressing room, then lock herself in this bedroom before Garret Stevenson returned. Not that a lock would keep him out if he were determined to get in. He was a strong man. He'd lifted her as if she were a bag of feathers.

She pulled on her fur-lined slippers and looked around. A wardrobe stood on the hall wall, with a dressing table beside it. It was in a good position, but would be of no use. She could never move that large a piece of furniture. A dresser and rocker sat against the long wall near the entrance. That was better. She could shove the dresser in front of the door and wedge it against the wardrobe if needed. The bed, small nightstand and heating stove, aligned as they were against the rear, outside wall, would be of no help.

The wind howled and rattled the small panes in the

window beside the bed. The pendulum on a wall clock hanging over the dresser ticked off the minutes. She snatched her nightclothes from the bag. Heat radiated from the stove.

You'll want to turn the draft down a bit more when that coal catches fire.

She dropped her garments onto the red-and-cream woven coverlet on the bed, stepped over to the stove and bent to examine it. Where was the draft? The pipe crackled. She looked up, spotted a handle on the side. That must be it. She turned the handle, leaned down and opened the door where Garret had put in the coal to check the fire.

"Oh! Oh…" She jerked back, coughing and blinking her stinging eyes, and waved her hands to dispel the smoke that puffed out into the room.

"Close that door!"

She whirled toward Garret, spun back and grabbed for the handle, touched the door instead. "Ow!" She shoved her fingertips into her mouth, blinked her watering eyes.

Strong hands grasped her upper arms and lifted her aside. She wiped her eyes, watched Garret close the stove door, then reach up to the pipe and turn the handle. "Why did you close the damper? Don't you know—" He stopped, turned and peered down at her through slitted eyes.

She pressed back against the wall.

"You *don't* know." He stared at her. "Have you ever tended a fire?"

"Not in a stove." She squared her shoulders and lifted

her chin to hide her trembling. "I have added wood to the hearth…on occasion."

A sound, something like a muffled grunt, came from him. "It's a good thing I came back." He turned to the stove.

She wiped her eyes, edged toward the door.

"This is the damper." He grabbed the handle on the pipe and twisted his wrist. "This is open. Leave it that way."

She froze in place when he glanced at her.

"This is the firebox door…where you add the coal or wood. This is the draft. When it's open wide the fire burns hot—too hot to be safe if no one is watching it. Adjust it about halfway or below so the fire burns constantly but safely. Turn it lower to keep the fire burning slowly all night. Don't close it all the way or the fire will go out." He glanced her way again. "Do you understand?"

"Yes." She took a breath. "I do not touch the damper, I add coal and adjust the burn there." She pointed to the fire box, then quickly hid her shaking hand in her long skirt.

He nodded, studied her a moment, then strode toward the hall, stopped and looked over his shoulder at her. "I returned because I forgot to tell you the linens for your bed are in the cupboard in the hall. Good evening."

He was angry. Was it because she didn't know how to use the stove? Or because of her reaction to him? The last thing she wanted was to make him angry. Emory Gladen had been charming and treated her well—until she had refused him. And then when she had obeyed her father and agreed to Emory's suit, the meanness she'd sensed in him had begun to show in subtle ways. He had demanded all her attention at social functions, become angry and cruel if she spoke to another man, even her oldest friends. And when her father had given Emory his blessing to ask for her hand, his subtle cruelties had become worse. And *she* was made to look foolish by his charming explanations.

And now she was married to Garret Stevenson. How did she know he wouldn't be the same?

She locked the door, sagged against it and listened to his footsteps fade away.

A fine situation he'd gotten himself into! Garret added coal to the heating stove, turned down the draft for a slow burn, stomped out of guest bedroom number one, and entered bedroom number two. He never should have signed that contract! But the lure of free land and free lumber to build with that John Ferndale had offered had reeled him in. He'd saved enough in costs to add a third floor to the hotel and purchase the furnishings. And he'd been certain he could find some way around the marriage clause.

Ha! He wasn't as clever as he thought. He'd delayed opening the hotel until his money started running low, hoping he'd find a way. But Ferndale had insisted he fulfill the contract to the letter. The man didn't care that he was reluctant to marry. He had started counting the days!

Thirty days to marry or turn his hotel and all its furnishings over to Ferndale. The memory of the posting of a cowboy for a mail-order bride in the *New York Sun* had saved him from that financial trap. He'd sent out his own postings to the New York City, Philadelphia and Albany newspapers to find a woman who would be interested in a business arrangement instead of a marriage. In two weeks he'd found his answer—Millie Rourk. She had seemed perfect. The maid had agreed to his in-name-only conditions for the marriage, *and* to cook and clean for his guests for a fair wage. It was perfect! And what had the maid done? *Betrayed him.* Just as his mother had. Just as Robert's wife had betrayed him.

Well, Virginia Winterman would not have that chance. She'd not find any opportunity to go sneaking off and leave him behind to try to find a way to save all he'd worked for. He'd see to that. He had worked and scraped and apprenticed himself to businessmen to get ahead since he was abandoned at ten years old. And he wouldn't lose all he had gained because of a woman!

He added the coal, adjusted the draft on the heating stove and strode the short distance to the public dressing room. The last train had gone through an hour ago. There would be no guests tonight. But it was too cold to shut down the water heater and the stove. He heaped coal into the fireboxes, adjusted the drafts and went back to the lobby. Now he was married to a dishonest impostor! A woman who didn't even know how to tend a fire!

I have added wood to the hearth...on occasion.

He let out a snort and sat on his heels on the hearth to bank the fire. Not only was his *bride* ignorant of tending a fire, she was so slight she could never carry the buckets of ashes that would have to be taken outside every day when the hotel had guests. He could blow her over with one good strong puff from his lungs. He would have to hire a Chinese laborer from the railroad work crews to handle the heavy work. If they weren't all off searching for gold.

He stilled, staring at the burning embers he'd gathered into a pile. Virginia was a plucky one, though. She'd gone out into the storm without complaint. And she was pretty, in a pale, scared, taut-faced sort of way. Did she know how her bright blue eyes reflected her emotions? They flashed with anger, darkened with fear, sparkled with interest and warmed with friendliness. And her long curls, so soft and silky even when they were covered with snow… His fingers twitched on the fire rake handle. *Keep your mind on your business, Stevenson!*

He frowned and hung the rake on its hook, lifted down the shovel and scooped ashes over the embers. He was a man. How was he supposed to forget the feel of her hair, or her lips? He should have made some sort of excuse to avoid that kiss. It would take some doing to forget how her soft lips had trembled beneath his. Five years…he had to stay married and live with her in Whisper Creek for *five years* before his hotel was safe. He never should have signed that contract!

The wind moaned outside. He rose, closed the damper to a narrow slit for the night and walked to the front windows. Splotches of light from the oil lamps on the porch roof glowed on the snow swirling at the caprice of the wind. But the storm was easing. Perhaps some of the passengers on tomorrow's trains would decide to stay over. That is, if the trains could get through the snow in the mountains.

He stared at the outer edge of the porch, watched the snowflakes falling through the sweeps of golden light. There must be close to twenty inches of snow by now, and the fall had to have been heavier at the higher elevations. And there was that big curve through the narrow gap in the mountains just before the trains entered the valley. If that filled in—no. The trains would plow through the snow with those big blades on the front of the engine he'd heard called "cow catchers."

He raked his fingers through his hair and went to snuff the wicks on the oil lamps of the chandelier over the lobby desk. Guests or not, tomorrow would be a busy day. He had a lot of shoveling to do to clear the porch and steps and walkway. Shoveling...

He looked back out the windows toward the railroad station. Who would clear the road so supplies or brave passengers still riding the trains could reach the stores and businesses? His lips curved in a wry smile. Given the limited population of Whisper Creek, he was fairly sure he knew the answer to that question. At least Virginia could prepare the rooms and tend to any guests while he was working outside. Maybe.

Could the woman cook? He'd gotten by with the few guests he'd had thus far by fixing ham, eggs and coffee for breakfast, and beef stew for dinner and supper.

The fresh-baked bread he bought from Ivy Karl was the saving grace of his meals.

He started for his office to make out an order for more supplies.

Virginia clasped her toilette items in her hand and pressed her ear to the door. All was silent. She lifted the latch, eased the door open and ran the few steps from the dressing room to her bedroom door, her heart pounding. The lock clicking into place calmed her. She hurried to the dressing table, set her things down and sank onto the matching bench. Garret had said the dressing room had every comfort, and he was right. Oh how she wished to have a long, hot soak in that big tub. But she didn't dare chance it.

Coward. She turned from her image in the mirror, reached up and pulled out the combs at the crown of her head. Her long curls tumbled to their full length halfway down her back. She ran her fingers into her hair at the roots, shook it loose and picked up her brush. The howling of the wind had stopped. She crossed to the window by the head of the bed, leaned over the nightstand and cupped her hands against one of the small glass panes. It was too dark to see if the snow had stopped. Not that it mattered. She had run from Emory Gladen and his veiled threats, had run as far as she could go.

You're mine now, Virginia. You have no choice. Your father has given his blessing to our marriage and will disown you if you defy him. I look forward to our union, my dear.

She shuddered, scrubbed at her mouth. Emory Gladen's

kiss had bruised her lips, made her sick. And the hurtful pressure of his hands gripping her, holding her tight
against him…she stared out into the darkness. Was he
searching for her? He'd warned her he'd never let her go.

*Well, you don't have to be concerned about the suitor
any longer.*

She closed her eyes, thought about Garret's words.
What he said was true. She was safe, even if Emory
found her. She was married. Emory was out of her life
forever. But Garret…

Her breath caught. So far, Garret had been polite
and thoughtful, in an impersonal way. Except for his
kiss. That was troubling. Why hadn't he made an excuse to avoid it?

She shoved the disquieting thought aside and brushed
her hair. What would happen tomorrow? When should
she rise? She was accustomed to being awakened by
Millie bringing her a cup of tea, then laying out a gown
for her that would suit her activity for the day. An image
of Garret carrying two cups of coffee into the sitting
room flashed before her. Did he even have tea? Of
course he did. This was a hotel.

Her hand paused midbrush. She'd forgotten that. Yet
she needn't concern herself about tomorrow morning.
Garret's hotel maid would start work early. She would
order her breakfast then. They served lovely breakfasts
at the Astor House, not that Garret's hotel compared to
the luxurious Astor House. Why, this room was—not
part of the hotel. These were his private rooms. Well,
no matter. She would manage in the morning and then

explain her likes and dislikes to his hotel maid over breakfast.

She went to the dressing table, put her brush down and tied her hair back at her nape with a ribbon that matched her velvet dressing gown. Exhaustion from the stress of the day hit her. She rubbed her tired eyes, snatched up the clothes she'd tossed onto the bed, and looked around. She would need to wear her brown wool gown again tomorrow. The dresses in the valise would be too wrinkled. They needed the maid's attention before she could wear them.

She carried her dress and petticoats to the wardrobe, opened the doors and hung them inside. Her valises she shoved against the wall. She pushed down on the bed, smiled at its softness, removed her dressing gown and pulled back the coverlet on the bed and stared. Where were the linens and blankets?

She frowned, grabbed her dressing gown and swirled it back around her shoulders. Where would she find a maid to make up her bed? Dare she go looking for one? She stared at the bare mattress, then glanced at the door. She had no choice.

She slid back the lock and opened the door a few inches to look out. Light from two of the sconces glowed on either side of the large, double-door cupboard. Garret's words popped into her head.

I forgot to tell you the linens for your bed are in the cupboard in the hall.

Why—she caught her breath. Surely he didn't mean for her to make her own bed! She couldn't do that. She fastened the buttons on her dressing gown, listened to the silence a moment, then stepped out of her bedroom. The hem of her velvet gown whispered against the floor. She hurried to the end of the short hall and looked out. The sitting room was empty. She stared at the open door beside the fireplace, tiptoed over and looked into the adjoining room. It was dark on her left, but she made out the form of a table with chairs. A dining room?

She edged forward and peeked around the shelves on her right. Dim light from two oil lamps over a large, heavy table gleamed on pots and pans, dishes, a fireplace with metal doors in the stone, a huge cooking stove, and cupboards and furniture she could not identify. There was another door on the far wall.

She crept between the fireplace and the table, slipped by a large cupboard, opened the door and looked into the next room. It was too dark to see anything but what looked like a server on her right and tables and chairs. The hotel dining room? She frowned and retraced her steps. Garret and his staff must have retired for the evening.

She opened the cupboard in the hall, stared at the shelves piled with bed linens. A quilt with red stars caught her eye. She grabbed it and two pillowcases, carried them to her bedroom and dropped them onto the bed. Tears stung her eyes. She blinked them away, shook out the pillowcases and stuffed her pillows in them. She folded the large quilt in half, wrapped herself in it and lay down, wishing for Millie.

The wind sighed at the windows. She turned onto her side and dimmed the lamp. Tears welled, then seeped from beneath her lashes and ran down her cheeks. She was frightened and helpless and all alone. No one but Millie even knew where she was.

I will never leave thee, nor forsake thee.

Peace stole through her. The tension in her body eased. She slipped her hand out of her quilt cocoon, wiped the tears from her face and looked at the dull light reflected on the plaster ceiling overhead. *Forgive me, Lord. I don't mean to sound distrusting or ungrateful. I know You are always with me. It's only that I'm afraid. Please grant me courage, and let tomorrow be a better day.*

Chapter Three

Garret popped the last bite of his buttered bread in his mouth, shrugged into his work jacket and squinted through the dim light to make out the face of the pendulum clock in the corner. *A little less than two hours until the first train.* He frowned, pulled on his hat and gloves, grabbed the lantern off the shelf and hurried through the hotel lobby to the front door. It inched outward and stopped. The snow fell through the narrow crack into a small pile. He lowered his shoulder and shoved the door against the snow until he could slip through the opening, then grabbed the lantern and pushed his way out. He brushed the pile of snow back out onto the porch and closed the door.

Light from the oil lamps that had burned all night flickered. Gray puffs of hot breath formed small clouds in front of his face and hovered there. Not a breath of wind stirred. That was good. At least he wouldn't have to deal with blowing and drifting snow. The cold nipped at his face and neck. He cast a thankful look at the copse of pines at the end of the building that had acted as a windbreak and kept the snow from billowing and piling in deep swells in front of the hotel. He tugged his collar up, grabbed the shovel he kept handy by the door and cleared a path across the porch to the steps. It was the work of a few minutes to shovel his way down them and clear his short walkway to the road.

"Morning, Garret!"

The hail carried sharp and clear on the still, cold air. He straightened, swiped his jacket sleeve across his forehead and looked over a high drift between his hotel and Latherop's General Store. Blake Latherop stood beside a lantern, his legs splayed and his hands folded on the handle of a shovel standing upright in the deep snow.

"Morning, Blake. You figuring on shoveling a path to the depot?"

The store owner nodded, tugged at his gloves and lifted his shovel. "There's no choice. I have to get the mail. And I'm expecting supplies for the store."

"I'll help. There may be some passengers who will want to stay over. That is if the trains are running." He frowned, glanced toward the surrounding mountains. "I was wondering if they might get blocked by drifts in some of those high passes."

"I guess we'll find out."

"Would you gentlemen like some help?"

He looked beyond Blake to the dark form trudging up the road from the parsonage, a lantern swinging from one hand, a shovel leaning like a weapon against one narrow shoulder.

"Good morning, Pastor. Blake and I were about to

start clearing a path to the station." He tugged his hat closer over his ears, then grabbed his shovel. "How about if I go first and scoop off the top ten or so inches, then you scoop off another shovelful, Blake, and you can clean and even the path, Pastor. That sound all right?"

"Lead on." Blake grabbed his lantern and shovel and trudged through the snow to join him. "Let me know when you get tired, Garret, and we'll switch places. We ought to make it all the way to the station in good time doing that."

"Fair enough." He whacked the snow off to the side ahead of him with the flat of his shovel and set the lantern on the firm surface, then scooped up a shovelful of snow and tossed it aside. Blake did the same. They fell into a rhythm, their heavy breathing and the swish of the shovels against the snow the only sound.

"If we're going to…have snow like this…" Blake's huffs and puffs came floating over his shoulder in small gray billows "…I'm going to…have Mitch make me a…snowplow. One I can hitch behind my horse to… clear the road."

He glanced over his shoulder and grinned at his neighbor. "Smart man." He scooped up more snow and cast it aside. "You'll be using your horse, Blake…so I'll pay for the snowplow. You plowing the road will…benefit the hotel, as well. That suit you?"

"Sounds…fair enough."

"And a whole…lot easier!"

"Well spoken, Pastor!" Garret chuckled, drove his

shovel into the snow and straightened to catch his breath. Blake followed suit.

"I have...my moments."

Like last night, when you performed my wedding? He watched Konrad Karl smooth out the path they'd shoveled, then turned and looked ahead. It was still too dark to see the depot, and there was no sign of a road to guide him, only flat white snow in every direction. He took a deep breath, pushed his shovel into the white powder and hoped he was on the right path.

Virginia bolted upright, startled by a whistle that sliced through the stillness and quivered on the morning air. "Oh!" She scrambled out of bed and grabbed for her dressing gown, her heart pounding. *The train.* No. She had reached her destination last night and— she was *married*!

Her knees trembled. She sank down onto the edge of the bed and looked around the strange room, casting back to yesterday and trying to order her thoughts. There was a snowstorm...

An image of Garret Stevenson standing strong and solid in swirling, blowing snow flashed into her head, followed by one of him kneeling in front of her and removing her boots. She shivered, fastened her dressing gown and looked at the small heating stove. The sleepy fuzziness in her head began to clear. He had taught her how to tend a fire. Yes.

She glanced at the stovepipe. She wasn't to touch that handle. She bent to open the small door on the front of the stove, remembered the smoke that had puffed out into the room and took a step back. No smoke. She glanced at the pulsing red coals, scooped coal from the box and piled it on top of the hot embers. Now she had to adjust the draft to burn hotter for the day...no more than halfway...she had done it! Her lips curved into a smile.

She stepped into her slippers and gathered her toilette items. If she remembered correctly, the dressing room was a short distance down the hall. She opened the door and peeked out. The way was clear. She ran on tiptoe, eased the dressing room door closed and slid the bolt, then hurried to perform her morning ablutions so she could get back to her bedroom before anyone came. She didn't want to miss Garret's maid.

There! Virginia turned before the long mirror fastened to one of the doors on the wardrobe. Her dress looked quite acceptable. She tugged the hem of the bodice into place at her narrow waist, shook out the long skirt, then checked to be sure the back of the high collar was in place. Memory stirred and her hands stilled.

Garret had slid his hands beneath her long curls and shook them. His spread hands had kept the snow from melting on her neck and sliding down her back. Her husband was a thoughtful man. So far.

Her face tightened. He was no stranger to ladies, for certain. Not given the practiced way he had removed her boots. The memory came bearing the sound of his laughter. It was infectious. She'd have laughed with him if she hadn't been so frightened. And she'd been even more so a few moments later when she'd mentioned

Millie. He'd been so angry. Had accused Millie of betrayal. And not only Millie.

Had Garret suffered the unfaithfulness of a woman? Would he be cruel? She shivered and rubbed her upper arms, where Emory Gladen had squeezed so hard she'd had to bite her lip to keep from crying out. Her face paled. Her eyes darkened with fear. He always had a charming reason for his "excesses;" as he called them—he loved her so much he forgot himself, he didn't know his own strength...

She whirled from the mirror, rushed to the bedroom door and hurried into the hall. She would breakfast early today. Garret's maid would be in the kitchen. Maids began their work early.

The sitting room was still dark, but for the flickering light from the fire. Outside the windows on the back wall, the sky was beginning to turn gray. She started across the sitting room, stopped when a log collapsed, sending sparks rising up the chimney. The fire needed wood. She moved to the wood cradle, lifted a small log, placed it on the fire, added another and poked them into place. The embers shot out tongues of flame and licked at the new fuel. The muted sound of stomping feet came from the front of the building. She turned toward the door.

"Good morning." Garret came into the room, tossed his hat and leather gloves onto the shelf and shrugged out of his jacket.

"You've been outside already?"

He nodded, rubbed his hands together briskly, then sat in the chair. "For a couple of hours."

"Whatever for?"

He tugged at one of his boots. "I had to shovel a path to the station in case the passengers want to come to town."

"You! Where is your help?"

He tossed his boot onto the small rag rug, rubbed his foot and looked up at her. "Blake Latherop—he owns the general store next door—and Pastor Karl helped me."

She stared. Last night he'd looked like a business-man who might be welcome in her father's club. Today, in a coarse-woven blue cotton shirt with a narrow band for a collar and a placket with buttons—one missing—he looked like a laborer. If a handsome one. "I meant your hired help."

He pulled off his other boot and stood. His brown twill pants were damp from midcalf to his knees. "Whisper Creek is a town in the making, Virginia. There is the general store, my hotel, an apothecary shop and soon-to-be doctor's office, the church and a saw-mill so far." He came to join her on the hearth, held his hands out to the fire. "I suppose you can add in the rail-road station and the laundry a Chinese family has out in the woods, though they're not rightly part of the town. The point is, the owners run their businesses. There's no one in town to hire. Mitch Todd—the sawmill owner and town builder—lures his construction workers from the railroad crews passing through." He grinned, obvi-ously amused at Mr. Todd's ingenuity.

Uneasiness spread through her, made her stomach flop. *There's no one to hire.*

"Fire feels good. Is there coffee?"

"I don't—" The unease turned to full-blown apprehension as understanding dawned. She took a breath and shook her head. "I thought you had a maid."

Anger swept over his face like a cloud and settled in his dark blue eyes. "Millie Rourk was to cook and clean for a wage, in addition to a good home and living." He blew out a breath, shoved his fingers through his hair and fixed his gaze on her. "It's getting late and I haven't shown you around the hotel yet. I'll make coffee when we come back. Have you breakfasted?"

"No. But I can wait until—"

"Follow me."

He headed for the kitchen. She looked down at the poker she'd been gripping, put it back in its place and trailed after him. Guilt tugged at her. He was right; Millie would have been the perfect wife for him. She on the other hand—

"Have a seat."

He motioned to the table and chairs along the back wall she'd noticed last night, pulled out an end chair and held it for her. He'd turned up the oil lamps hanging above the massive table in the center of the kitchen. The light gleamed in the polished wood of the bare table in front of her. She glanced up at the window—also bare.

"Here we are." He set two small plates, napkins and flatware on the table, left and returned quickly with two glasses of water and a towel-covered basket. A small crock dangled by its bail from his little finger. "I'm sorry there's not time to have a real breakfast, but this is delicious bread. Ivy Karl bakes it, and she's kind enough to sell me some." He handed her the basket, then sat in the chair at the other end of the table.

She unfolded the towel, and a mouthwatering aroma of freshly sliced bread rose. She placed one of the slices on her plate, handed him the basket and picked up her knife to dip into the butter in the crock he'd opened. The first bite of bread was better than the smell. She took another bite.

"Be careful of the water. It's from the waterfall and icy cold."

"There's a waterfall?" She took a tentative sip from her glass and shivered.

"On the mountain out back." He took another bite of his bread and nodded toward the window. "That's why John Ferndale located the town here in this valley. If you like, I'll take you to see it one day when the weather warms." He took another bite of his bread and glanced at her plate.

He was in a hurry. She applied herself to finishing her slice, wished she had time for another. "I'm ready for the tour of the hotel."

"Time is getting short. We'll leave these dishes here." He rose and came to pull out her chair. "I'll show you what you need to see for today. The rest can wait until later tonight or tomorrow. We'll go through the kitchen. This dining table is for the help—when I have some." His lips curved in a wry grin that tugged her own lips into a responsive smile, even while her stomach sank. She had ruined Garret Stevenson's plans.

"This room is huge."

"It will need to be when the hotel is full. There are

twenty-six rooms. Add in mates and children, and that's a lot of people to be fed."

It was indeed.

"And then, of course, there will be those who come only to dine. Passengers first, but residents, too, as Whisper Creek grows."

He would need to hire a cook. And meantime…her stomach tensed. He ushered her to the door she'd peeked through last night, and they entered a large dining room. She caught her breath at the beauty of the Hepplewhite servers, tables and chairs. A corner cupboard, painted a darker gray than the dove-gray plastered walls, stood on the outside wall on her left. A long banquet table and evenly spaced small tables filled the room. Extra chairs sat in the corners. Red-and-white patterned china and a pewter chandelier and sconces added bright touches that caught the eye. But it was the paneled fireplace wall that held her gaze. The workmanship quality was equal to that in her father's library. "It's a beautiful room, Garret."

Pleasure flashed across his face. "I studied some of the best hotels and restaurants before I left New York. I want people to be so comfortable in my hotel they don't want to leave." He pushed open one of the doors flanking the fireplace and stepped back.

She entered the hotel lobby and looked around to orient herself. In a cozy corner on her right was a game table and bookshelves. On her left was the fireplace with two padded chairs facing it. Beyond that was the hotel entrance. An aura of welcome and comfort impressed itself upon her.

She moved ahead to stand by the long paneled desk, her hems whispering across the polished wood floor.

"Are you familiar with the procedure for staying at a hotel?"

"I know one must register and pay. I've never done so."

He gave her a measuring look. "Your maid registered for you, while you were escorted to your room by the concierge."

She treated his statement as a question. "Yes."

His face went taut. "This is where the guests sign their name and address. Like this…" He opened a leather register resting beside a bell and a pewter pen and ink holder, and turned it so she could see.

She glanced at the few names entered and nodded.

"The fee is one dollar and a half per night. When they pay they are assigned a room, their money is placed in the till on the shelf under the counter, and they are given the key to their room. The keys are there." He pointed behind the desk to numbered cubbyholes holding keys. "Duplicate keys are in my office—through that door under the stairs."

"Your office also has a door from the hall in your private quarters."

"Yes. It's convenient to be able to enter or exit from either side. Now…any additional charges for the guest are noted beside their name in the ledger, and a note specifying the charge is placed in their box. Also, any messages they may receive during their stay are placed in their boxes. This—" he turned a small leather folder her way "—contains all of the other services offered by the hotel along with their costs." His lips lifted into that wry smile that was so contagious it pulled the corners of her own mouth upward. "You'll note there are few at the moment."

She glanced at the list of services, her mind playing with an idea. Perhaps she could act as a hostess. She was skilled at that. She had performed that service for her father often.

Hotel
Meals served in your room: 5 cents
Checking daily for telegrams or posts: 1 cent
Maid service—bed made, rooms swept or dusted:
2 cents per service
Fresh towel: 3 cents

Dining Room
Breakfast served at six-thirty
Dinner served from twelve o'clock until three o'clock
Supper served from six o'clock until eight o'clock
Meals: 50 cents
Extra dessert: 5 cents

"I'll show you the upstairs rooms later. That way…" He motioned her toward the stairs, which turned and ran a short distance to an arch in the opposite wall.

Her breath caught. Her fingers twitched. She stopped and stared. Close to the front corner of the room stood an upright Steinway piano. A padded settee and several chairs were clustered around the instrument.

"Is something wrong?"

"What? Oh, no. It's only...do you play the piano?"

"Not so anyone would want to hear." His eyebrow lifted, his gaze fastened on hers. "Do you play?"

She tipped her head and answered him in kind. "Well enough that people like to listen."

He chuckled, a low masculine rumble that made her smile. "Good. You'll be able to entertain our guests."

At last, something she could do to repay him for her escape from Emory Gladen. The cost of the ticket and the money she had used weighed heavily on her. The tension across her shoulders lessened.

"This hallway leads to the guests' dressing room—" he gestured toward the door at the end of the hall on their right "—and two guest bedrooms. These are the rooms I want ready in case any passengers decide it's too dangerous to travel farther and choose to stay overnight." He opened the doors. "I tended the fires earlier. You've only to make up the beds and set out the towels in the dressing room. You'll find the linens in the cupboard in the hall. I've got to finish shoveling. Oh, and when you finish the rooms, you'll find beef stew in the refrigerator to be heated for dinner."

She stared after him, wanting to tell him she didn't know how to make a bed or cook. But the thought of the anger that shadowed his face and eyes whenever he mentioned Millie held her silent. What if he annulled their strange marriage? She had nowhere to go. And she was indebted to him for the ticket and money she had used.

Tears stung her eyes. She blinked them away and

squared her shoulders. She wasn't helpless. Surely she could make a bed. She would worry about the cooking later.

She opened the cupboard in the hall, stared at the shelves piled with sheets and blankets and pillowcases. She closed her eyes and thought about her bed at home, then filled her arms with the items she needed and carried them to bedroom number one. She dropped them onto the seat of a chair and faced the bed. What did Millie do?

Tears welled again. So did her anger. One thing was for certain—Millie didn't cry. Was her maid more capable than she? Of course not! It was only a matter of applying oneself. She blinked the tears away, pulled the coverlet off the bed and tossed it over the chair back. First she needed a sheet for the guest to lie on. She pulled one from the pile, laid it on the bed and unfolded it. It was too big. She folded the extra length out of her way at the bottom, but that did not work on the sides; they simply fell down. She let them hang, and unfolded the second sheet on top of the first and repeated the process.

It looked quite good.

She smoothed out every crease and wrinkle, unfolded and placed two blankets on top of the sheet. A smile curved her lips. This wasn't so difficult. She stuffed the pillow into the case, remembered Millie pummeling hers, and punched and fluffed it. The blue-and-white coverlet finished her job.

She stood back and examined her work. There was not a wrinkle showing anywhere. She let out a long, relieved sigh and hurried to the cupboard in the hall to get the linens for bedroom number two.

Garret stomped the snow from his boots, wiped them on the rag rug and hurried across the lobby. Finally, he was through shoveling for possible guests. With all the narrow connecting paths, the town looked like a rabbit warren. But at least people could get around. He opened the door to his private quarters and froze. *Smoke!* He bolted for the kitchen.

"Oh...oh..." Virginia stood in front of the stove waving a towel through the air. Smoke billowed and curled from a large pot sitting on the front burner plate. The smell of burned stew mingled with the stringent odor.

He leaped forward, snatched the towel from her hands and lifted the pan off the hot surface.

"Oh!" She whirled around, bumped into him and rebounded toward the stove.

"Careful!" He grabbed her with his free hand, pulled her against him and backed toward the sink, bringing her with him. He set the pan in the sink and turned on the tap. Cold water rushed out and covered the burned stew. The pot hissed. The smoke stopped. He looked down into her watering eyes. Tears? Or stinging smoke? "What happened?"

"I—I don't know." She placed her hands against his chest and pushed away. "I—I put wood in the stove, then found the refrigerator and the stew in it."

She *found* the refrigerator?

"I put the stew in a pan and was heating it as you asked. I stirred it with a big spoon the way I've seen

Martha do, but it started bubbling and splashing out of the pan." Her eyes watered more.

Tears. He held back a frown and waited for her to finish her explanation. "Some landed on my hand and I went to wash it off and put lotion on it. When I came back the stew was burning and smoking, and I couldn't make it stop." She lifted her chin and squared her shoulders. "I'm sorry."

He didn't know which was more pathetic, the way she looked or her story. "Who is Martha?" He had a sinking feeling he knew the answer before she spoke.

"Our cook."

"And Millie helped her in the kitchen."

"Yes. Garret—"

He shook his head, set his jaw and looked at the scorched mess in the pot. There went the possibility of stew for today's dinner or supper for any guests... or them. "We'll talk later. First I'll..." He lifted his head, looked toward the sitting room. "There's the bell. I have a guest." He looked down at his rough clothes and scowled. "The way I'm dressed, it would be best if you register him and show him to his room to make certain everything is satisfactory. Can you do that?" She seemed capable of that much.

She straightened, brushed back a curl that had fallen free to dangle in front of her ear. "Yes."

"All right then. I'll tend to the fireplace, to stay close in case you need my help." He snatched up the towel he'd dropped and handed it to her. "Wipe your cheeks and eyes." The bell rang again. He waved her forward and hurried through the sitting room after her, hoping he wasn't making another mistake in trusting her to handle the guest. He eyed her golden-brown curls falling from her crown to her shoulders, the way her expensive gown fitted her slender form, and the graceful way she moved even when she hurried. She certainly looked the part of a successful businessman's wife. But he needed help, and there was no one to hire. Maybe she could learn.

He opened the door and Virginia swept through it, her long skirts floating across the floor. She smiled as she moved behind the desk. His pulse skipped. He'd never seen her look so composed, so capable, so... beautiful.

"May I help you, madam?"

Madam. He'd assumed the guest was a man. He stepped into the lobby, glanced toward the woman standing in front of the desk. The woman looked his way and stared. Great. He probably had soot from the pan on his face. And his clothes! He sure didn't look like a successful hotel owner.

"Madam?" Virginia's soft voice called the woman's attention back to her.

"Yes, I'm sorry, I—" The woman covered her mouth with her gloved hand, coughed. "I'd like a room, please."

He strode to the fireplace and squatted to add wood to the fire and scrape at the ashes. He'd clean up as soon as he'd shoveled the snow from the back porch.

"Would you like a room here on the first floor, madam? It's very convenient to the sitting area and the dining room. But if you would prefer a room upstairs, that can be arranged, also."

What was Virginia doing? He'd told her to assign the two down—

"The downstairs room sounds convenient." The woman coughed again, cleared her throat. "I'll take it."

"Wonderful." Virginia smiled and turned the register around. "Sign your name and write your address here, please."

"I don't have an address at the moment. I've been traveling."

Traveling? The woman didn't look that prosperous. Her cloak and hat were worn. So was the old carpetbag sitting on the floor at her feet. Of course, he didn't look like a hotel owner in the clothes he had on.

"No matter. Just write 'traveling.'"

He sneaked a look over his shoulder at Virginia. She was doing a good job handling the registration. He glanced back at the woman, noted the awkward angle of her hand while she signed in.

"And how long will you be staying with us, Mrs. Fuller?"

"I don't know. It depends…on the weather. At least two nights."

"That will be three dollars, please."

The woman ducked her head, pulled the reticule from her wrist. There was the dull clunk of coins hitting against one another.

"Here you are."

"And here is your key. If you'll come with me, I'll show you to your room, Mrs. Fuller. I've put you in room number two. I think you'll find it quite comfortable."

The woman bent and reached down.

He stood, shook his head, gestured at the bag, then pointed to himself.

Virginia gave a small nod of understanding. "Leave your bag, Mrs. Fuller. It will be brought to your room."

He waited until she stepped out from behind the counter and led the woman to the short hallway off the lobby, then moved to the desk and picked up the woman's bag.

"The sign says the Stevenson Hotel. Is that the proprietor's name? I always think it's nice when people call their businesses by their name."

The woman's quiet voice floated out of the hall. He stepped to the edge of the arched opening and waited for them to enter bedroom number two.

"Yes, it is. My husband is Mr. Stevenson."

Husband. His heart jolted. He'd never wanted that word applied to himself.

"Here we are. This is your room, and that is the dressing room. You will share it with the occupant of room number one, if I rent it out tonight."

Good! Virginia had thought to tell the guest about the dressing room. He hurried forward, stepped into the bedroom doorway. "Madam's bag." He set the patched carpetbag on the floor and backed out.

"What a lovely room."

He paused to listen, pleased by the woman's approval.

"I'm looking forward to sleeping in a bed that doesn't rock back and forth beneath me."

The bed springs squeaked.

"I'm sure you'll find it quite comfortable. I'll—I'll send someone by later to tend the fire."

It was the first time Virginia had hesitated. His fault. He should have told her—

"No need, my dear. I see there's a coal box. And I've been tending fires all of my life. But I'm afraid there is a problem with the bed. It's...undone."

Undone! He'd told her—

"I'm so sorry. Let me fix it for—"

The door closed, shutting off Virginia's voice. *Fix it! What*—? He stared at the knob, clenched and unclenched his hands, then spun on his heel. He stalked to his office, strode straight through it to the door that led to the hall by their bedrooms, and yanked it open. Three long strides took him to her bedroom door. He opened it, stared at the quilt in a pile on the bare mattress. The woman couldn't even make a bed!

He drew a deep breath, clamped his lips closed on the words scorching his tongue and strode back down the short hall. Going back to the guest's room would only make things worse. And he hadn't time. The woman would expect dinner to be served and, thanks to his *bride*, the stew he'd prepared was an inedible burned lump! He'd have to apologize to the woman, go to her room and make her bed while she was eating her midday meal. If he could even feed her! He was no cook.

He stomped through the sitting room into the kitchen, grabbed the ruined panful of burned stew out of the sink and threw it out the back door with all his fury propelling it. He watched it arc into the air, then stared at the dark hole in the snow where it landed.

If only he could get rid of his bride as easily! He wanted no part of her! Even if she was beautiful. If it weren't for that contract...

He left the door open to get rid of the smell and headed for the pantry. He had to find something to feed his hotel guest. It would have to be cold food. He had no time to make more stew.

And his *bride* would be of no help. That was certain. He'd be better off with a cookbook!

Chapter Four

*P*lease don't let her leave on the next train out of town, Lord! Virginia turned from the door she'd hastily closed and faced the guest. "I'm sorry your bed isn't properly made, Mrs. Fuller. I'm afraid I—" she took a breath and threw herself on the woman's mercy "—I'm to blame. We are only just married and Garret doesn't know that I can't make beds or…anything." She straightened under the woman's stare. "But I will learn."

Mrs. Fuller nodded, placed her fisted hands on the mattress and pushed up from the bed. "There's no maid?"

She shook her head, hurried to the side of the bed and pulled off the covers and sheets. "Whisper Creek is only coming into being. Garret says there is no one in town to hire."

"I see…"

She glanced from Mrs. Fuller's back to her reflection in the mirror. The thin, lined face was pensive, and one hand fiddled with the cuff of a glove. Was the woman trying to decide if she would stay or go back to the depot and wait for the next train? Her stomach knotted. If Mrs. Fuller left, Garret Stevenson would likely pack her and her belongings off to the station, as well. She yanked a sheet from the pile of linens she'd tossed on a chair and spread it on the bed, but could think of nothing to do with the extra length except fold it out of the way at the bottom as she'd done before. Her situation was hopeless. She couldn't do this work! Tears welled.

Mrs. Fuller's long skirts rustled and her boot heels clicked against the floor.

Her stomach sank. The woman was leaving. She blinked away her tears and squared her shoulders.

"Not that way, dear. Like this..."

She stared, rendered speechless as Mrs. Fuller stepped to the other side of the bed, took hold of the top edge of the sheet and tugged. The fabric unfolded.

"Now center the sheet so there is extra length all around—at the top and bottom and sides."

She swallowed back a fresh spate of tears at the woman's kindness, grabbed hold of the sheet and copied Mrs. Fuller's actions. "But what do I do with all of this extra fabric?"

"Have you ever wrapped a present?"

"Yes, of course. But..." She stared at the bed, then looked up at the woman standing across from her. "You're saying I should *wrap* the mattress?"

The blue eyes fastened on her warmed. "Exactly. Let me show you."

She could have hugged the woman. "How very kind of you."

"Not at all, my dear. I'm happy to help. First, you tuck the extra length of sheet at the top between the mattress and the one beneath it that rests on the ropes." Mrs. Fuller slid her arm under the top mattress, lifted it, then used her other arm to sweep the extra linen between that mattress and the one beneath it. She copied the older woman's actions on her side of the bed.

"Good! Now, we go to the bottom of the bed, pull the sheet nice and tight, then tuck it under as we did at the top. And then we'll do the same on the sides." Mrs. Fuller edged along between the bed and the wall smoothing the sheet with one hand and tucking it under the mattress with the other.

She glanced over at the wrinkle-free linen on Mrs. Fuller's side of the bed, frowned down at her side. "What did you do at the corners? Mine are all puckered."

"I folded them—like you do on a present." The older woman came to her side and demonstrated.

"Oh. I see." She fixed the other corner, slid her palm over the perfectly smooth sheet and smiled. "And I do the top sheet and blankets the same way?"

"Yes, except you tuck all of the extra length under at the bottom."

She nodded and spread the other sheet over the bed. Making it even with the edge of the mattress at the top, she tucked the extra length under at the foot of the bed. Satisfaction surged when Mrs. Fuller nodded and smiled. She reached for a blanket.

The older woman removed her hat and cloak and

placed them in the wardrobe. "Whisper Creek must be a very small town if there is no one to hire for a maid."

"Yes. I only arrived last night, but Garret said there is a general store, an apothecary shop, a church and—" she finished tucking the blanket in and straightened "—and something else...oh yes, a sawmill. And a laundry in the woods at the edge of town."

"Well, that's helpful. There are a lot of linens to be washed for a hotel of this size."

She shook the coverlet out over the bed, then stopped and stared at Mrs. Fuller. "I hadn't thought of that." *Thank You, Lord, for the laundry.*

The older woman smoothed back the dark, graying hair at her temples, tugged at her faded dress. "It's getting close to midday. What time is dinner served?"

"I don't know. I'll have to ask Garret." Her cheeks heated. Mrs. Fuller must think her a complete dolt. "As I said, I only arrived in Whisper Creek last night. We were married shortly after my arrival."

"Last night..." The woman blinked, held a hankie to her mouth and coughed. "May I offer my best wishes on your marriage. I hope you will both be very happy."

Impossible. "Thank you." She smoothed the coverlet on the bed, put the pillows in place and turned toward the door. "If you'll excuse me, I'll go and see about dinner." She stopped, glancing over her shoulder. "Thank you so much for teaching me to make the bed, Mrs. Fuller. I'm very grateful. And I know Garret will be grateful, also."

The woman nodded, turned to gaze out the window.

"You're welcome to come to the lobby and sit by the fire. I'm sure you'll be comfortable there."

"Thank you, dear." Mrs. Fuller coughed again, then cleared her throat. "I'll do that a little later. I want to unpack my bag first."

"Of course." She took another quick look at the bed, smiled and slipped out of the room.

Garret worked quickly, the light from the oil lamps hanging above the worktable flashing on the sharp knife he wielded. He glanced at the clock again. Two minutes. His jaw clenched. He slipped the knife beneath the ham slices and lifted them onto a platter, speared a few pickles and placed them beside the meat. It still looked bare. What else…*corn relish!* He'd included some in the last order he'd placed with Blake Latherop. He rushed to the pantry, grabbed a can of the relish and hurried back to the worktable.

The slam of his palm on the handle of the can opener was satisfying. He hit it again for good measure, then pumped his wrist up and down, slicing around the tin top. He spooned the yellow corn relish onto the empty space on the platter, pushed it aside and grabbed a loaf of Ivy Karl's fresh-baked bread.

The door from the hotel dining room opened. He looked up, caught a glimpse of his bride hurrying toward him. Her small, perfect nose wrinkled.

"It still smells of smoke in here."

Because of you! He pressed his lips together. There was no point in castigating the woman for her helplessness. It wasn't her fault she had no housekeeping skills.

But she would have to learn. Perhaps Ivy Karl would teach Virginia how to cook. He would ask Ivy after he was through with the shoveling. And he would buy a cookbook—

"Mrs. Fuller would like to know when dinner is served?"

"At twelve o'clock." He drew the knife through the bread, tossed the slices into the basket he had ready and pulled the towel over them. "It's ready now. All but the tea. I'll pour the water in the teapot and let it steep while I…" He glanced down at his rough clothes, looked across the worktable at her. "I don't want a guest to see me dressed like this. Do you think you could set the table and carry in the food?" *Without causing another disaster?* He pushed away the thought and shook his head before she could reply. "Never mind. I—"

She stiffened, reached out and snatched up the bread basket and the small dish of butter. "I may not know how to cook, Mr. Stevenson, but I am an expert at overseeing our help. And that includes planning menus and creating lovely settings for my father's dinner parties! Of course I know how to set a table!" She whirled and hurried toward the dining room, glanced over her shoulder. "And I suggest you burn a few candles in here. It takes the smell away. Martha always burned candles if the smoke from the hearth blew into the living room." She pushed the door open and disappeared.

He held his breath, waiting for the sound of dishes breaking or crashing to the floor. All was quiet. He poured the steaming water into the red-and-white china teapot sitting on its tray, then picked up the knife to slice ham and bread for their own meal. If he hurried, he could be through eating his sandwich and be back outside by the time Virginia was finished preparing the table for their guest.

He scowled, shoved some ham and a pickle between two slices of Ivy's bread and took a bite. The thought he'd been holding back shoved to the fore of his mind. What about supper? He chomped down another bite of his sandwich and looked at the deep drifts of snow outside the back windows. He would have to forget about the rest of the shoveling and make stew. There was time if he started fixing it right away.

The dining room door pushed open and Virginia appeared, her long skirts swishing over the floor. "Mrs. Fuller is on her way to the dining room." She grabbed the prepared platter, rushed back to the door then slowed to a sedate pace.

The soft murmur of voices reached him. He strained to catch any negative comments the guest might make about being given a cold meal—a result of Millie Rourk's and Virginia Winterman's treachery. Along with an unmade bed! He had to make that right, too.

He scrubbed a hand over the back of his neck and headed for the refrigerator. At least he didn't need to get another block of ice. He'd done that yester—

"Mr. Stevenson..." The door in the sitting room slammed against the wall.

Eddie! His heart jolted at the desperation in the child's breathless voice. He strode to the sitting room, stared at the boy's pale, frightened face. "What is it, Eddie? What's wrong?"

"Minna's trapped in the cave!" The boy swiped his sleeve across his tearing eyes and gulped for air. "We was playin' Injuns was chasin' us, an' I told her to hide, an' then all the snow fell an' I couldn't get her out!" The boy gulped air again. "Pa says come quick!"

"Show me where the cave is!" He tugged on his boots, grabbed his jacket and hat and ran through the lobby after the youngster. He caught a glimpse of Virginia's startled face in the dining room doorway as he yanked the front door shut and grabbed his shovel.

He raced behind Eddie down the shoveled pathway toward the church, and followed when the boy veered off toward the new doctor's office and clinic being built across the main road from the parsonage.

A broken path through the snow led to the towering pines at the foot of the mountains. He sucked his lungs full of the cold air and ran on, ducking and dodging the limbs Eddie ran under with ease. At least the snow was less deep among the trees. A glimpse of the ice-covered pond that supplied their water glittered on their left. He took note of their direction and lunged over ice-coated rocks and slapped snow-covered branches out of his way, keeping his gaze fastened on the nine-year-old ahead of him, who never stopped or wavered from his path.

They burst out of the trees to the right of the pocket in the mountain that held the waterfall. A patch of bare stones showed gray on the mountainside, a huge pile of snow below it. Pastor Karl, Blake Latherop and Dr. Trace Warren were digging frantically, their efforts deepening a narrow tunnel they'd started in the hill of white that towered over them. Ivy Karl stood to the side, her eyes closed, her lips moving. She clutched a blanket in her gloved hands. Two lanterns sat at her feet, mute testimony to the few hours that remained until nightfall. A chill chased down his spine. Prayer didn't help anything. It would be up to them to save the girl. "Where is the cave, Eddie?"

The boy lifted a shaking hand. "At the bottom of the mountain, beneath that big stone."

He followed the direction of the boy's pointing finger upward, above the top of the heaped snow. There was a narrow crack in the mountain face beneath the projecting rock where Eddie pointed. If it supplied air to the cave…and if the cave was deep enough for Minna to have escaped being buried…there was a chance.

Hope rose, warred with reality. He moved closer, glanced into the tunnel. If it collapsed—He broke off the thought, gripped Eddie's shoulder. "Run to the sawmill and get Mit—Mr. Todd. Tell him to bring his men and any logs his horses can drag through the snow. Tell him we'll need them to support a snow tunnel. Hurry!"

He watched Eddie dart back into the trees, then ran to the packed white mass of snow and joined the others.

Virginia finished making the bed in room number one, spread the colorful quilt over it and left the room. There would be no more complaints about her bed making—thanks to Mrs. Fuller.

A train whistle sliced through the silence. It was the third, no, the fourth time today. She was becoming accustomed to the sound, but she couldn't help but wonder where the train was going, who was on it and why. Every passenger had a reason for their journey—as she'd had for hers. Her steps faltered. She still couldn't believe she was married. Of course she wasn't...not truly. Her marriage was a business agreement. And she intended to uphold her—*Millie's*—end of the bargain. She'd already learned to register a guest, make a bed and serve a meal. And to clear away the dirty dishes and put the table back in order.

A twinge of guilt pricked her at the thought of the dirty dishes sitting on the worktable in the kitchen. She shoved it away and glided through the archway into the lobby, smiled when Mrs. Fuller looked up from the book in her hand. "Are you finding the fire comfortable?"

"Very much so, dear. And I'm sure it will be very welcome to any train passengers who may decide to spend the night in your hotel instead of rocking back and forth on the train while they try to sleep." The older woman shook her head. "Those cars are not as warm as one expects they will be."

Passengers. Garret had gone off somewhere. What if—she caught her breath, hurried to a front window and looked toward the station. The train engine sat puffing smoke toward the overcast sky. She slid her gaze to the passenger car. A man stood on the small platform. Her stomach tensed. Was the man getting off the train? What if he came to spend the night? Or what if more than one came? What was she to do?

There was only one room prepared. She hadn't even *been* upstairs. Where was Garret? How dare he leave her here alone and helpless!

"Is there something wrong, dear?"

"What? Oh. No…" She glanced over her shoulder. "I'll be right back." She opened the door and stepped out onto the shoveled porch. Cold air penetrated her wool dress. A chill slithered down her spine. She hurried to the railing and looked down the shoveled path toward the church and parsonage. Nothing stirred. She brushed snow from the railing, leaned out over it and drew her gaze back to her side of the road. But she could see nothing beyond the building beside her. No voices floated on the still, cold air. Where was Garret? "Please, Lord, let him return!"

She glanced back at the train. The man was no longer there. He must have only wanted a breath of fresh air. She shivered, brushed the snow from her hands and hurried back inside.

"I hope whatever the emergency was, it's better now." Mrs. Fuller peered at her over the top of the book she held. "I'm not prying, dear, truly. But I was sitting by the window in the dining room when your husband went running down the street with that young boy, and I saw the look of urgency on his face. I've been praying that whatever was wrong would turn out well."

"That's very kind of you. But I've no idea where Garret went, or why. I couldn't see or hear anything outside." She pressed her lips together before she blurted out her unease, and went to warm herself at the hearth. The fire needed wood. She lifted a piece from the wood cradle and frowned—only two pieces of split log remained. They wouldn't last long. And then what? She massaged her temples, stared down at the flames. Garret must have a supply of wood for the fires, but she had no idea where it was. And with the deep snow covering everything outside...

She straightened, shot a glance toward the door to the private quarters. She could use the wood for the sitting room fire to keep the lobby fire going. And the dining room fire, also. It would make it cold in the living quarters, but the public rooms had to be kept warm and comfortable. She would spend her time here in the lobby. She glanced at the piano, stretched her hands out toward the fire and flexed her fingers.

The train whistle echoed through the room, the sound repeating a moment later. Mrs. Fuller turned her head toward the windows. "That is such a lonely sound..."

A *welcome* one. There would be no new guest to— Boots stomped outside the door. The tension across her shoulders eased. Garret was back. He would handle all these problems. The door opened. She turned, stared.

A short, portly man stepped inside, swept a quick glance over the room and removed his hat. "Ladies..." He dipped his balding head their direction and strode toward the desk. A leather valise dangled from his hand.

Her stomach flopped. She drew in a breath and hurried forward, her long hems swishing across the floor. "Good afternoon, sir." She glided behind the desk, fastened a polite smile on her face. "Welcome to the Stevenson Hotel."

The man set his valise on the floor and straightened. "Where is the proprietor?"

"Mr. Stevenson is out." She opened the black leather

ledger and turned it toward him. "I will be pleased to register you. The rate is one and a half dollars a night."

"And you are…"

"Mrs. Stevenson." It was getting easier to say. She slid the pewter pen and ink holder closer to his hand and smiled. "Write your name and address, please. I'll give you room number one." *As if there was a choice.* She turned to the cupboard on the wall and reached into the cubicle for the key. "The room is here on the first floor and handy to the lobby and dining room. I'll show you the way."

The man nodded, slid the ledger back and handed her the money. "What time is supper?"

Supper! What if Garret didn't return in time to cook supper? Panic snatched the air from her lungs. She closed her eyes, tried to think of an answer. Her mind went blank.

"The menu card says supper is served from six o'clock until eight o'clock."

She opened her eyes, looked at Mrs. Fuller. The older woman smiled, gave her a small nod. The pressure on her lungs lessened.

She took a breath and moved toward the archway. "Your room is this way, Mr. Anderson. I'm sure you'll find it comfortable." *Thanks to Mrs. Fuller.* She opened the door of room number one, glanced at the dim light coming in the window and hurried to the bedside table to light the oil lamp. "You will share the dressing room at the end of the hall with the guest in bedroom number two. And, of course, you are welcome to relax by the fire in the lobby."

"There's an indoor necessary?"

Her cheeks burned at the indelicate reference. "Yes." She adjusted the flame to quell the smoke, lowered the lamp chimney into place and hurried back to the door. "You will find the latest of comforts provided. Including hot running water."

"Well, well… I didn't expect to find such luxury out here in the wilds. How's the bed?" The man plopped down on the edge of the mattress and bounced.

She held her breath, released it when the linens stayed in place.

"Feels comfortable." Mr. Anderson slapped the mattress beside him and rose. "I'll settle in and then come out and sit by the fire until supper."

Her stomach tensed. "Enjoy your stay, Mr. Anderson." She pasted on another smile and backed out of the room before he could ask her any more questions. Her temples throbbed. She rested back against the wall and rubbed at the ache. It was foolishness to get upset. It would be dark soon and Garret would come home. He would cook supper, and she would serve the guests.

Everything would be fine. Perfectly fine.

Chapter Five

Plop.

Garret threw his shovelful of snow into the gathering box, canted his head to the right and listened. *Trickle. Plop.* He glanced over his shoulder. Snow drifted down onto a small pile forming in the middle of the smoothed surface of the tunnel floor. Another clump of snow fell on top of the pile. He looked up, braced himself and pushed the back of his shovel blade against the beginning of a crack at the top of the slanted wall. *If that snow gave way...*

He gathered breath and turned his head toward the opening of the long, narrow tunnel through the snow. "We need logs, Mitch!" He sucked another breath into his straining lungs. "We have a weak spot!"

Blake Latherop stopped shoveling on the opposite side of the box, grabbed one of the lanterns, came and held it up to where the two slanted walls of snow met overhead. "It's...small. You've got...most of it...covered. Call if...need me."

He nodded, closed his mind to the ache in his back and shoulders, and watched the shadows of Pastor Karl and Dr. Warren dance against the snow. Blake stepped back to his side of the tunnel, set the lantern down and resumed shoveling.

"Logs are on their way!"

Boots crunched against the snow. Logs banged against logs.

"Careful, Tom! We don't want the bottoms of those standing logs to kick out of place. Hang on, Garret! We're almost there…"

He had no breath to waste on an answer. They were all past the point of exhaustion, but there was no one to relieve them. He hung his head and forced the quivering muscles of his upstretched arms to keep the pressure of the shovel blade against the snow. The sounds grew louder. Brown twill pants stuffed into black, calf-high boots straddling the angled ends of a bundle of logs came into view. A beautiful sight.

"Hold on, Garret…"

Mitch Todd dropped to his knees, untied the bundled logs and dragged one to his left. He stared at the butt end of the log as Mitch shoved it into place at the bottom of the wall and heaved. The rough bark snagged at the wool of his jacket, but stopped as Mitch pushed the log higher.

"Ready, Tom…" Another log was dragged by, maneuvered into place at the bottom of the wall on his right, the angled end hefted.

"Brace yourself, Garret. I have to…lean against you to…fit the logs together."

He stiffened his legs and listened to Mitch's huffing and puffing as the sawmill owner leaned against his shoulders, reached overhead and shoved the angled ends of the logs into place against one another.

"Got it! 'Nother log, Tom."

"Right here…"

He watched the men's boots, the ends of the logs being set in place, and ignored the increasing weariness in his body. Mitch moved in front of him.

"We're…ready to set the next log. When I tell you… lower your shovel and…step back out of the way."

He nodded and unlocked his knees, waited…

"Hold the snow, Lord. Hold the snow."

Konrad Karl's prayer floated to him, brought a rise of irritation. *Did the man really think God answered prayers?*

"Move, Garret!"

He lowered his shovel and stepped back, rolled his cramped shoulders and watched Mitch align the slanted tops of the opposing logs. Tom had another timber already in place. The snow was holding.

Garret rubbed the stiff muscles at the back of his neck, shoved his hand back in his glove and resumed shoveling. Blake had gained a lead on him. He quickened his pace, cleaned the wall and bottom on his side of the tunnel. The gathering box filled to overflowing. He leaned his shovel against the wall and grabbed the pull rope, slung it over his shoulder. The other men gave the box a shove, and he started for the tunnel opening, Blake pushing the long, narrow sled box from behind.

Lanterns flickered outside. Horses loomed out of the

darkness, stomped and tossed their heads while their handlers hurried to unhook the chains wrapped around the logs they'd dragged in. Men stopped sawing timbers and rushed forward to help overturn and empty the gathering box.

How much farther? He looked at the massive mound of snow left by the avalanche, but could see nothing but the dim light of the tunnel entrance. There was no way to tell how close they were to their goal. The snow was so deep they couldn't set any markers to indicate their progress. He glanced to where Ivy Karl sat on a log, holding the folded blanket...waiting. His heart squeezed with pain for her.

If You do ever answer a prayer, Lord, please answer hers and return her child to her. Let Minna be all right.

He frowned, chided himself for being caught up in the foolishness of Pastor Karl's constantly murmured prayers. He knew they were useless. He'd learned that when he was ten years old. He would serve Ivy Karl better by getting back to work on the tunnel.

The men thudded their fists against the bottom of the box to loosen any clinging snow.

"That's it. Box is empty."

He nodded to Blake. They tipped it upright, grabbed the pull rope and dragged it back into the tunnel.

Virginia turned from staring at the darkness outside the window and cast another look at the clock hanging on the lobby wall. The ticking of a clock had always been a friendly sound. But not tonight. Tonight it made her stomach churn.

Ten minutes until five o'clock, and no sign of Garret. No sign of anyone. There wasn't even a light glowing in a window at the church or parsonage. She closed her eyes and rubbed at the ache in her temples. Supper was to be served at six o'clock. What should she do? She couldn't send their guests elsewhere. There *was* no elsewhere.

"You look troubled, dear."

The soft words tightened the pressure in her chest. She opened her eyes and looked at Mrs. Fuller. Tears clogged her throat at the kindness in the woman's eyes.

"I wish I could help, but—"

"*Would* you?" The words popped out, needy and irretrievable. Where were her manners and her pride? Her cheeks burned. She bit down on her lower lip and looked away from Mrs. Fuller's startled expression. "I'm sorry. Please forgive my ill manners. I—"

"There's no need for you to apologize, Mrs. Stevenson." Mrs. Fuller set her book aside, rose and came to stand beside her. "I don't understand how I can ease your worry over your husband's absence, but I'll be pleased to do what I can."

"It's not that I'm worried about Garret, Mrs. Fuller. It's—"

Snort! "Harrumph!"

She glanced at Mr. Anderson, asleep in a chair with his legs stretched out toward the fire. The portly man blinked, smacked his lips, then crossed his hands on his ample stomach. She held her breath and waited. Soft bursts of air puffed from the man's mouth, and his relaxed lips fluttered when he drew in more. His snoring resumed, punctuated by the crackle of the fire.

She looked back at Mrs. Fuller and lowered her voice. "If you will come into the dining room with me, I'll explain." *Please, Lord, let her agree.*

"Of course, dear." The older woman nodded. "There's no point in interrupting Mr. Anderson's nap with our chatter."

With my *begging*! The thought flooded new warmth into her cheeks. She led the way into the dining room, stopped by the fireplace and added another small log to the fire. The wood should last until suppertime. "I told you this morning that I am newly married and that there are many household chores I do not know how to do."

"And that there is no maid to do the work." There was a question underlying Mrs. Fuller's soft words.

"Yes." She pushed back a strand of hair and rose, smoothed down her skirt. "And now Garret is gone. And I don't know where he is or when he will return. And it will soon be suppertime and I—I—" She choked on the humiliating words.

"Do not know how to cook?"

She nodded, squared her shoulders. "Would you be willing to help me? To show me what to do? I'm sure Garret will pay you for your—" She halted her plea, caught her breath and stared at the older woman. There was an odd expression on her face. Panic struck. "You *do* know how to cook?"

"Yes." Mrs. Fuller pulled a handkerchief from her long sleeve, held it to her face and coughed. The clock struck the hour. "Time is running short. We'll have to hurry. If you will show me to the kitchen…"

Her held breath gushed from her lungs. "Thank you, Mrs. Fuller! This way." She lifted her hems and hurried to the double doors, stepped through into the kitchen and stopped. There was a definite chill in the room. She looked back at the older woman, mindful of her cough. "I'm sorry, Mrs. Fuller, I didn't realize how cold it is in here." A soft sigh escaped her. She motioned toward the ashes in the fireplace. "I don't know where Garret keeps the wood outdoors, so I've been using this wood to feed the fires in the lobby and dining room. Perhaps you had best go back and sit by the hearth. I don't want your cough to worsen."

"I'm fine, dear. It's a nervous condition." Mrs. Fuller gave a distracted nod, looked around. "I've never seen such a kitchen! Why, there's everything a woman could want in here." The rustle of the older woman's long skirts blended with her awed whisper.

"I suppose…" She tried to see the kitchen through the older woman's eyes, but it was simply confusing to her.

"Well, standing here admiring things won't get supper on the table. Though I may not have to do that much cooking, supper being a light meal. The ham and bread from dinner are still here on the worktable. I can use them…" Mrs. Fuller bustled to the cookstove. "The first thing I have to do is get a fire started."

She rushed to the woman's side. "Tell me what to do."

Astonishment swept over Mrs. Fuller's thin, lined face, but was quickly erased. "Well, we need kindling and stove wood. That box under the window looks a likely place to find them."

"All right." She lifted the slanted lid of the large box, eyed the newspapers, twigs and different sizes of wood contained in compartments.

Mrs. Fuller reached up and twisted a handle in the stovepipe, then opened the firebox. "Now, wad up a piece of newspaper and place it just inside the door. Pile some of the kindling on top and then lay on a few small pieces of wood. And here are the matches."

She averted her gaze from the awkward angle of Mrs. Fuller's hand and struck a match. The paper caught fire, the kindling flared. "What now?"

"We'll leave the firebox door open until the wood is burning hot. Meanwhile, Mrs. Stevenson, I will have a look in the refrigerator. And then, if you will show me the pantry, I'll see what there is on hand that I can fix to go with the ham. It will have to be simple. There's no time for the oven to get hot enough for roasting or baking."

"Please call me Virginia, Mrs. Fuller." *Where was the pantry?* She opened a door and peered inside then moved on to the next cabinet.

"That's a lovely name, dear." The refrigerator door squeaked open. "Hmm...well, there's some meat. And a bit of cheese..." Mrs. Fuller glanced her way. "What is in that small room, Virginia?"

She moved beyond the sink and opened a door, stepped into a small room lined with shelves. "It's the pantry. There are some potatoes and onions and carrots in here. And quite a few tins of food."

"Good. I can make potato pancakes. I'll need three or four potatoes and a small onion. Is there a can of pineapple? And a bottle of vinegar?"

"I'll see." She lifted potatoes and an onion out of baskets on the floor into a large bowl, scanned the shelves, found a tin of pineapple and the vinegar, and carried them to the worktable. Mrs. Fuller was carrying the dirty dishes from dinner to the sink. The day was holding one humiliation after another. She sighed and hurried to the sink. "I didn't know how to clean the dishes. I'll do it now if you will show me."

"We'll do them all after supper, dear. Time is too short to do them now. I need your help with the cooking." The woman smiled, bustled back to the worktable, opened a drawer and peered inside. "One of the first and most important things to learn about preparing a good meal is the timing. So, if you would please add more wood to the stove, then close the door and adjust the draft so it burns hot, we'll get started on your first lesson—peeling and grating potatoes. If I can find—ah, there you are!"

Virginia glanced at the object Mrs. Fuller pulled from the drawer, then hurried to the stove. The draft was similar to those on the heating stoves in the bedrooms. At last, something she knew how to do! She made quick work of her assigned task and hurried back to the worktable. Light from the oil lamps overhead flashed on the small knife Mrs. Fuller slid around a potato. A thin strip of brown skin curled off and fell onto a small pile.

"I found a grater. That will be your part—like this…"

Mrs. Fuller rinsed the peeled potato in a bowl of water, set a piece of curved metal full of holes on the table and slid the potato from the top to the bottom. Small shreds of the white flesh fell onto the table. "Now you try it, dear."

She copied Mrs. Fuller's actions, smiled when potato shreds dropped onto the others. "I did it!" She slid the potato down the grater again.

Mrs. Fuller smiled back and reached for another potato to peel. "Mind your fingers, dear—that grater is sharp."

Peeled potatoes piled up in front of her. She finished the first and began grating the others. The pungent odor of onion stung her nose. Her eyes smarted and burned. She blinked and glanced over at Mrs. Fuller, met her watery gaze. The woman chuckled, stopped chopping at a pile of small pieces of onion and wiped away the tears running down her thin cheeks turning her wrist to compensate for its limited use. "I don't know what I was thinking, Virginia. I should have given you this task."

"Indeed. Thank you for your kindness." She laughed, grabbed the last potato and continued her grating.

Mrs. Fuller finished the onion, scooped it into a bowl with the grated potatoes, then carved slices from the ham. "We want to brown this meat a bit before we add the sauce. A bit of the fat will serve." The older woman placed a thick lump of fat she'd trimmed from the ham in a cast-iron frying pan and carried it to the stove. "Bring the slices of ham and come watch, dear. Timing is one of the most difficult things to learn about cooking. It depends on so many things. Because our fire is new, without hot coals, we must use the flames."

She watched carefully as Mrs. Fuller rested the edge of the skillet on the stove, removed the cast-iron circle above the firebox and lifted it aside. Flames shot up out of the opening. She gasped and jumped back.

Mrs. Fuller shoved the frying pan over the hole, stuck a fork in the fat and wiped it around the bottom of the pan. The fat sizzled. "Time for the ham. Put those slices in the pan, Virginia. And mind the fat doesn't spatter up on your hands."

She stared at the fork Mrs. Fuller held out to her.

"Turn the slices when they get a nice color to them. I'm going to open the pineapple tin and see if I can find some spices."

She caught her lower lip in her teeth to keep from calling the woman back. The fat popped. She tipped the plate until the ham slid into the pan, then poked at the slices with the fork to spread them. The smell of the browning meat made her stomach growl.

"Ah, here they are! And I found the sugar and flour and such in these crocks."

She kept her gaze fastened on the meat, pierced one of the slices of ham with the fork and turned it over. *Brown.* She hurried to turn the rest of them.

Mrs. Fuller bustled back and emptied the contents of her arms onto the small table beside the stove. "Time to add the sauce. Slide the meat to one side."

"*Me?* But—"

"Hurry now, we've potatoes to make."

She caught her breath, pushed the ham into a pile.

"Now, pour in the pineapple chunks. And be careful, the juice will spit and steam when it hits the hot pan. Good. Now we'll add a little sugar…a splash of vinegar…some cinnamon and a pinch of cloves…"

Her mouth watered. "That smells wonderful!"

Mrs. Fuller smiled. "Stir it up, spread the ham out, then slide the pan back a little so the sauce will cook but not burn—we want it to be like a syrup. Then add a couple small pieces of wood and cover the fire with this griddle. We need it hot for the potato cakes. Come to the worktable when you finish."

She did as she was bid, then stared at the bowl of grated potatoes and onion Mrs. Fuller shoved in front of her. Her shoulders tightened.

"Sprinkle some flour over the potatoes and add some salt and pepper. That's good. Now give them a stir and we'll add this egg…"

Mrs. Fuller brought an egg down sharply on the edge of the bowl, emptied the contents onto the potato mixture, tossed the shell away and picked up a tin pail. "Stir the egg into the potatoes, then bring them to the stove. You have to stir the sauce and turn the ham so it doesn't burn."

She caught sight of a colorful bird and the words *PURE LARD* on the pail before Mrs. Fuller snatched a wood spoon from a crock bristling with utensils and headed back to the stove. Her stomach clenched. She couldn't do all these things! Tension traveled from her shoulders down her arm and drove the spoon she held in swift circles. *Done!* She gripped the bowl, spun about and hurried back to the stove, her skirts swirling around her. "Mrs. Fuller, I—"

"Set the potatoes here, dear, while you stir the sauce and turn the meat."

She fought down the urge to run to her bedroom and cry, grabbed the fork and turned the ham slices over. The sauce clung, sliding off in strings. "It's thick, like syrup…"

"Exactly as we want it. Slide the pan to the far side to stay warm, and we'll start the potatoes. Put a bit of lard on the hot griddle and spread it around. When it's melted, add four good spoonsful of the potatoes and flatten them out a bit with the spoon. When they're nicely browned turn them and cook the other side— add more lard should you need it. I'll slice some bread and find some preserves."

The clock donged. She glanced at it. Her stomach sank. Fifteen minutes until six o'clock, and she still had to set the tables! *Please make Mr. Anderson sleep until everything is ready, Lord.* She checked the potatoes, flipped the cakes over and tapped her foot.

"Here are serving plates for the potato cakes, dear. And more for the ham and pineapple. Keep the food up here in the warming oven until you're finished cooking and ready to serve. It's time for me to join Mr. Anderson in the lobby. I'll delay him a bit, if possible." Mrs. Fuller touched her arm briefly, then walked from the kitchen.

She was alone. Panic swelled. *Help me, Lord! Please help me!*

His shovel blade hit something solid, the shock of the blow vibrating up Garret's arm. Hope swelled his chest.

He scooped up another shovelful of snow, grabbed the lantern and stared at the dark spot he'd uncovered. He caught his breath and brushed at the surrounding snow. The rock went off to his left. "Konrad, I've uncovered some rock over here. We may have to change our direction a little."

All sound stopped. Silence filled the narrow white tunnel. And then there was a rustle of clothing, the thud of boots. Konrad Karl fell to his knees beside him, tears sliding down his cheeks, his gloved hands digging at the snow around the stone. Blake and Trace crowded in behind them.

He laid his hand on the pastor's shoulder. "Easy, Konrad, we don't want to make a mistake now. Use the probe." He handed Konrad Karl the long, thin metal rod they'd been using to try to stay on the right path to the cave.

"Guide this rod, Lord!" Pastor Karl drew the rod back, then thrust it forward into the snow in front of them. The other men grabbed hold and, adding their waning strength to his, pushed the rod in to half its length. They took a step forward and shoved harder, fell in a heap. They glanced at one another, untangled themselves and grabbed the rod to try again. There was no resistance. They'd found the cave. But what of Minna? Was the little girl alive? The thought hung in the air, heavy and unspoken.

"Please, Lord, spare my Minna's life."

Konrad Karl's words spurred them to action. Garret pushed his shovel into the gathering box and tossed the snow in it to the side of the tunnel. One way or another, they would use the sled to move the little girl out through the tunnel. *Please, Lord...* He didn't believe in it, but he couldn't stop the silent prayer.

"*Minna!* Minna, my child…my dear child…"

They'd found her! His stomach knotted. He grabbed the sled's pull rope and watched Konrad Karl turn from the dark hole, his small daughter in his arms. Leaves tumbled from the hole, clung to Minna's clothes. Trace Warren ripped off his glove, raised the child's eyelids, felt her neck.

"She's alive, but barely. Thank God for that pile of leaves! Get into the sled, Konrad, and hold her close. We need to get her warm." Trace pulled off his jacket and covered the child. Blake gave the sled a shove.

Garret gripped the rope and hurried toward the light at the end of the tunnel.

Chapter Six

Garret raised a hand to bid Blake farewell, winced and lowered it to his side. Every muscle in his body reminded him he'd been shoveling snow since long before dawn. And it wasn't over yet. He had to shovel out the woodpile and coal bin before he could stop. And then he would have to do what he could to repair any disasters his bride had caused while he was gone. Including making Mrs. Fuller's bed—if the woman hadn't left in a huff.

Weariness dragged at him. He frowned and turned onto the path he'd shoveled that morning to the hotel. What had Virginia done about the fires without him to bring in wood? The place was probably as cold as an icicle. And supper—what had she done about supper if Mrs. Fuller had stayed? He gripped his shovel tighter and glanced at his hotel looming in the darkness ahead of him. At least she hadn't burned it to the ground. And she'd kept the lamps lit in the lobby. That was more than he'd expected.

He trudged up the steps and across the porch, stomped the snow from his boots and opened the door. Warmth hit him like a sledgehammer. He shot a glance toward the fireplace, blinked, shook his head and blinked again. Mrs. Fuller was sitting in a chair by the hearth, and a portly man was playing Patience at the game table. *Another guest!* He met their startled gazes, hid his surprise at their presence and dipped his head in greeting.

Soft footsteps blended with the hiss and crackle of the fire. "Oh! You've returned."

There was accusation, irritation and a wealth of relief in the voice. He figured the last would overcome the others. At least he hoped so. He was in no mood for a sparring match with the spoiled Miss Winterman. Correction, the spoiled Mrs. Stevenson. He shifted his gaze to his bride standing in the dining room doorway with her arms full of wood. *Stove wood.* She was more industrious than he'd thought. And obviously desperate to keep the guests warm. He nodded, quickly wishing he hadn't when a twinge of pain shot from his neck into his shoulders. "Yes, Minna is safe." He stepped around Mrs. Fuller's chair, leaned his shovel against the fireplace and took the wood from his wife.

"Minna?" Delicate eyebrows arched over shadowed blue eyes.

"Sorry. I forgot you don't know her."

"Or anyone else in town but the pastor and his wife." She followed him to the hearth and brushed clinging bits of sawdust off her dress, annoyance in every quick flick of her hand. Her message of disgust with him was clear. Not that he could blame her. He'd left her in a tough situation.

He knelt in front of the fire. Steam rose from his wet pant legs. "Minna is Pastor Karl's daughter. The oldest one. She's six or seven..." He laid the wood on the fire and reached for the poker. "The doctor thinks she'll be all right."

"She is ill?"

"What? Oh, no—not exactly." He brushed his hands off and rose, looked down. He was so close he could see tiny dark flecks deepening the blue in Virginia's eyes. He stepped back. "She was trapped in a cave by an avalanche. We've been shoveling all day to get her out."

"The poor child!"

The compassionate whisper brought the tightness back to his chest. He glanced over at Mrs. Fuller. The woman looked down at the book in her hand.

"She must have been terribly frightened."

He turned back to Virginia. "I'm sure she was at first. But she was sort of...sleeping when we reached her. Dr. Warren says it's because of the cold. There was a pile of leaves in the cave Minna huddled in. Trace—that's the doctor—thinks they helped keep her alive. He thinks she'll be all right once she gets warmed up."

He rubbed the sore muscles at the back of his neck, rolled his shoulders and stole another look at his bride's eyes. The shadow of annoyance was gone. They looked like two bright spots of summer sky. "I'll bring in a load of firewood as soon as I clear the snow off the pile." He grabbed his shovel and headed for the dining room doorway. Her skirts rustled behind him.

"I'm afraid we'll need more than one load." She rushed by, turned and faced him at the kitchen doors. "I used all of the wood for your setting room and kitchen fireplaces to keep the lobby and dining room warm—until after supper. Since then, I've been burning the stove wood in the lobby."

"Ours."

"What?"

"*Our* setting room and kitchen. We're married."

"Oh. Well, yes…" Her face went taut. "But not really."

"Real enough." He frowned, stretched out his arm and placed his hand on one of the doors. "I'm sorry I had to leave you in such a trying situation without any explanation, but there wasn't any time to spare for talking."

She nodded and stepped aside. "I understand…now."

He studied her tense posture, listened to the underlying strain in her voice. Did she think he was angry with her? "You did a good job of keeping the guests warm and comfortable today. I was concerned over how you would manage with no wood supply. Thank you. It was very resourceful of you." He didn't have the courage to ask what she had done about supper. He shoved open the door and took a surreptitious sniff. There was no odor of burned food in the air. Only a hint of something spicy. His stomach growled. He frowned and stalked the length of the cold kitchen, shoved open the back door and kicked his way through the piled snow onto the porch.

* * *

Virginia slid behind the dining table and peered out the window. Light from the kitchen lit the center of the porch, glittering on the snow that flew off of Garret's shovel into the darkness. Frosty air issued from the window. She frowned and drew back a little. Curtains would stop some of that chill, but there was no seamstress in town. No wonder all the windows were fitted with shutters.

She shivered and rubbed her upper arms to create warmth. Garret's pant legs were wet. Were his socks wet, too? The thought sent another shiver coursing down her spine. How cold he must be! And strong—shoveling snow all day to save the pastor's young daughter. That was a noble thing to do. And...surprising.

She leaned back against the table, lifted her hand and ran the curls dangling behind her ear through her fingers. Was she being unfair to Garret Stevenson? Was he an honorable, decent man? Dare she stop looking for hidden meanings in the things he said and let down her guard around him? Yet how could she when he said things like their marriage was "real enough"? Emory Gladen had acted honorable, too. In public.

She straightened, leaned close and squinted out the window. Garret had disappeared into the darkness at the other end of the porch. How could he see to work? She inched out from behind the table and hurried into the pantry she had explored earlier. There had been a lantern on the shelf by the door. And matches beside it. Yes, there it was. She lit the wick, adjusted the flame and lowered the chimney back into place.

A gold circle appeared on the floor, swung beside her as she went back and stepped out onto the porch. The cold penetrated her wool dress and prickled her flesh. The lantern shook with her shivering.

"What are you doing out here?" Garret rushed toward her out of the dark. "Get back inside before you catch your death."

"I thought a l-lantern would h-help."

"It will. Thank you." He grasped the handle and opened the door. "Now go and sit by the fire to get warm."

She needed no coaxing. She stepped back into the kitchen and rushed toward the dining room to go to the lobby. The overhead lamplight threw her shadow on the cooking stove as she hurried by. She stopped, glanced back toward the porch. Garret had been out in the cold all day. What if *he* took sick? The least she could do was make certain he had hot food to eat when he came in.

She touched the cold stove, lifted the front plate and peered in. A few embers glowed among the ashes. She slipped in some kindling and opened the draft and the firebox door as Mrs. Fuller had done. The embers flickered, turned red. Small flames licked at the new fuel, caught hold and flared into a fire. She added the few pieces of stove wood left in the box, waited until they caught fire, then closed the door. She'd done it! All by herself! She put the stove plate back in place and smiled. If only she could tell Millie of her newly acquired skills. How surprised her maid would be.

She pulled down the door of the cold warming oven and lifted out the covered plate of food Mrs. Fuller had put in there after supper. "In case Mr. Stevenson comes home cold and hungry," the woman had said. A frown stole her smile. She should have thought of that herself. It was her wifely duty to see to her husband's comfort—even if theirs was not a real marriage. And it wasn't. But it was real enough for them to require and to expect certain…considerations of one another. That must be what Garret had meant earlier. Well, he'd not find her wanting. She knew what was required to run a household efficiently; she simply didn't know how to do it. But she would learn the skills she was lacking.

She set the plate of food on the stovetop to warm, and eyed the granite pot sitting at the back. An image of Garret cradling a cup of coffee in his hand flashed into her mind. A hot drink would be welcome to him, she was sure. How hard could it be to make coffee?

She whirled and headed for the lobby, her long skirts billowing at her quick movements. Hopefully, Mrs. Fuller had not retired for the evening…

Garret turned sidewise and fumbled for the door-knob. It pulled away from his groping fingers, and light flowed over him.

"I thought I heard you." Virginia swung the door wide open.

He stepped into the kitchen, stopped and sniffed. "Coffee!" He shook his head and sniffed again, looked over his shoulder. "Do I smell coffee, or have I been wishing I had a cup for so long my imagination is playing tricks on me?"

Virginia laughed and closed the door. "It's real coffee. I thought you might like something hot to drink when you finished shoveling snow."

She had made coffee? "Smell's good. But it will have to wait until I carry in enough firewood to warm it up in here and see us through the night." He stomped his feet and headed for the sitting room, dumped the wood in his arms into the cradle and hurried back outside for more.

The coffee smelled better with every trip he made in and out, carrying the firewood. And there was something else. That faint spicy smell he'd noticed earlier was stronger. He was practically drooling by the time he had all the fires going. He rose from starting the kitchen fire, brushed off his hands and tugged off his hat. "I'll be right back for that coffee. I need to get out of these wet clothes."

His bedroom was cold. Not that he expected any different, but had she thought to add coal to her own bedroom stove throughout the day? He didn't want another disaster if she tried to light one. He yanked off his boots, changed into dry pants and socks, and hurried back to the kitchen, his taste buds begging for that coffee and his stomach demanding food.

"Virginia, did you keep your bedroom fire going or—" He stopped, stared at the table. "What's this?"

"I thought you would be hungry, so I heated your supper for you."

He gazed at the plate of potato pancakes nestled against slices of ham with pieces of pineapple clinging to them. "*You* made *this*?"

"Yes. With help, of course."

"Help?" He watched her hurrying toward him with

the coffeepot in her hand. His pulse quickened. There was no denying the woman was beautiful. He jerked his thoughts back from that direction. "I don't understand. Who—"

"Mrs. Fuller."

"Our *guest*?" He caught back his words, looked down and watched her fill his cup. "Why don't you join me at the table? I'd like to hear the story of how this came about." *And make certain it doesn't happen again.*

"Very well. Let me get a cup."

He stood by a chair and waited to seat her. But she gave a little wave toward the table. "Please sit down and eat before your food gets cold. I'll be right back."

He sat, picked up his coffee and took a tentative swallow. The dark, rich brew washed over his tongue, slid down his throat. *Perfect!* He took a full swallow, put down his cup and picked up his knife and fork. If the food was as good as the coffee...

"I don't blame you for being displeased about my asking Mrs. Fuller for help, Garret. But I assure you, it all came about accidentally."

What was on the ham? He took another bite and all but smacked his lips at the delicious taste.

"She was so kind to me when she taught me how to make her bed this morning, that when—"

His head jerked up. "Mrs. Fuller taught you how to make her bed?" Well, that was one job he wouldn't have to do tonight. But his hotel's reputation! He scraped back his chair, shoved his hands through his hair. "Virginia, if you have a problem, I want you to come to *me*, not some strange woman who happens to be a hotel guest!"

"I would have, but when she said her bed was *undone*, and I apologized and told her it was my fault, that we were newly married, and that you didn't know I had no housekeeping skills, she came to the bed and showed me what to do. She was most kind and understanding about it."

"Nonetheless…if she mentions your incompetency to others—"

"I am not incompetent!" Her eyes flashed blue sparks. "Ask Mr. Anderson. I made his bed the way Mrs. Fuller showed me, and he's very pleased." Her shoulders stiffened like a soldier's at attention. "And with his supper, too!"

"Which you made with Mrs. Fuller's help?"

"Yes."

He pulled in a breath, looked down at his plate and picked up his fork. "And that came about accidentally?"

"Well, I *did* ask her, but I didn't intend to. I was… distraught over everything." She looked down, traced the rim of her coffee cup with her fingertip.

"Everything?" He took a bite of potato, cut off another.

"Yes. Mrs. Fuller had stayed, which was good. But then you ran out without a word—and she saw that."

Busybody. He scowled, took another bite of ham and potato.

"And then Mr. Anderson came. And the firewood was almost gone. And I didn't know where it was outside or how to find it in the snow, so I used yours—I mean *ours*—and these rooms got colder and colder. And I kept thinking about the disaster I had caused at dinner and worrying about what I was going to do about supper. The mere thought of it made me feel ill."

Me, too. But all his worrying was a waste of time. The food was wonderful. He took the last bite and reached for his cup.

"I kept hoping you would come home in time, but the clock kept ticking and it got dark, and though I tried my best to keep my distress hidden, Mrs. Fuller sensed that I was upset and said she wished she could help."

And what business was it of hers?

"And that's when I blurted out, 'Would you?'"

Her cheeks turned pink. Her gaze dropped to the table. His irritation sputtered and drowned. He really had left her in an untenable situation.

"Mrs. Fuller thought I was worried about you, but when I explained it was dinner that concerned me, she agreed to help." Her teeth caught at her upper lip again. "I told her you would be happy to pay her. I'm sorry. I know I have no authority to do that, but I was desperate."

He nodded, took another swallow of coffee and focused on her words. "I'll pay her. But no more help from Mrs. Fuller." He didn't want the woman involved in his life. And he sure didn't want to be embroiled with his bride any more than necessary—it was dangerous. "Unless there's another emergency, I'll be here. You come to me."

"Very well."

She rose and gathered his dishes.

He clamped his mouth shut to keep from asking what she was doing, and watched in silence as she carried them to the sink and slipped them into the dishpan. She was *washing* them! Was that more of Mrs. Fuller's teach—

"I shall meet you here in the kitchen at dawn."

"What?" He stared at her over the rim of his cup, grappling with the twinge of unease seeing her being so...housewifely caused. "Why?"

"Mrs. Fuller made dough and put it in the fireplace oven for overnight. She was going to show me how to bake bread and rolls in the morning." She rinsed and dried his dishes, then glanced over her shoulder at him as she carried them to the large corner cupboard. "You *do* know how to bake bread?"

"No. That's not one of my...talents." He refilled his empty cup, thought about that ham. Mrs. Fuller was staying at his hotel only one more day. And if she baked as well as she cooked... He rose, carried the coffeepot to the stove to stay hot, and sniffed. He didn't smell any bread dough. He reached for the fireplace oven.

"Don't open that door, Garret!"

He halted, frowned as she hurried toward him. "Why not?"

"We only had wood enough to make a small fire, and the oven didn't get as warm as it should. But Mrs. Fuller said it should stay warm enough to make the dough proof—that means rise up—" she gave him a pleased look "—if the door stays closed tight."

"I see." He stepped back, leaned against the work-table and uttered words that somehow had the feeling of a trap. "I suppose Mrs. Fuller teaching you to bake bread will be all right. But that's all."

"As you wish. Good evening, Garret." She smiled and left the kitchen.

He watched her walk away, the short train of her skirt floating over the floor behind her, and had a sudden, intense wish to call her back, to talk with her and get to know her.

A dangerous inclination.

He scowled, drank his coffee and warmed himself by the fire until she retired for the night.

Chapter Seven

Garret frowned and shoved his chair away from his desk. The aroma of baking bread was everywhere, even his office, and it was wreaking havoc with his concentration. He kept thinking about a hot cup of coffee and a slice of that fresh-baked bread slathered with butter.

He blew out a breath, drummed his fingers on the chair arm. How much longer before Mrs. Fuller would leave the kitchen? Not even the lure of the bread and whatever smelled of cinnamon could tempt him to go to the kitchen with that woman in there. She looked about the age his mother would be—if she was even alive. And he'd been reminded of his mother enough yesterday. Every time he'd seen Ivy Karl sitting outside that tunnel, waiting and praying for her child to be alive and safe, he'd remembered how his mother had deserted him, and the anger and resentment had stirred and boiled to the surface.

What sort of woman walked away and left her child behind? Or betrayed her husband? He'd vowed way back when he was ten years old that he would never give a woman the opportunity to do that to him. And now, eighteen years later, he had been forced to place himself in that position. *Marriage!* He'd been a fool to sign that contract!

His face tightened. He glanced at the clock: twelve minutes until six. He couldn't delay starting breakfast much longer. He rose, stretched the kinks from his abused muscles and crossed to the door that opened onto the lobby. There was no sign of Mr. Anderson. The man must be a late sleeper. Still, Mr. Anderson didn't look the sort to miss any meals. He checked the key box for room number one. There was no note to wake the guest. Was that because Mr. Anderson wanted it that way? Or was it an oversight on Virginia's part when she'd registered him? He would have to find out. He couldn't have a guest missing a meal or a train connection because of their error.

Virginia. He scrubbed his hand over the back of his stiff neck and strode into the dining room to feed the fire and light the oil lamps on his way to the kitchen. He wasn't eager to see his bride this morning. In spite of his physical exhaustion, she had caused him a good deal of tossing and turning before he could get to sleep last night. The image of her being all *housewifely* wouldn't leave his head. He didn't want a wife. But he was stuck with one for five years. Five *long* years—less two days.

He stopped by the hearth and stared. The oil lamp sconces on the paneled wall above the mantel were already lit. Golden light flowed over the two tables that cozied up to the warmth of the fireplace. The flickering flames of the fire cast a dancing reflection in the red-and-white dishes and pewter flatware set for the two guests. A tall pewter candlestick holding a white taper stood guard over a sugar bowl and creamer in the center of each table.

The kitchen doors swished open. "Thank you for showing me how to make the bread and rolls, Mrs. Fuller. Though I'm afraid I will never master—oh! You startled me, Garret. Good morning."

He pivoted, skimmed his gaze over Mrs. Fuller and fastened it on Virginia. His pulse jumped up a notch. The blue plaid gown she wore made her eyes brighter than ever. His sour mood worsened. If he had to be stuck with a wife, why couldn't she be an unattractive one? "Good morning."

"If you'll excuse me, I'll go freshen up for breakfast now, Virginia." Mrs. Fuller came to the tables, set the small dishes she carried on one of them and dipped her head in his direction. "Mr. Stevenson."

He looked up from eyeing the dishes of butter and preserves she'd put down, nodded and stepped aside. She hurried by him into the lobby.

"I'm so glad you said Mrs. Fuller could show me how to make the bread, Garret. I've had a piece and it's the best I've ever eaten. She puts potatoes in it!" Virginia glided up to the other table, set down matching dishes of butter and preserves and smiled up at him. "I'm certain you will be very pleased with it. I know Mr. Anderson will be pleased, as well." She gestured toward the tables. "Are these dishes suitable? I didn't know what you're cooking for breakfast for our guests, so I wasn't sure what to set out…other than a plate and cup and saucer."

"They'll need a bowl for oatmeal. And also, a small dish of molasses to spoon over it or spread on their bread." He looked away from the enticing curve of her mouth and strode toward the kitchen. "Did you ask Mr. Anderson if he wanted to be awakened in time for breakfast?"

"Yes. He said there was no need, that his stomach was his clock." A soft laugh escaped her.

He gritted his teeth, shoved open one of the double doors and held it for her. She smiled her thanks and walked to the dish cupboard, her long curls bouncing, the fabric of her gown rustling. He grabbed a pan from a shelf and carried it to the sink, ran some water in it and turned to the worktable. She set a cup before him, held the coffeepot poised over it. "Would you like a cup of coffee to drink while you're cooking?"

The steam carried the aroma to his nose. His mouth watered. He'd *kill* for a cup of coffee, but not from her hand. That was too…cozy. "I'll wait. I'm going to be busy now."

"Of course." She put the coffeepot back on the stove.

He glared at his empty cup, pushed it aside.

"Is the molasses in the pantry?"

"A small keg of it, yes. But I keep some handy here on the table." He pointed toward a crock among a cluster of them at the end of the worktable, then grabbed another and scooped dry oatmeal into the pan of water, added some salt.

"How do you know how much oatmeal to cook?"

She leaned forward and peered into the pan, her curls mere inches below his nose.

He jerked back. "I make it almost every morning for breakfast."

"Did you put in extra for Mr. Anderson?" She smiled up at him. "He has a healthy appetite, judging by the supper he ate last night."

Her nearness made his pulse pound. "There'll be enough." *Would there be?* He scowled down at the pan. He should have spent more time with the cook at his hotel in New York City. He added more oatmeal and water, then turned to check the fire in the stove. It was burning slow. He opened the damper to make it burn hot, shoved the oatmeal pan toward the back and stalked to the refrigerator. She was slicing bread onto napkin-covered plates when he returned to the table. Molasses gleamed like dark shiny pools in two small red-and-white bowls sitting on saucers with sugar spoons beside them. She might not be able to cook, but she knew how to serve the food in an attractive manner.

The clock chimed the hour. He unwrapped the slab of bacon, sliced thick rashers onto the cast-iron griddle and placed it on the stove. The oatmeal was boiling. He gave it a stir and shoved it farther back to simmer before going to the pantry and grabbing the bowl of eggs.

There was a scraping of chairs and muted voices from the dining room.

Virginia pulled the napkins up over the bread and slid the plates on the tray beside the bowls. "I'll be back for the food." She grabbed the coffeepot with a padded holder and headed for the dining room. He told himself not to look, but his obstinate gaze locked on her, followed her to the door.

The bacon sizzled on the griddle. He turned to tend it, slid the griddle toward the side, then cracked eggs into a large bowl. He added a bit of salt and pepper and stirred.

The door swished open. He frowned, but kept his gaze fastened on the bowl in his hand. Her soft footsteps approached, stopped. The coffeepot clinked against the stove.

"I told our guests they were having oatmeal and bacon for breakfast." Her skirts rustled as she turned back to the table. "What is that you're making?"

"Eggs."

"Eggs?" She leaned over to peer in the bowl. "Why do you make them all frothy? I've never had them like that."

"Your cook could probably fry eggs without breaking them. I can't. So I break them before I fry them."

"Oh. That's a clever solution." She laughed, picked up the tray holding the bread and molasses. "What do you call them?"

"Broken."

Her laughter died. She gazed at him a moment, then looked away. "That doesn't sound very appealing. I'll think of something."

The look on her face said clearly that she didn't deserve his surly attitude. And she was right. He scowled, picked up the fork and turned the bacon. She was only helping him—which was what he wanted. Just not in the same room. She was hard to ignore.

"I'll be back for the oatmeal."

That's what he was afraid of.

"Oh, bother!" Virginia set the rinsed dishpan in the sink and grabbed the towel.

"What's wrong?"

"I've splashed water all over me." She swiped the towel over the wet splotches on the front of her dress, looked toward the sitting room door and froze. Garret was wearing his jacket. "Are you leaving…again?"

"No. Mr. Anderson is on his way to the depot, and Mrs. Fuller is sitting by the lobby fire knitting, so I went to their empty rooms and gathered the ashes from their stoves to dump outside. Then I'll bring in coal to refill the bins in their rooms." Garret pulled on his gloves. "That towel won't help much. You'll dry faster if you stand in front of the fire."

A train whistle blasted through the predawn stillness.

"The 7:10 is late. Could be it's still storming up in the mountains." A frown drew Garret's dark eyebrows down. "I hope we don't get any bad weather today. I shoveled enough snow yesterday to last me all month."

She glanced toward the windows, but it was still too dark to determine the weather. She tossed the towel on the drying rack and went to stand in front of the fire.

"When your dress is dry, the bed in room number one needs to be made. I want the room ready for the next guest."

"All right." She was earning her way! Satisfaction as warm as the fire's caress swept through her. She was no longer helpless in her role of pretend wife and helpmate to Garret Stevenson—thanks to Mrs. Fuller's kindness. She would miss the older woman when she left tomorrow.

A sigh escaped her. She glanced toward the loaves of covered bread on the worktable. That lesson had not gone well. She could never make bread. At least not without a lot more instruction. Cooking and baking were hard, but she was determined to learn. She had hoped Mrs. Fuller would give her a few more lessons, but Garret did not want the woman in the kitchen.

The oil lamps on the back porch flared. She slanted a look that direction. He seemed to have taken an immediate dislike to Mrs. Fuller. And there seemed to be no reason, since the woman was so kind. She smoothed the dried front of her dress and started for the lobby, on her way to bedroom number one. Perhaps when Garret came in, she would ask him to reconsider. It would benefit him if she could learn to cook, even a little.

Boots stomped on the front porch. Oh, no. A new guest had arrived and the bed was unmade! She hurried from the sitting room into the lobby, stopped and stared at the people coming through the front door carrying valises. Why, there were a dozen or more! And some with children! And Garret was outside.

She took a deep breath, patted her hair and stepped forward. "Welcome to you all. May I help—why, Mr. Anderson! I thought you were leaving us today."

"So did I, Mrs. Stevenson, so did I." The portly man snatched his hat from his head with his free hand and frowned. "The snow is too deep in the mountains ahead. The train can't go forward till the engineer gets the word. They figure it will be tomorrow or the next day before they get the tracks cleared, so here I am." He smiled and held out his hand. There was a dollar and fifty cents in it. "You can just give me back the key to my room, and I'll get out of your way so you can register the rest of these fine people."

"Thank you, Mr. Anderson." She stepped behind the long desk and opened the register. "I'll just add another day to your previous visit. Here is your key."

She smiled at the next man standing in front of the desk. "May I help you, sir?"

The door to their sitting room opened. She met Garret's shocked gaze and smiled. "You were right about the snow in the higher mountains blocking the Union Pacific tracks. The train is to stay here in Whisper Creek until workers are able to clear the way forward. I was about to register those who wish to stay here meantime." She looked back at the young man in front of the desk. He put down the two valises he held and took a small child from the woman beside him. An older child pressed back against the woman's skirts.

"I'll take a room. And that Anderson fellow said that you serve breakfast until eight o'clock. I'd like to order breakfast for my family, please. My wife's not been well, and she needs food to get her strength back."

"I'll have breakfast for my family, too, please."

"Coffee would be just the thing…"

"I'll have breakfast, too."

The chorus of requests for breakfast grew. So did her panic. She shot a look at Garret.

He put down the bucket of coal he held, moved to

stand beside her and held up his hands. The chorus dropped to a murmur.

"Ladies and gentlemen, we will take care of you all as quickly as possible." A friendly grin warmed his face. "I know there's nothing like a good hot cup of coffee to make a situation look better. Now, those of you who want rooms, line up in front of the desk, please. You need to be registered before you have your breakfast."

What breakfast? Her stomach clenched.

"Those of you interested only in purchasing coffee or breakfast, please have a seat in our warm, comfortable dining room. It's through those doorways." He swung his arm to his left. "My wife will be with you as quickly as breakfast can be prepared."

She stiffened, caught her breath. What was he doing? She turned her back to the people and looked up at him, mouthed, *I can't—*

He gripped her shoulders and squeezed. "It's all right. I'll take care of the registering, dear." He leaned down, hissed, "Go and get Mrs. Fuller. Tell her you need help, and that I will pay her to cook breakfast for these people."

She looked into his eyes—he was not happy at being forced to ask for the woman's help. And it was her fault. She nodded, slipped out from behind the desk and hurried to Mrs. Fuller's room, his voice following her.

"Just sign here, sir. Your name and address, please. And then, if you and your family will have a seat here in the lobby, or if you wish breakfast, in our dining room, we will get the fire going in the stove to prepare your room for occupancy. It's a dollar and fifty cents per night. Or twenty-five cents more if you'd like one of our larger corner rooms with two beds."

"I'll take the corner room."

Beds! Who was going to make all those beds? She would be busy in the kitchen and she had to serve all those people, as well. Her stomach roiled. How could Garret be so calm? She fisted her hand and rapped on the door of bedroom number two. *Please, Lord, let Mrs. Fuller agree to help me again. Please!*

Garret grabbed a fork, the plate with his apple pandowdy on it, and left the room. Even sitting at the eating table by the back wall was too uncomfortable when Mrs. Fuller and his bride were in the kitchen. Just the sound of their voices made his anger rise and boil in his gut. It was unreasonable and unfair, but the feeling was there and too deep to be ignored. He left them to their chores, walked through the sitting room into the short hallway and entered his office.

Mrs. Fuller could cook. There was no denying that. Breakfast was a triumph over time and the grouchy, out-of-sorts people who had filtered into the dining room. The bread was perfection. And the bacon with eggs, and pancakes served alongside, had his guests asking for more. And how had she turned that pot of stew he'd started that morning for dinner into a delicious beef and vegetable soup that had served all their guests? It seemed impossible, but she'd done it. And the hash she'd made from tinned corned beef for supper! And the corn pudding. And…everything. The woman had made three excellent meals from the meager supplies he had on hand. It made his mouth water to think of what she could do with a full pantry and fresh meats. If only she were a man.

He flopped down in his chair, set the plate on his desk and took a bite of the pie. Flavors exploded in his mouth. He scowled, stabbed the fork back into the pie and ate another bite. It was as good as the first. So the woman could bake, too. He finished the pie, drummed his fingers on the desk. He desperately needed a cook. Today had proved that. And he'd looked in the kitchen often enough throughout the day to realize that while Virginia tried hard to learn, she just wasn't a cook. But she was wonderful in the dining room or behind the desk. She was very good at soothing the guests. And she could make beds.

He grinned at the memory of her flapping the sheets and blankets through the air, tucking them in with the corners neat and tight, then adding the pillows and quilts before running to the next room. He'd been hard-pressed to keep up with her while starting fires in the heating stoves.

And tomorrow would be another busy day. There had been no word from the railroad about the train moving on.

That was it, then. His grin died. He shoved his chair back, picked up his plate and headed for the kitchen. Like it or not, he would offer Mrs. Fuller the position of cook for his hotel. But people traveled for a reason. There was always a possibility that she would refuse.

For the sake of his business, he hoped she would ac-cept. For his peace of mind, he hoped she traveled on.

* * *

Garret scrubbed his hair dry, draped the towel over the rack and left the dressing room. He glanced at Virginia's bedroom door—then stopped and looked again. It was ajar. It had been closed tight when he'd gone to take his bath. He stepped close and listened, frowning at the silence. "Virginia, are you all right?" There was no answer.

He turned and hurried down the short hallway into the sitting room. She was standing on the hearth, looking down at the fire. Her hair, encircled by a ribbon at the nape of her neck, hung in a thick cluster of dark blond curls down the back of her purple dressing gown.

"You're up late."

She turned, met his gaze. "I couldn't sleep."

Neither would he...now. He should have gone to his room and let her fend for herself. "Are you overtired or sore? I know you worked hard helping with the cooking, serving our guests and making beds. It must have been exhausting for you."

"A little. But mostly I found it—" she frowned, tapped her chin with a piece of paper in her hand "—I don't know the exact word I want...perhaps...exhilarating."

"Exhilarating! Making beds?" He half snorted the words. She went as stiff as the poker hanging on the cast-iron hook on the fireplace behind her.

"I realize that for someone as talented and skilled as you, Mr. Stevenson, cooking or serving tables or making a bed seem common, mundane tasks. But for me, with my lack of skills, they are an accomplishment! And that, sir, is exhilarating!"

He looked into her beautiful blue eyes, now throwing angry sparks his way, and raked his fingers through his still damp hair. "I didn't mean to demean your accomplishments." *Best to get off that subject.* He gestured toward the paper in her hand. "Is that the list for me?"

"Yes. After supper, Mrs. Fuller and I made a menu for the coming week. And then we made a complete inspection of the pantry and refrigerators and cupboards and drawers as you instructed. We even looked in the crocks and baskets to be sure we didn't overlook anything. This is the list of provisions we will need. I waited to give it to you, as we'll need some of them to prepare breakfast in the morning." She held out the paper, slanted a look up at him. "I'm quite certain Mrs. Fuller was being frugal with your money. I added aprons to the list. Martha always wore an apron."

He nodded, glanced at the long list. "With the trains not moving, it may be hard to get some of these things in the quantities listed. Especially the fresh meats. I'll go to Latherop's store first thing tomorrow morning and get what I can." He shoved the list in his dressing gown pocket and scrubbed his hand across the back of his neck. His shoulders were tightening. "Mrs. Fuller will simply have to change the menu if I can't get the supplies."

"I'm sure she will do her best."

He wasn't. He let it alone.

"Why don't you like Mrs. Fuller, Garret? She's been very kind and helpful."

He glanced at her, skirted the truth with his answer.

"It's nothing personal. She puts me in mind of some-one I once knew."

"Someone you disliked?"

"Not then."

She studied him, sighed, lifted her hand and twisted the top button on her dressing gown back and forth. "I thought, when I came, that my stepping in to fulfill Millie's arrangement with you would help both of us out of our dire situations. It has helped me, but I seem to have made yours worse. I'm sorry that my lack of skills has forced you to employ someone you don't care to have around."

He shoved his hands in his pockets and looked down at the fire. "There's no need to apologize. I realized dur-ing the rush of guests this morning that it would be im-possible for one person to do all of the work required. I should not have put that burden on you." He fingered the list in his pocket, hoping he hadn't made another mis-take, though he'd had no choice. "Mrs. Fuller is a good cook. And her skills are helping me out of a very diffi-cult situation. I'm grateful she accepted my offer." The bitterness rose, tainted his words. "But she's a woman. I dislike having to wonder when she will walk away."

"But why—"

He gave her a look that said he didn't want to dis-cuss it, and walked over to wind the clock on the wall. "You're not without skills, Virginia. You have a natu-ral gift for putting people at ease, and that is a valuable asset in this business. One that can't be learned—like making beds." He put the key back and closed the glass over the clock face. "It's been a strange day without whistles blasting out the notice of a train's arrival or departure. And a busy one, with the eight rooms on the second floor all full. And it seems as if it may be the same tomorrow. We'd best get some rest." It was a mistake, one he knew would cost him sleep, but he turned and looked at her. She was smiling. "Good night, Virginia."

"Good night, Garret." She crossed the room and disappeared into the hallway.

Five years.

He sucked in air and went to bank the fire.

Chapter Eight

Virginia waited by the door, pulled it open at the thud of Garret's boot against it. Cold air rushed in, chilling her hands and face. Garret edged through the doorway into the kitchen. She shut the door, reached up and snatched the bulging burlap bag off the top of the barrel he carried. "Ugh!"

"Careful, that's heavy. You'd better put it down before you hurt yourself. I'll come and get it as soon as I put this flour with the rest of the stuff." He stomped his boots on the small rug and headed for the pantry.

"I'll manage." She took a firmer hold on the neck of the rough sack and followed him, the cans inside bumping against her knees. She willingly relinquished her hold when he grabbed the bag and swung it to the top of the barrel he'd shoved into the far corner.

"This is the last of it."

"I should hope." She glanced around, her gaze skipping from barrels to crates to overstuffed burlap bags. "There isn't room for anything more."

"That's good, because there's nothing much left to buy. I about cleaned out Blake's reserves. The back room at his store is almost empty."

"It must be. I'll help Mrs. Fuller put these supplies on the shelves when we have time." She hurried back and picked up her knife to finish dicing the potatoes Mrs. Fuller had peeled for breakfast. There was a steaming cup sitting at the end of the worktable. "What's this?"

The older woman glanced up from slicing ham into three large, cast-iron frying pans. "I thought perhaps Mr. Stevenson would welcome some hot coffee after being out in the cold."

"I'm sure he would." She looked over at Garret, caught a glimpse of a frown. He tugged off his hat and gloves, shoved them into his jacket pockets and came to the worktable, his boots thudding against the floor.

"Virginia told me you helped her plan a menu, Mrs. Fuller. But there are a few things I couldn't get. Mostly the fresh meat." He placed the list on the table and picked up the cup. "Blake is supposed to get in a supply this afternoon, but it's snowing, and the trains may be held up again today. I bought an extra ham, two more boxes of dried cod and some tinned stewed beef to take the place of the fresh meat. It was all Blake had on hand. I should have prepared better for an occasion like this." He blew on the coffee, took a swallow.

"It's difficult to plan when the number of people staying in your hotel changes from day to day, Mr. Stevenson." The older woman pushed the ham aside, scooped a dollop of lard from a can and began to grease two large crockery baking dishes. "I'm sure Mrs. Stevenson will adjust the menu accordingly."

"With your help, Mrs. Fuller. Oh!" She jumped back out of the way as a wet potato slipped from her fingers and dropped back into the bowl of water. "Did I splash you?" She glanced across the table. There were wet splotches on the bodice and right sleeve of Mrs. Fuller's plain green cotton dress. "I'm sorry."

"It's no matter, dear. This is an old dress." The women turned toward the stove and tugged at the wet fabric clinging to her forearm.

She stared at Mrs. Fuller's face. The woman was as gracious as ever, but there was an underlying stress in her voice. An image of the older woman's mended carpetbag flashed into her head. Mrs. Fuller could not have many dresses with her.

She glanced at Garret. "Were you able to get the aprons I asked for?"

He lowered his coffee, swallowed and nodded. "They're in one of these bags." He put his cup down and spread open the neck of one of the burlap sacks he'd set on the floor by the worktable.

"I'll help you look."

"No need. Here they are." Garret straightened, folded white fabric clutched in his hand.

"Oh, good! They should help. Thank you." She took the aprons, handed one to Mrs. Fuller and smiled. "This should protect your gowns from my clumsiness."

"Thank you, dear. But you're not clumsy. Wet potatoes are slippery. I've dropped more than a few in my day." Mrs. Fuller patted her on the arm, turned and shook out the apron.

The movement of the older woman's right hand was limited, though she did her best to hide the fact. She squelched an offer to help in order to spare Mrs. Fuller any embarrassment and held up her own apron. The fabric unfolded, the length cascading toward the floor. "Now, let's see…" She lifted a narrow strap, frowned.

"Like this…" Garret took the garment and held it by the straps. "Slide your arms through the holes, then turn around. It ties in the back."

Warmth stole into her cheeks. What a dolt he must think her. "I know that!" She slipped her arms through the straps, smoothed the bib, then reached behind her and fumbled for the apron strings. "Martha and Millie wore aprons…and I'm perfectly capable of—there!" She smiled in satisfaction, snatched another potato from the water and resumed her slicing and dicing.

"There what?"

She stopped her work and looked at him. "I beg your pardon?"

He gestured toward her waist. "You've tied your apron to your dress sash."

She glanced down. One side of the apron hung askew, and the waist of her gown was sagging. "Bother!" She flexed her fingers. They were covered with potato juice.

"Allow me."

He grabbed the free apron tie and drew her up short, stepped behind her. A chill slithered down her spine. The waist of her gown pulled taut, went tighter still. She peered over her shoulder, caught a glimpse of his frown. Had her ignorance angered him? Another chill slipped down her spine. Would the little acts of cruelty start now? "What's wrong?"

"You've got the ties tangled."

Heat from his fingers penetrated the light wool of her gown and made warm spots on her back. She sucked in her stomach and leaned forward to get away from them.

"Hold still. There! That's got it."

The waist of her gown relaxed. His hand slipped around her side, grabbed the dangling apron tie again and pulled it to her back. She caught and held her breath, then released it and stood quietly, suddenly mindful that while he was strong, his touch was gentle and respectful. Not at all like Emory Gladen's.

"Finished."

"Thank you." She picked up her knife, wishing she had time to go to her room and think. Garret Stevenson confused her.

The clock chimed the hour.

She glanced up at the sound of movement and found Garret looking at her, his gaze as warm as his fingers. He looked away, shrugged out of his jacket and ran his fingers through his hair. "It's time for me to start knocking on the doors of the guests who left requests for me to wake them. I hope I haven't ruined your plans or delayed things by not getting all the items you needed for your menu. But I have to know before I start waking the guests—will breakfast be ready on time?"

She looked across the table. "Mrs. Fuller?"

"It will be ready, Mr. Stevenson." The woman

coughed, lifted her apron skirt and wiped at her eyes. "Sorry…onions…"

"Mrs. Fuller, I was supposed to chop the onions this time!" She reached across the table for the diced onions. "You're too kind."

"An odd objection as that works out in your favor, Virginia." Garret started for the sitting room. "Make sure there is plenty of coffee."

"We will." She pulled her gaze from him and looked back across the table. Mrs. Fuller was cracking eggs into a bowl. "I've finished the onions. What do you want me to do now?"

"Mix the onions into the potatoes, then spread them in those baking dishes. I'll pour these eggs over them, and then we'll put them in the oven to bake."

She did as directed, then watched her mentor add salt and pepper and a little water to the eggs before picking up a fork and whipping them. She slid the filled baking dishes to the other side of the table so the woman wouldn't have to stretch out her arms to reach them. The golden froth poured over the vegetables, filled the spaces. "Garret makes eggs like that. He calls them 'broken.'"

The bowl jerked. Eggs spilled over the side of the dish onto the table. "I'm sorry, dear. That was clumsy of me."

"No bother, Mrs. Fuller." She wiped the dish and table, went and rinsed the cloth at the sink while Mrs. Fuller put the potatoes in the oven. "What's next?"

The older woman straightened, closed the oven door and adjusted the damper on the firebox. "I've only to make oatmeal, start the ham frying and slice bread. And make coffee. Four pots should be enough."

"Then, if you don't need me, I'll get started on setting the tables. I've butter, preserves and molasses to set out before the guests come to the dining room." She piled small bowls from the corner cupboard onto a tray, carried them to the worktable and reached for the crock of molasses.

He couldn't stop looking at her. He'd taken every opportunity throughout the day to watch his bride. Garret gave up any pretense of work, rose from his desk and went to stand in his office door. It wasn't only Virginia's beauty—though that took his breath away. It was her willingness to learn and to work. She'd sailed between the kitchen and dining room serving their guests today as if she'd been doing so for years. And in between meals, she'd switched back and forth from helping Mrs. Fuller in the kitchen to playing hostess to the guests. And everyone, from the oldest to the youngest, responded to her natural charm and graciousness. She'd entertained the snowbound, bored older children by organizing dominoes and jackstraws tournaments. She'd even tied a blue hair ribbon into a fancy bow for the winner. Her ease with their guests of all ages intrigued him. It was a definite asset in the hotel business.

And she was smart, seemed to have an intuitive mind for business. He'd noticed that the first night, when he'd explained to her that Whisper Creek was dependent on the train for their food supply. Her immediate response that he should buy a ranch to have his own source of food for the hotel was a good one. He'd been seriously considering it ever since. The deep snow and the stalled trains made it more sensible than ever.

He swept a glance over the people who remained in the lobby—Mr. Anderson, three young men and an elderly woman. The families had retired. Mr. Anderson and the woman were holding books, but had stopped reading to listen to Virginia play the piano. The young men simply sat and stared at her. Not that he blamed them. Still...

He scowled and moved out of the shadowed doorway to the desk, flipped open the register and pretended to look for something in it. The men glanced his way, stirred in their chairs. *Message received.* He hid a smile and looked back at Virginia. His gut tightened. She had an exquisite profile. She'd done something with her hair that held it in a pile of curls at the crown of her head, and it made her fine-boned features look even more delicate. And her neck, bent slightly forward as she played, a graceful curve revealing creamy skin between her high collar and her upswept hair...his fingers tingled to touch it—to find out if it was as soft and smooth as it looked.

The clock chimed.

The elderly woman rose, picked up her cane and poked the young man in the chair beside her. "Time I was in bed, Albert."

"Yes, Grandmother." The young man rose, took the woman's arm and helped her to the stairs.

Mr. Anderson yawned and got to his feet, walked to the hallway and disappeared.

Virginia stopped playing, lifted her hands from the keys and stood. The two young men left in the room bolted to their feet. She dipped her head. "Good night, gentlemen."

"Good night, Mrs. Stevenson."

She started toward the door to their sitting room, saw him standing behind the desk and smiled. "I didn't know you were still working, Garret. Would you like me to bring you a cup of coffee?"

Her smile shook him. "No need. I'm through here." He closed the ledger, opened the door and held it while she glided by. A hint of roses teased his nose.

He closed the door and followed her into the room, reminding himself that it was her graciousness and her ease with their guests that intrigued him. Nothing more.

Sleep wouldn't come. Virginia donned her dressing gown and slippers and looked out into the hall. The oil lamps were dimmed. She brushed her hair back over her shoulders and made her way to the sitting room. Flickering firelight lit her way to the kitchen. The yeasty smell of bread dough proofing greeted her.

She glanced around, turned up the wick on the oil lamp left burning over the worktable, and smiled. The kitchen had been completely foreign to her only a few days ago, and now it felt like home. She filled the teapot, opened the damper and added wood to the stove.

Had Garret been pleased with her work today? She hoped so. But it was hard to tell. He was smiling and friendly with the guests, but he was all business when he was around her or Mrs. Fuller.

She spooned tea in her cup and leaned back against the worktable to wait for the water to heat. Why was Garret so distrustful of women? What had he said the night she came—*betrayal comes easily to women*? Yes, that was it. And then last night, when she'd asked why he didn't like Mrs. Fuller, he'd said, *She's a woman. I dislike having to wonder when she will walk away.* Who had betrayed him? Who had—

She stiffened, jerked upright as the idea struck her. Had Garret been married before? Had his wife left him? Was that why he'd wanted a marriage in name only? Why he always seemed angry when he was around her? That seething anger kept her uneasy, wary. She kept waiting for it to surface in acts of cruelty. Like this morning. She'd been standing right here when he'd grabbed her apron and pulled her close. She had refused his help and tied it wrong. It had been the perfect opportunity for him to teach her to do as he said, and she'd thought...

She rubbed her shoulders, shuddered. When Emory Gladen was displeased with something she said or did, he would step up behind her, rest his hands on her shoulders and press his fingertips against her collarbones. And if she cried out, he would act contrite and claim it was his ardor that had made him grip her too hard.

She lifted the steaming teapot and filled her cup, then closed the stove damper back down for a slow burn. Helping her with her apron had been Garret's chance to exhibit his control over her, to exhibit his anger, but all he'd done was tie her apron strings. Gently.

She sighed, left her tea to steep and walked to the window to look out into the darkness. Even her father spoke harshly when he was angry with her. And though he'd never physically hurt her, he used the power of his purse to make her obey his wishes. She understood such behavior, knew how to respond. But Garret...

She shook her head, reached up and absently twisted a button on her dressing gown. Garret bewildered her. He truly had reason to be angry with her. He had been forced by circumstances to accept her as his bride in Millie's place. And then, through a series of disasters of her making, he had learned she had no housekeeping skills. Yet even though the anger was there whenever she was in his presence, he treated her gently and with respect.

Another sigh escaped her. She turned and walked back to the worktable, the hem of her dressing gown whispering softly over the polished wood floor. Today had gone well—thanks to Mrs. Fuller's kindness in teaching her. And tomorrow she would learn even more from the woman she was beginning to consider her friend.

"Thank You, Lord, that Garret overcame his reluctance and hired Mrs. Fuller. And please, Lord, help me to continue to learn the skills I need to be a good wife and helpmate to Garret Stevenson. Even if our marriage is only pretend."

She took a sip of tea, stared down into the clear brown liquid in her cup. Garret was wonderful with his guests, gracious and charming. And when he smiled...

She leaned back against the worktable and took another sip of the hot, comforting tea, letting the wish surface.

Perhaps one day he would smile at her.

Chapter Nine

"All of our guests are at breakfast in the dining room, Mr. Busby. Right this way."

Garret strode through the doorway, stopped and rang the bell he'd taken from the lobby desk. The clink of flatware against china and the murmur of voices stopped. "Ladies and gentleman, quiet please. Conductor Busby has an announcement."

The slender man in the black uniform standing beside him cleared his throat and stepped forward. "Ladies and gentlemen, the engineer has just learned that the Union Pacific tracks are clear ahead. Therefore, the train at the station will be leaving for parts south and west at eight thirty of the clock. I repeat, the train presently at the station will be leaving at eight thirty o'clock. If you wish to continue your journey, be on the train with your baggage at that time. Any latecomers will be left behind. That is all."

Silence fell, followed by the ring of flatware hitting against dishes and the scraping of chairs against the floor. Mothers implored their children to finish eating. Dresses rustled and boots thudded as people headed for the lobby, on their way to their rooms.

The conductor stepped back and gave a brief nod. "Thank you, Mr. Stevenson. I wish I had time to have some of whatever smells so good."

He smiled and ushered the man back to the front door, out of the way of the rushing guests. "Come by the next time your train stops at Whisper Creek, Conductor Busby. I'll give you a serving of whatever our dessert is that day." He pulled open the front door.

"I'll do that, sir." The conductor hurried across the porch and down the steps.

He closed the door and turned. Mr. Anderson stood in front of the desk with his valise in his hand. He hurried behind the desk, checked the man's account and accepted the room key.

"I've enjoyed my stay at your establishment, Mr. Stevenson. Splendid food. Splendid! My compliments to your missus." The portly man slapped his hat on his head and walked to the door. "I'll be stopping with you whenever my travels bring me by Whisper Creek. And I shall tell my colleagues of your fine accommodations."

"I'll look forward to your next stay, Mr. Anderson." He slipped the key in the proper box on the wall behind him and turned back. "Ah, Mr. Holmes—" he shifted his gaze to the elderly woman leaning on her cane "—and Mrs. Holmes." He flipped the register to the right page and checked their account: two rooms, an extra blanket.

"I must echo Mr. Anderson's sentiments, Mr. Stevenson. You have created a fine establishment here in this *uncivilized* territory. The food and service is most satisfactory."

"Thank you, Mrs. Holmes." He smiled and accepted their keys.

The woman stuck her nose into the air. "I shall tell any of my friends who are forced to travel through this remote area that they must take the opportunity to stay in your excellent hotel."

"That's very kind of you." He looked away. The lengthening line allowed him no time to chat. "I believe you are next, Mr. Moore." The woman held her ground.

"Grandmother, it's time to leave. Mr. Stevenson has other guests to serve."

The woman glared. "I've paid my money and I'll have my say!"

The clock chimed. *Eight o'clock!* How would he ever—the faint scent of roses floated to him. *Virginia.* He watched her glide up to the robust woman, touch her arm and smile.

"I know you are in a rush to claim a seat of your choosing on the train, Mrs. Holmes—the good ones are taken so quickly. But I wanted to tell you how much we have enjoyed having you as our guest. Please come again."

"I hope to never see this *wilderness* again, Mrs. Stevenson. Now, if you will excuse me…stop dillydallying, Albert! I want a seat close to the heating stove." The woman's cane clicked against the floor as she hurried across the room, her grandson following with their bags.

Virginia turned toward the desk. He shot her a look

of gratitude, then returned to business. "Thank you, Mr. Moore. Come again." He accepted the man's key and turned, bumping against Virginia as she stepped between him and the cupboard. He froze, unwilling to lean over her to reach the box. She was already too close for his comfort. "What—"

"The departures might go faster if you handle the accounts and I take care of the keys." Her soft fingers brushed against his clenched hand. "What room number?"

"Five." He turned to check the next account, felt her arm brush against his as she came to stand beside him. He shifted his position. "Thank you, Mr. and Mrs. Bradley. I hope you have enjoyed your stay with us. Mrs. Stevenson will take your key." The name came quite easily to his tongue, brought warmth to his chest. He frowned, stole a glance at her standing beside him, then turned to the next guest. "Mr. Edwards…"

The line moved smoothly and swiftly. The clock ticked, the minute hand jerking forward. He glanced up at it. Five minutes until the train left. And one family remained. They would never make it. Footsteps pounded on the stairs. The young husband rushed up to the desk.

"My wife needs a doctor! Is there one in this town?"

"Yes. A very good doctor. You'll find him two doors down."

"Thank you." The young man pivoted, ran for the door.

"Mr. Tanner—" he hurried from behind the desk "—you stay with your wife. I'll go for the doctor."

* * *

Virginia jiggled the toddler on her hip and looked out the back window. There was no sign of Garret and the other men of the town who were shoveling out the service road that ran in back of the stores. Had they reached the depot yet? She glanced at the toddler and smiled. "See the snow, Wally?"

The toddler squirmed, pointed a pudgy finger at the window. "Me play."

"Not now, Wally. Perhaps when your papa comes to get you."

The toddler's lower lip pouted out, trembled. Tears welled into his big brown eyes. "Want M-Mama."

She cuddled him close. "Shh, don't cry, Wally. You'll see your mama soon." *Please, Lord.* She turned and looked at Mrs. Fuller. "What should I do?"

"Mama gives him a toy when he fusses."

She shifted her gaze to the five-year-old putting her doll to bed in a chair on the hearth. "Thank you, Rachel, that's a good idea. A toy..." She glanced around the kitchen, looked again at Mrs. Fuller.

"Wooden spoons work well." The older woman smiled and added a bit of water to the soup she was making for dinner. "Little ones like to chew on them and beat on things with them."

"Beat on things?"

"Pans and such." The woman stilled, then grabbed a bowl from the pile sitting on the worktable and scooped flour into it from the large crock on the bottom shelf. "Anything that is handy will do. They're not particular. A wooden bowl is good. It's not as noisy as a pan."

"It sounds as if you've had experience, Mrs. Fuller." She hurried across the room and pulled a wooden spoon from the crock on the worktable. "Have you chi—"

"Mine!" Wally grabbed the spoon in his chubby little hand, drew it to his mouth.

The older woman tossed some raisins into the flour. "You don't get to be my age without having experience at most everything."

"I suppose—oh!" She jerked her head back out of the way of the wildly waving spoon, grabbed a small wooden bowl and lowered the toddler to the floor. "Here, bang on this bowl, Wally." The toddler plopped down on his well-padded bottom and banged away. She looked at Mrs. Fuller and grinned. "It worked. Do you think he will be all right here? I haven't had a chance to clear the dining room tables."

"I'll see to Wally. It's one of my chores at home. He's good most of the time."

"Oh. Well, thank you, Rachel." She smiled down at the little girl, who came and sat on the floor by her toddler brother, her dolly cuddled against her shoulder. She looked back at Mrs. Fuller.

"We'll be fine, dear."

She nodded, grabbed a tray and a bucket and hurried to the dining room, her steps accompanied by Wally's enthusiastic banging.

The fire was dying. She added a couple logs, poked them into place, then hurried to clear the tables. The muted banging accompanied the rasp of the knife she used to scrape the uneaten food from the plates and bowls into the bucket. The clink of the dirty china being stacked on the tray added to the discordant tune. The thud of boots added a bass note. She paused in her work to listen. The footsteps were coming from the lobby. Was the doctor leaving?

She wiped her hands on her apron, patted her hair and started toward the doorway. It was Mr. Tanner. She stopped and stared at their guest's pale, taut face. "How is your wife, Mr. Tanner?"

"Not well, Mrs. Stevenson. The doctor is still with her. She—she lost the baby, and—" He stopped, shook his head.

Her stomach flopped.

"I came to check on the children, to ask if they might stay down here with you for a bit longer. I want to stay upstairs close to my wife in case—"

Her throat tightened at the man's fear. She forced out words. "Of course the children may stay with me. Don't give them another thought, Mr. Tanner. You go back to your wife. And, as my husband said, use whatever linens you need. If the doctor needs anything you cannot find in the linen wardrobe or dressing room, you've only to ask."

"Thank you, Mrs. Stevenson. I brought some diapers for Wally." He handed her a small valise and hurried back into the lobby.

She listened to his footsteps running up the stairs and to the muted banging from the kitchen. Tears welled into her eyes. "Please, Lord, help the doctor to save Mrs. Tanner. Please restore her to her husband and children. Wally and Rachel are so young. Please heal their mother for their sake. Amen."

* * *

"Now you pin the diaper."

Virginia shook her head and backed away from her bed. "You do it, Mrs. Fuller. My hands are shaking, and he's wiggling. I might prick him with the pin."

"No, you won't, dear. Just slide the fingers of one hand between his skin and the diaper, push the pin into place, and then you have both hands free to fasten it."

"Well…hold still, Wally." She took a deep breath and slipped her hands in place. "I did it!"

Mrs. Fuller smiled and nodded. "You can carry on from here. I have cookies ready to come out of the oven."

"I'm going with you, Mrs. Fuller!" Rachel scooched to the edge of the bed and dropped over the side, holding her dolly by one arm.

"Very well, come along." The older woman held out her hand. "But mind you, I expect you to help me make the next tray of cookies."

Rachel took hold of Mrs. Fuller's offered hand and skipped out the door beside her. "I'll help. I *want* to. How come your hand looks funny?"

The words floated into the bedroom from the hallway. She caught her breath at Rachel's question, tipped her head toward the hallway and strained to hear the answer. She'd wondered about Mrs. Fuller's hand herself.

"I hurt it a long, long time ago."

"Sissy…" Wally stretched a pudgy hand out toward the hallway.

"Yes, Rachel is your sister. And I'm Virginia. Can you say Virginia?"

"Gin…" The toddler yawned and rubbed at his eyes. "Gin…"

She smiled at the way his little mouth puckered, then finished buttoning on his soaker and lifted him into her arms. "That's not a very flattering name, young man." She carried him back to the kitchen, put him in the high chair she had brought in from the clean dining room and gave him the wooden spoon. There were dishes on the table. "What's this?"

"Wally looked about ready for a nap, so I ladled out some soup to cool for him." Mrs. Fuller looked up from the cookie dough Rachel was dropping on a tray. "He's a might young to be eating by himself, so you'll likely have to feed him."

Her stomach clenched. "Mrs. Fuller, I've never fed a child. Why don't you—"

"There's nothing to it. You just spoon in the soup. He'll take care of the rest."

"But—"

"If you give him that piece of bread and butter to hold, it will keep him occupied while you feed him. And it's a lot less dangerous than that wooden spoon."

"I'm done, Mrs. Fuller." Rachel dropped the spoon she held back in the bowl. "Can I put the cookies in the oven?"

"Not until you grow up a bit more, Rachel. Your arms are too short. You'd burn yourself. But I need you to watch the clock and tell me when…um…eight minutes have gone by."

Mrs. Fuller was obviously finished with their conversation about feeding Wally. Virginia looked back at the dishes, sat and pulled Wally's high chair close. He dropped the spoon and made a grab for the bowl. "No, Wally, that's hot! Here, you can have this." She gave him a piece of the bread and butter, then picked up the spoon.

"Touch the soup to your lips to make sure it's not too hot for him to eat."

Her heart squeezed. It was the sort of everyday advice mothers passed on to their daughters. She glanced at Mrs. Fuller and nodded, smiled at Rachel standing on a chair by the worktable, staring intently at the clock, then turned back to Wally. A giggle bubbled up her throat. The toddler had butter all over his face. She wiped him off with a napkin, then offered him a spoonful of soup. He opened his mouth and leaned forward. She tipped the soup in and scooped up another spoonful. His little mouth opened again.

A train whistle blasted in the distance. The first train arrival since the snowstorm had stalled them.

"T'ain!" Wally wiggled and beat on the high chair tray with his pudgy, buttery hands.

The porch door opened. Cold air poured into the room, touched her face and neck and hands with its icy fingers. She shivered. The soup in the spoon rippled. She tipped it into Wally's opened mouth and looked up. Garret was staring at her. Her pulse skipped. "You've finished shoveling the road?"

"Just in time." He pulled off his gloves. "That train will be carrying the supplies and food this town needs to survive."

"Eight minutes, Mrs. Fuller!"

He yanked his gaze from hers, looked toward the worktable, then back, pulled off his hat and frowned. "What's all this?" There was an odd sound to his voice.

"Mrs. Fuller and Rachel are making cookies for today's dessert. And I'm feeding Wally his dinner before I put him down for a nap." She gave a soft laugh and fed the toddler another spoonful of soup. "I never expected this to be a part of my duties. It seems the hotel business is one of surprises."

"So it seems. What's wrong with the boy? Is he sick?"

"No, he's fine. Aren't you, Wally?" She gave him more soup, then looked up. "Why do you ask?"

"He's all shiny—like he's sweating or something."

"That's butter." She laughed and dipped her head toward Wally's pudgy, pint-sized hand clutching a piece of bread so hard bits of it stuck out between his little fingers. "You must be cold. Would you like a hot bowl of soup? Mrs. Fuller has made some for dinner."

He looked toward the older woman and shook his head. "I'll wait. I need to carry out the ashes from the heating stoves and close down the fires in the upstairs rooms. I imagine they'll be empty again for the most part—now that the trains are moving."

She studied his taut face. Was he upset because of the lack of custom, or because she'd not yet cleaned the used rooms? "I'll take care of the beds as soon as I put Wally down for his nap."

He nodded and strode into the sitting room.

She looked after him, then shrugged and gave Wally

another bite of soup. Rachel ran up to her and held out her hand.

"Here's a cookie for Wally when he's through with his soup, Mrs. Stevenson."

"Thank you, Rachel."

"Cookie!" The toddler leaned forward and grabbed for the cookie. The squashed piece of bread he'd been holding fell to the floor.

She picked up the bread and offered him more soup. He turned his head away.

"Cookie!" His feet drummed against the footrest.

Obviously, he would eat no more soup. She handed him the cookie, picked up the dishes and carried them to the sink. When she returned to the table the cookie was gone. She washed his chubby face and pudgy little hands with a clean dishcloth she'd rinsed in warm water, and lifted him from the chair. His head drooped against her shoulder. His eyes closed, and soft puffs of warm breath feathered against her neck as he drifted off to sleep.

She carried him to her bedroom, laid him on the bed she had pushed up against the wall at Mrs. Fuller's suggestion, placed the pillows on the outside edge and covered him with a blanket.

For a long moment she stood gazing at his sweet little face, then turned and left the room. She had work to do while he slept—just like a mother. An odd, empty feeling swept through her. Her steps faltered. She glanced back toward her bedroom, fighting the sting of tears.

What had she done? She would never be a mother.

Chapter Ten

The clock chimed the hour. Virginia rose and put the Bible back on the shelf. She could find no solace in reading the Scriptures tonight. The sense of family that had settled over her while caring for Wally and Rachel in the kitchen with Mrs. Fuller had brought a hunger to her heart that left her disquieted in a way she couldn't shake off. She sighed, ran her fingers through the curls dangling behind her ears and glanced toward the hallway. It was late. She should go to bed.

She started for her bedroom, paused and looked at her coat and hat hanging by the door to the lobby. Perhaps a walk would help. Both her situation and the deep snow had kept her indoors since she had walked with Garret to the church to get married on the night of her arrival. She glanced at the sliver of light showing beneath his office door. Was it truly only a few days ago she had become his bride? So much had happened, and her days had been so full it seemed longer. Not that it mattered. They weren't really married. It was all a pretense. She'd never be truly married.

Tears stung the backs of her eyes. She grabbed her boots, sat in the chair by the door and took off her shoes. An image of Garret kneeling before her to remove her boots that first night flashed before her. He'd been thoughtful but grim. And then he'd grinned...

She closed her mind to thoughts of Garret's charm, buttoned on her boots, grabbed her garments and pushed through the sitting room door into the lobby. Fluffy snowflakes floated through the circles of light thrown by the oil lamps on the front porch. She donned her red velvet coat, freed her hair from inside the collar and tied on the matching hat. A couple of quick tugs, and she'd pulled on her black leather gloves.

She opened the door and stepped out onto the front porch. The hush of the night closed around her. There was no hustle and bustle and noise of city life here. Small gray clouds of breath formed in front of her face, then drifted away. The cold nipped at her face and neck. It was like a winter evening at home in New York.

No, not home. Not anymore. She lived here now. She didn't have a home. A home meant family, people you loved who cared about you. Her throat constricted. Tears made icy streaks on her cheeks. She wiped them away and strolled across the porch and down the steps to the walkway Garret had shoveled to the station road. A quick look around gave her her bearings. Small blotches of yellow glowed in the distance beyond the copse of pines on her right. That would be the train depot.

She straightened and stared into the darkness, arrested by a sudden thought—perhaps some of her restlessness was because the trains were running again. She had felt safe, hadn't given a thought to her father and Emory Gladen searching for her when there had been no way for them to reach her, even if they somehow discovered she had come to Whisper Creek. But now...

She shivered, pushed Emory Gladen from her thoughts. He frightened her. But not her father. Not any longer. Her father might be a stern man who seldom showed his feelings, but he did care about her— if only in a proprietorial way. And while she hated to lose her father's regard and the little affection he had shown her, his threats of disowning her no longer held power over her.

Her fear of being homeless was gone. She had a safe place to live, even if it was based on her deception. Garret might be angry about her coming to marry him in Millie's place, but he was a man of honor. He would live up to their agreement. And so would she. No matter the cost. And that was the last time she would think about her situation tonight!

She took a deep breath of the cold, bracing air, turned left and started down the road, the falling snow kissing her cheeks, the packed snow crunching beneath her boots. Moonlight bathed the buildings, overlaying them with silver. She stopped and read the sign that proclaimed the one beside the hotel to be Latherop's General Store, then lifted her gaze to the windows above the porch roof. Garret had mentioned that the proprietor and his wife lived above the store. Perhaps she would have an opportunity to meet Mrs. Latherop one day soon. She still had some of the allowance her father had given her the day she'd run off to board the train for Whisper Creek in Millie's stead.

She brushed snow from her shoulders and glanced back at the hotel. That rash decision had gotten her into this strange marriage that wasn't a marriage. But she'd had no choice. At least her guilt over her deception had faded a bit, thanks to Mrs. Fuller. The woman had taught her enough housekeeping skills that she was able to earn her way and live up to Garret's expectations when he'd sent the ticket and money to Millie for her journey to Wyoming. Except for the cooking.

An idea struck her, curved her lips into a soft smile. At the first opportunity, she would enlist Mrs. Latherop's help in buying Mrs. Fuller a thank-you gift... perhaps a lace collar to add a touch of elegance to her out-of-style worn dresses.

She blinked snowflakes from her eyelashes and continued down the road to the next store, considering various styles of lace collars and imagining Mrs. Fuller's pleasure. A single oil lamp burning in a window drew her attention. She scanned a display of various-sized bottles of different colors on a small stand and read the tasteful sign that announced the establishment to be an apothecary shop. *Two doors down.* This must be where the doctor—

"Virginia!"

Her name carried sharp and clear on the still, cold air. She turned. Garret was walking toward her, his long, confident strides eating up the distance between them. Her stomach fluttered. She stood and waited for him, told herself it was the anticipation of whatever message he was bringing her that caused her pulse to race. She blinked snow from her eyes and straightened when he came near. "Is there something wrong? Does Mrs. Tanner or the children need me?"

"No." He stopped and looked down at her, his eyes dark and unreadable in the moonlight. "I went to the sitting room to bank the fire and noticed your coat and hat were gone. When I checked the porch, you weren't there, so I came looking for you."

Her heart skipped. "And why would you do that?"

"Because it's not safe for you to be out at night on your own." He tugged his hat closer over his ears and looked off toward the mountains. "There are wolves and other animals in the area that are having a hard time finding food in this deep snow. I wouldn't want them to decide you would make a good supper."

"Oh." She stepped closer to him and glanced out into the darkness.

"What are you doing out here at this hour?"

"I wanted some fresh air, and I've been busy until now. And I've always liked snow." She tipped her head up and raised her gloved hands, catching some of the large, fluffy snowflakes drifting down out of the night sky. "Do you?"

"Do I what?"

He sounded irritated. Did he think her foolish? She lowered her hands. "Do you like snow?"

"As long as I don't have to shovel through a mountain of it."

She nodded, then shivered when snow fell off her

hat. She wiped the cold flakes from her cheeks and gave him a sideways look. "I guess that would make a difference in your outlook toward it. Have you heard how Pastor Karl's little girl—Minna, is it?—is faring?"

He reached up and brushed the rest of the snow from her hat. "As I understand it, her biggest problem is that the doctor insists she continue to rest by the stove and eat lots of nourishing soup." He lowered his hands to her back, shook the snow from her hair. She lost her breath. "Minna, of course, wants to play with her brother and sister."

She inhaled, coughed when the cold air hit her lungs. "I'm sure her mother is taking excellent care of her. It would be terrible to lose a child."

"Or a mother." He stepped back, shoved his hands in his jacket pockets.

There was something in his voice… She glanced at his taut face. Was he thinking of this morning? "Yes. I'm so glad that the doctor was able to save Mrs. Tanner. Wally and Rachel are so young. They need their mother." She stomped her cold feet, started walking again. "But I'm sure she must be sad to have lost her baby." She cleared a lump from her throat, stopped and looked at the raw lumber attached to the apothecary shop. "What is this new building?"

"That will be Dr. Warren's office and clinic when it's finished." He placed his hand at the small of her back. "We'll turn back here."

He lowered his hand to his side, and it brushed against hers. Hope rose, sudden and intense. Would he take hold of her hand? She kept her fingers still, waiting. He jammed his hand back into his jacket pocket and the foolish, unexplainable hope died.

"It was kind of you to watch the children for Mr. Tanner. You didn't have to do that."

"I'm glad I could help." She glanced up at him, confessed the truth. "I couldn't have done it without Mrs. Fuller. She told me what to do. I'm very thankful that you hired her."

"She's a good cook."

It was a statement of fact uttered in a tone as cold as the night. "She's much more than that. She's taught me so much that I can, at least, help you enough to pay you back for the ticket and money you meant for Millie to use. And to earn my way."

He caught hold of her shoulders, turned her toward him. "You do *not* have to pay me back or earn your way, Virginia. You're my wife. It's my duty to take care of you. As for Millie, she had entered an additional agreement with me to act as a maid and cook for a wage. I do not expect you to do the same."

You're my wife. Her heart pounded. If only she *were* his wife. His loved wife. Instead of merely a *duty*. She lowered her head lest he discern the turmoil of emotions his words stirred within her. Emotions that unsettled and confused her.

"Do you understand?"

"Yes. I understand." *What you are saying. Not what is in your eyes.*

He stood there a long moment looking down at her, his fingers working on her shoulders, and then he released his grip and stepped back. "We'd better go in now. Before you get cold."

She wasn't at all cold. She was warm from his touch and the look in his eyes. She nodded, and they started forward side by side. She looked at the road ahead and fought back tears. It was both too long and too short. Nothing was simple anymore.

Garret dumped a shovelful of coal into his heating stove, turned up the damper and scowled. It was too early to rise, but if he was going to be awake, he might as well be comfortable. He flopped back onto his bed and laced his fingers behind his head, the thoughts and images that had stolen his sleep throughout the night playing against the darkness. *Pay him back for using Millie's ticket...earn her way...*

The woman had no business being so upright! And beautiful. He'd almost kissed her. Had come within a hairbreadth of doing so. How could he not, with her face tipped up toward his and the moonlight shining on her while the snow fell all around? He was a man, after all. One who was running out of weapons.

He lurched to his feet and ran his hands through his hair. He couldn't even fault her for incompetence any longer. She was cleaning rooms and making beds, helping to cook and serving guests in the dining room, washing dishes, helping him at the desk, caring for children...

His chest constricted. He strode to the window, gripped the frame and stared into the night, his stomach knotting. He didn't want a wife. He didn't want a family. He'd decided long ago that he wasn't going to father a child so its mother could abandon it and crush its heart! But when he'd come into the kitchen this morning and seen Virginia sitting there at the table feeding that toddler, for an instant—a wild, irrational instant—he'd wanted... Ah, it didn't matter what he'd wanted! What mattered was that those moments of wanting the things he knew would lead him down a dangerous path were happening too often.

The muscle along his jaw twitched. He fought it, but the image of his best friend and business partner slumped on his desk, holding a pistol in his hand, swept into his head. He still found it hard to believe that Robert had taken his own life, but the bloodstained suicide note telling of Robert's wife's betrayal confirmed it. His shock and fury at such a tragic, wasteful end of his friend's life struck anew, reinforced his determination. He would not end up like Robert. He would not give any woman such power over him. And that included Virginia—no matter how drawn he was to her.

His clock chimed four o'clock. He shoved away from the window, shrugged into his wool vest and headed for the kitchen. There was no point in trying to get back to sleep now. What he needed was some coffee. He strode into the kitchen and stopped short, met Mrs. Fuller's startled gaze and barely held back a frown. He was in no mood to be in the woman's company, but it was too late to back away now. If he'd been paying attention, the glow from the oil lamps over the worktable would have warned him the woman was there. "Isn't it early for you to be up and working?"

"A little." She bowed her head and continued rolling out the dough on the table. "But it's been snowing quite heavily all night, so I thought I'd come and make another pan of cinnamon rolls to proof—just in case the early train was stalled again here at Whisper Creek." She put aside the roller and reached for the crock of butter. "And even it if isn't, some of the passengers may want to come and breakfast on a fresh sweet roll and a hot cup of coffee. Cold, stale food is not that satisfying on a winter's day."

"A good plan." It was. So why did it irritate him? "I won't get in your way." He turned to leave.

"Was it coffee you wanted? There's a pot ready. It would only take me a minute to stoke up the fire."

Something in her voice drew him back. "You go on with your work. I'll take care of the fire." He strode to the wood box, took out a few pieces and lifted the burner plate, stealing a look at Mrs. Fuller while he fed the fire. His mother had the same dark hair. If she was alive, would it be streaked with gray? Would she be shy and withdrawn as this woman was? She'd always been quiet and reserved.

Anger stirred deep. He didn't need to be wondering about the woman who had abandoned him. He pulled the pot forward to start the coffee brewing, determined to stay facing the stove, but something drew his gaze to the older woman. He watched her sprinkle the buttered dough with sugar and cinnamon and then roll it up into a log shape. With quick strokes, she sliced it into rolls, put them into a baking dish and covered them with a towel. Her crooked arm didn't seem to hinder her work.

"Pardon me, Mr. Stevenson, but I need to set these in the warming oven to proof."

He stepped back.

She moved to the front of the stove, opened the warming oven, and with an awkward twist to her shoulder raised the baking dish high enough to slide it inside. She closed the oven door and hurried back to the worktable, began to scrape the flour residue into the waste bucket. "Would you like some bread with your coffee, Mr. Stevenson? I made some apple butter."

"Apple butter! That's my favorite." He looked at her, but she was carrying the dirty dishes to the sink.

"How nice. I hope Mrs. Stevenson likes it."

Mrs. Stevenson. It didn't even jar him to hear it. But that fact jarred him to the bones.

Chapter Eleven

Virginia glanced at the clock ticking away the minutes, looked back at her few dresses in the wardrobe and sighed. She needed to make a decision. She'd already taken too long with her morning toilette. Her hand hovered over the cream-and-dove-gray-striped dress. It was the best one she had brought with her. The pointed bodice above the two-tiered full skirt fitted her small waist in a most flattering way. And—

No! That dress was for church and other social occasions. She was only being vain wanting to wear it this morning so Garret would see her at her best. He didn't care, anyway. He didn't find her attractive, or he would have tried to kiss her last night. Not that she would have let him! Still, he'd had the perfect opportunity. The image of him standing in the snow, holding her shoulders and looking down at her, flashed into her head, brought with it the sting of his indifference, the hurt of his rejection. She pushed it aside. It was the memory of that moment that had stolen her sleep last night. She'd stared into the dark and gone over and over it, wondering why…

Enough! She was glad Garret hadn't tried to kiss her. It would only complicate their pristine, in-name-only marriage. If one could even call it that.

She took a deep breath and fastened the waist of her quilted silk petticoat. What was wrong with her, anyway? It was foolishness to waste her time reliving the incident. She didn't want Garret to be attracted to her. It was only that her pride was hurt. It wasn't pleasant being…rebuffed.

She snatched her dark green wool dress with the ecru dots off its hook and slipped it on, puffed out the gathered fullness at the top of the sleeves and fastened the small buttons that closed the bodice. It was a nice, sensible dress.

Sensible…

Hmm. Perhaps if she looked older… She gazed into the mirror, removed the added ecru lace collar and cuffs, and ran her palms down over the wide pleats that flattened the front and left the fullness at the sides and back of the long skirt. That was better. Now, she had only to do her hair and she would be ready for the day.

She hurried to the dressing table, brushed her hair back and up to her crown, stopped and stared at her long, bouncy curls. They looked like a young girl's. She frowned, turned her head this way and that. There had to be some way to—her gaze lit on the dark green braid that formed the short stand-up collar on the dress. Of course! She divided her hair into three sections, braided them together into a loose coil at her crown and studied the effect in the mirror. Yes, she looked older with her curls contained by the braid. She hurried out into the hallway.

She glanced toward Garret's office. Was he there? Or in the lobby? Now that the snowstorm was over and the trains were running again, she needed to talk to him about her work—find out exactly what he wanted from her and establish a routine. She would be completely businesslike.

The smell of coffee brewing drifted through the sitting room. Was he in the kitchen? Her stomach fluttered at the thought of facing him. Warmth stole into her cheeks. Though why it should was beyond her. Nothing had happened between them last night. There was absolutely no reason for her to feel shy.

She squared her shoulders and walked into the kitchen. He wasn't there. She fought down a rush of what felt suspiciously like disappointment. "Good morning."

"Good morning, dear." Mrs. Fuller looked up from her work and smiled. The woman's hands stilled. "You've changed your hair."

"Yes." She lifted her apron off its hook on the pantry door and tied it on. "I'm sorry I'm late. But breakfast should not be so rushed today. The only guests we have are the Tanners."

"Unless some of the passengers on the morning train decide to come to the hotel for a hot breakfast." The older woman diced some cooked potatoes and placed them in a bowl. "Twenty minutes is not a very long time to enjoy a meal. But it's long enough for coffee and fresh bread and preserves. Or cinnamon rolls. Or pancakes with eggs."

She pulled up a smile. "And we have all of those things. Thanks to the trains bringing in supplies yesterday. Do you need me to do something?"

"No. The rolls are in the oven and I have everything ready to put on the stove when it's time. I only need to know how many to cook for. And if Mrs. Tanner wants anything special on her tray."

"I'll go to their room and ask her wishes when it's time." She shifted her gaze to the table in front of the windows along the back wall, thought of sharing breakfast with Garret that first morning.

This dining table is for the help—when I have some.

Well, he had help now. She went to the dish cupboard, gathered settings for three and put them in place. "Will you need a bowl for oatmeal, Mrs. Fuller?"

"Me?" The woman stared at her, looked down at the table and back up again. "You haven't set a place at the table for me?"

"Yes. This is where the help eat."

"But Mr. Stevenson—I can't—"

"That is his wish, Mrs. Fuller. And mine, also."

The woman stared at her, then turned and gathered the dirty dishes into a pile. "Very well."

She watched the older woman carry the dishes to the sink and slide them in a dishpan of soapy water. It was the first time she'd ever seen Mrs. Fuller look flustered.

The whistle sliced through the early morning darkness, quivered in the air. The train would pull into

Whisper Creek Station in five minutes. He was finishing just in time. Garret poured oil into the last lamp's small reservoir, lit the wick and replaced the glass chimney. The flame flickered. He turned the wick up a bit, waited until the lamp settled to a steady burn, then closed and latched the small, lead-framed glass door. That did it. All six of the lamps were filled and burning, the hotel's front porch bathed in their golden light. If any of the Union Pacific passengers were interested in having breakfast while the train was stopped at the station, they would be able to find their way.

He put the container of oil in its storage box at the end of the porch, took a deep breath of the cold, fresh air and went inside. It wasn't likely he would have any customers from the trains until daylight, when the passengers could see the hotel and read its sign, but it didn't hurt to be ready.

He wiped his boots and glanced toward the door to his living quarters. He was longing for a hot cup of coffee and some of those cinnamon rolls he'd smelled baking earlier. But it would have to wait. A lot of soldiers rode the trains, and quite a few of them came to town to buy chewing tobacco and other necessities at Latherop's General Store. Also Audrey Latherop's biscuits. But Dr. Warren had told Audrey to rest as much as possible while she carried her baby, and she'd stopped baking. Blake Latherop had told him he'd send the soldiers his way.

He lowered the chandelier over the desk, turned up the wicks and raised it back into place. Once those soldiers discovered his dining room was open for business and a few of them had tasted Mrs. Fuller's cooking and baking, his trade would grow. The soldiers would talk about Mrs. Fuller's good food with their fellow troopers while out on patrol. And that was for certain. Cavalrymen often ate jerky and hardtack. They seldom got a decent meal. Even at the forts.

Firelight flickered on the hearth. A log fell, sent sparks flying up the chimney. He grabbed the poker and shoved the log back into place, then straightened at the sound of voices coming from the dining room.

"I'll be back, Wally. And if you eat all of your oatmeal, and your papa says it's all right, I'll give you a big, sweet cinnamon roll."

Virginia. He tugged off his hat and ran his fingers through his hair.

"Me, too?"

"You, too, Rachel. As long as your papa gives his permission."

"Which you have, as long as I'm included, Mrs. Stevenson. Wally, stop that banging and eat. I want one of those rolls."

The soft tap of Virginia's footsteps approached the dining room doorway. He stiffened, listened—her long skirts rustled, the hems brushing against the floor. Why was she coming into the lobby? Did she have a problem? He took a breath, braced himself for the sight of her after last night. That moment in the snow hadn't seemed to affect her, but it had shaken him to his toes. He couldn't resist many more moments of temptation like that. He scowled and poked at the fire.

"Oh. Good morning, Garret." She paused, glanced at

his coat, with his hat sticking out of its pocket. "You've been outside already. Is it snowing again?"

What had she done to her hair? "No. I wasn't shoveling snow. I had to fill the porch lamps." He looked down at the towel-covered tray in her hands to keep from staring.

"I'm taking Mrs. Tanner her breakfast." She moved on toward the stairs, glanced back over her shoulder. "When you're ready to eat, I've a place set for you in the kitchen."

"Thank you. But it will have to wait until—" Two quick blasts of the train whistle drowned out his voice. He shrugged and lifted his hands. "—the train leaves."

She nodded and hurried up the stairs.

He dragged his gaze from her, stepped into their sitting room and hung up his coat and hat. The smell of coffee was inviting. And the scent of the cinnamon rolls tantalizing. He took a deep sniff, straightened his tie and shrugged into his suit coat.

The bell on the lobby desk rang. "Yo! Anyone here?"

A cavalryman. He grinned and went back to the lobby. "May I help you, Lieutenant?"

"The store owner next door told me I could get a quick, hot breakfast here."

"Indeed you can. It will be seven cents for coffee and bread and preserves, fifty cents for the complete meal, five cents for any added items." He looked up at Virginia, who was coming down the stairs, and motioned to her. "The lieutenant would like a hot breakfast—fast. He has to be aboard when the train leaves."

"Of course." She smiled at the cavalryman, who had

whipped off his hat. "If you will follow me, sir." She turned toward the dining room.

The lieutenant tossed a coin onto the desk and grinned. "My pleasure, Miss…"

His face went taut at the soldier's flirtatious tone. He scooped up the coin, clenched his fingers around it. "*Mrs.* Stevenson, Lieutenant." He dropped the coin in the till, watched the cavalryman follow Virginia through the dining room door, and listened to her voice floating back to the lobby.

"If you will take a seat here at the table by the fire, I will be right back with your breakfast."

The door opened. Two more soldiers entered, looked his way. "This where we can get a hot breakfast, fast?"

"It is." He repeated the prices.

The older soldier glanced at his watch. "Sixteen minutes. I can eat a horse in that length of time. Here's my fifty cents."

"And mine."

The coins hit the counter. He hurried around the desk. "Follow me, gentlemen." He led them to a table between the doors to the kitchen and the fireplace. "Have a seat, gentlemen. My wife will serve you in just a moment."

He caught Virginia's arm as she hurried into the room carrying a tray loaded with coffee and bread, a plate of corned beef hash, two eggs and a cinnamon roll. "These gentlemen will have meals, also."

She nodded, placed the lieutenant's meal on his table. The cavalryman leaned forward, sniffed at the roll and smiled. "I'll have another of these rolls, please."

"That will be another five cents, sir."

"And from the looks and smell of this roll, it will be money well spent." He dug a nickel out of his pocket, tossed it on the table and picked up his fork.

"I'll bring your extra roll as soon as I serve these other gentlemen their meals, sir." She turned toward the kitchen, holding the empty tray.

He caught her arm again. "Do you need me to help you?"

"No. I can manage—as long as the food holds out." Her blue eyes sparkled up at him. "I'll be serving these gentlemen our breakfasts." She grinned and hurried back to the kitchen.

Our. He clenched his jaw, stared at the swinging kitchen door.

The desk bell rang. He picked up the nickel from the lieutenant's table and hurried back to the lobby. Three soldiers stood by the desk. "How can I help you, gentlemen?"

"This where we can buy breakfast?"

He looked at the grizzled older trooper. "It is, Corporal." He glanced at the clock—ten minutes. "But I'm afraid there isn't time—"

A young trooper with a bloody bandage on his forearm stepped forward. "We'll take some hot coffee and bread, if you got it. We been out on patrol and—"

"Say no more. We'll be happy to serve you. That will be seven cents apiece." He held up his hand as they dug into their pockets. "You can pay me after you've been seated. That will give you a bit more time to eat. Follow me."

The influx of customers stopped. The clock ticked off the minutes. The train blew its whistle, and boot heels thudded against the floor as troopers raced from the dining room to the front door, all of them with cinnamon rolls clutched in their hands.

"You almost lost your cinnamon roll, too. There are only three left. Here is the money."

He turned and Virginia smiled at him. He held out his hand, and her soft fingers brushed against his palm, sent warmth shooting up his arm.

"There is hot coffee—if you have time for some." Her gaze fastened on his. "Mrs. Fuller and I would like to discuss some things with you before the next train comes."

He nodded, tossed the handful of nickels in the till and followed her to the dining room and on to the kitchen. "You wanted to speak with me, Mrs. Fuller?"

The woman looked up, then returned to slicing bacon into a cast-iron frying pan. "I'm sorry I don't have any hash left for your breakfast, Mr. Stevenson. I wasn't prepared to feed so many people. I'm wondering if it will be like that with every train? Should I plan on having to feed that many regularly? I don't want to disappoint you." She laid down her knife and wrapped paper around the bacon. "Are you ready for breakfast? Should I put the bacon over?"

He glanced at the three cinnamon rolls left in a baking dish on the table. He might not want to be around the woman, but she had questions he needed to answer, and his stomach demanded he stay.

"I'm ready to eat. As for running out of food, that

was my fault, not yours. Blake Latherop told me he would send some customers my way, but I had no idea how many to expect. I imagine it will be the same with all of the trains, now that the dining room is open. There may be more when the sun comes up and the passengers can read my sign." He grabbed a cup, strode to the stove and poured himself some coffee. "There's simply no way of knowing how many passengers are on a train, or how many of them might want a good, hot meal—though the short length of time will likely discourage most."

"Do you believe so?" Virginia came from the dining room carrying a tray loaded with dirty dishes. "People from the cities are accustomed to meeting friends for tea and a sweet while they are out shopping. And from what I saw this morning, soldiers will eat anytime and anywhere. And they *love* sweets. Every soldier bought at least one extra cinnamon roll. They took them with them so they wouldn't miss the train. There was a tremendous rush for the door when that train whistle blew."

"A stampede, to put it in cavalry parlance."

She laughed and unloaded the tray onto the sink cupboard. He grabbed one of the cinnamon rolls and took a bite to keep from staring at her. "Those soldiers weren't the only ones rushing."

"That's true. I was unprepared, as well. But I won't be the next time." She put down the tray and came to stand beside him. "It struck me, as I was running around, that if I set the four tables closest to the fireplace with cups and saucers, napkins and flatware, and bread plates along with butter and preserves in the lull before the trains arrive, I will only have to carry plates of food and pour coffee or cider during the rush. I will be able to serve the patrons much faster. And every minute is important when they have so little time to eat their meal."

He nodded, his throat too constricted to chance speaking. How much she had changed. How willingly she had gone from a pampered rich daughter to a hard-working...wife. His stomach knotted.

"From what you say, I'd best get to cooking and baking as quick as I finish your breakfasts." Mrs. Fuller glanced up at him. "There are no more rolls for the soldiers to take with them, and it's too late to set the dough. Perhaps cookies..." The bacon sizzled. "This bacon will be ready in a minute. How do you want your eggs fixed, Mr. Stevenson?"

"Broken."

She nodded, grabbed a small bowl, broke eggs into it, added water and beat them with a fork.

"You know how to make 'broken' eggs?"

The older woman's hands stilled. "Mrs. Stevenson told me the other day." She cleared her throat, poured the beaten eggs into a frying pan and removed the pan of bacon from the stove. "Perhaps I should plan soups and stews for meals the next few days until we learn how many diners to expect. Cold as it is, there'll be no waste if I set any extra out on the porch to keep."

He finished the roll, took a swallow of coffee and nodded. "That's an excellent idea. And your rolls are excellent, too."

A look of pleasure swept over her face. "That's nice to hear. Eggs are done."

"Here are our plates." Virginia held out three plates and looked up at him, a challenge in her eyes.

He glanced over at the table set for three and winced inwardly. It was too cozy. But there was no getting out of sharing a meal with them this morning. It was too late to make an excuse, and they had business to discuss.

But this would be the last time. He'd make certain of that.

Chapter Twelve

Virginia slipped into her best dress, buttoned the pointed, waist-hugging bodice and straightened the scalloped edges on the sleeves and stand-up collar. It was a beautiful dress. The wool was so lightweight, the long, gathered top tier of the full skirt fell like cotton. She skimmed her gaze over the scalloped hems of the two tiers to make sure they were straight, then stood back and studied her reflection in the mirror. She'd lost a little weight due to all her hard work, and the dress fitted a little more loosely than the last time she'd had it on. A smile curved her lips. She ran her hands down the diagonal dove-gray stripes that joined in a V pattern at the centered buttons. They made her small waist look even smaller.

She turned and glanced over her shoulder, shook the skirt's top tier to make the fabric hang right, then lifted her gaze to her hair. Curls cascaded from the constraining gray velvet ribbon at the crown of her head to the middle of her back. She frowned, caught at her bottom lip with her teeth. She should brush them into an up-sweep. She would be meeting the people of Whisper Creek at church, and she wanted Garret to be proud of her. *Please, Lord...*

She hurried to the dressing table, removed the ribbon and brushed her curls up into a cluster and pinned them in place. The wide ribbon fastened under the curls insured they would not fall free.

There was a sharp rap on her door. "Virginia, are you ready? It's time to leave."

"I'm coming, Garret!" She slid hairpins on the underside of the bow to hold it in place, slipped a lace-edged handkerchief in her gray velvet reticule and hurried to open her bedroom door. "I'm ready."

He stared. Warmth crawled into her cheeks. She reached up to make sure her curls were still in place. "Is there something wrong?"

"Nothing you can do anything about." He growled the words under his breath, stepped back and walked down the hallway.

Now what did that mean? What had she done to make him angry? She sighed, closed her door and hurried after him.

He held out her coat. She slipped her arms in the sleeves, and he dropped it on her shoulders. He grabbed her hat off its peg and handed it to her. "Do you want your muff?"

"No. It will only be in my way at church."

He shrugged into his coat and opened the door to the lobby.

"Oh, my!" Mrs. Fuller smiled and set aside the Bible she was reading. "You look beautiful, Virginia. And you are quite handsome, Mr. Stevenson. You make a lovely couple."

"Thank you, Mrs. Fuller." *A lovely couple.* She glanced at Garret. He was looking at her. Warmth stole across her cheeks. She settled her hat on her head and tied the ribbons beneath her chin to hide a sudden swell of shyness.

"Well, I'd best go check on the stew I'm making for dinner." The older woman rose from the chair by the hearth. "Don't you be concerned about your guests, Mr. Stevenson. I'll listen for the bell and do my best to take care of them, have they a need."

He nodded, put on his hat and tugged on his gloves. "We'll be back before the next train comes. And I'll pay you extra for your help, Mrs. Fuller."

The woman paused in the dining room doorway. "There's no need of that, Mr. Stevenson. I'm pleased to be of help." Her soft words faded away with her footsteps.

"Until the day you leave."

Virginia caught her breath. The words were bitter and so quiet she wasn't sure she heard him right. She looked at Garret. He was staring at the empty dining room doorway, his face taut. *Lord, please heal whatever has hurt Garret. Please heal his heart, Lord.*

He turned and opened the door. Cold air swept into the room. "Shall we?"

She nodded and took hold of his offered arm.

"My text for today is taken from Matthew chapter five. Verse forty-eight says, 'Be ye therefore perfect, even as your Father which is in heaven is perfect.'"

Pastor Karl grasped the sides of the altar, looked out over the people in the church and smiled. "I figured I was safe in using this text, as I know most of you sitting here this morning, and I know you're not perfect."

"You are, Papa."

Ivy Karl gasped, leaned down and whispered to the small towheaded child sitting on the bench next to her.

Laughter burst from the congregation.

Garret chuckled, an infectious rumble from deep inside him that she could almost feel. Virginia looked up at him, caught her breath. His eyes were twinkling, his mouth slanted in a crooked grin. The hint of a dimple indented his cheek, as if someone had lightly touched him there with a fingertip. Hers twitched. How would it feel?

"Ah, out of the mouth of babes." The pastor laughed, then sobered and looked down at the first bench. "Don't speak out in church again, Nixie." He looked up and the laughter stopped. "To continue…the word that bothers me the most in this verse is that word *therefore*. It harks back to all of the previous verses. And if you read…"

Heat from Garret's arm warmed hers. He was perfectly still, but there was something about him that made her very aware of him. Everyone here thought he was her husband. What would that be like? Her chest tightened. The pastor's voice drifted into the background. She looked at Garret's hand resting on his thigh, so close to her own. If she shifted her position a bit…

Her stomach fluttered. She resisted the temptation, lifted her gaze to his face. He looked different. Rather…rakish, handsome and dangerous. The way he had looked when he was removing her boots that first night.

He looked down. He'd caught her staring at him! Heat flooded into her cheeks. She jerked her gaze forward.

"'—pray for them which despitefully use you.'" Pastor Karl swept his gaze over the people, rested it on her for a moment, then moved on. "This is a hard command to follow. Most of us want to get even if we are insulted or injured or otherwise mistreated."

Emory Gladen flashed into her mind. She hadn't wanted revenge. All she'd wanted was to escape him. And that had brought her to Whisper Creek to become Garret's wife—his *pretend* wife. But it didn't feel that way anymore. She felt as if she belonged to him.

Tears stung her eyes. Her throat closed. She loosened the drawstring, slipped her handkerchief out of her reticule and stole a sidelong glance at Garret from beneath her eyelashes. His face had that closed, taut look again. She bowed her head and surreptitiously dabbed at her eyes, held them wide to stop the flow of tears.

Lord, please help Garret. Heal his heart and make him happy, I pray. And please help me to be the best pretend wife he could have.

Garret shut his ledger and shoved away from his desk. It had been another prosperous day. People had to eat and sleep, even on Sunday. The dining room had been visited by passengers from every train that came to town until it closed. Mrs. Fuller had cooked delicious meals. And Virginia had been busy all day helping in the kitchen, serving the customers in the dining room, then cleaning up the tables and washing dishes between trains.

He wished she would complain. Her composure kept him off balance. He kept waiting for her to leave—to abandon him. To run off with one of those cavalrymen who flirted with her, though he'd never seen or heard her do anything but politely remind them she was married. But then, none of them could offer her a decent lifestyle. She might work hard here, but she had a comfortable place to live. Of course, if a wealthy man came along…

He lurched to his feet, shoved his hands in his pockets and paced around his office, the images he'd been warding off all day flooding his mind. The way she had looked when she opened her bedroom door that morning—he'd been hard-pressed not to take her in his arms and—

Stop it, Stevenson! Don't even think about it! He yanked his hand from his pocket and scrubbed the back of his neck. It had been torture sitting beside her in church, with her hand so close to his and that look in her eyes he didn't understand, but sure wanted to explore. It had been the longest morning of his life. He'd thought the pastor would never stop preaching! And then—

He had to get out of here—go outside where he could stretch his legs and breathe some cold air.

He strode to the sitting room, tugged on his boots and yanked his coat off its hook. "Virginia!" He jammed his arms into the coat sleeves and fastened the buttons.

"Yes?"

He glanced at her, standing in the kitchen doorway, wearing her apron and drying a plate. She'd let her hair down when she'd changed out of her church dress. He clenched his hands. "Are you still working?"

"We're almost finished. Mrs. Fuller is setting bread dough for tomorrow, and I'm finishing up the dishes." She glanced toward the windows, then back at him. "I see you're going out. Did you want me to get you the lantern?"

"No. The moonlight is sufficient. I only wanted you to know that I'm going out and will be back shortly."

"All right. I'll listen for the bell."

Her smile took him like a fist to the stomach. He frowned and hurried through the lobby to the front porch. It had started snowing in a desultory way. He trotted down the steps and started down the road, his long strides eating up the distance. The moonlight filtered through the tops of the towering pines at the foot of the surrounding mountains and glazed the snow with a silver sheen. Even with the falling snow, it was bright enough to see. He frowned, walked faster. He might as well turn all this excess energy into some purpose.

He left the road at the edge of the trees and followed a narrow path through the darkness beneath the overhanging branches to a small clearing. Flickering firelight beneath large laundry tubs led him to a patched canvas tent in front of a snow-covered shanty. Ah Cheng came forward to meet him.

"Meester Garret, welcome. Ah Cheng come see you tomorrow."

"You've found me a worker?"

The Chinese man bobbed his head. "Ah Cheng sister number three come tomorrow from bad house. Li Min be glad to get free. She learn fast. Work hard to no go back to bad men."

"That's good news, Ah Cheng. I will pay you for finding help for me when you bring her to the hotel tomorrow." *If she is able to get away from the man who is selling her services to the railroad workers.*

"That very good. Money help Ah Cheng bring family from China. Need to pay bad man much to let family come."

"Perhaps I can help you reach your goal. I don't want to endanger anyone, but have you any more…sisters who would like to come to work for me? My business has grown faster than I expected, and my wife needs more help than I anticipated."

"Ah Cheng will find. Tell Li Min. Maybe so she bring sister number four with her."

"All right. I'll see you tomorrow." He started to leave, then turned back. "Be careful, Ah Cheng. I don't want to be the cause of you or your wife or your sisters being hurt."

The Chinese man's black eyes glittered. He patted what was obviously the handle of a knife beneath his tunic. "Ah Cheng, get free bad man in China. No bad man hurt me here. You make good work for sisters, Meester Garret. You save them from hurt."

He dipped his head. "I'll see you tomorrow." He started back up the path, focusing on his conversation with Ah Cheng to hold thoughts of Virginia at bay. Maybe he'd get some sleep tonight.

The snowfall increased. He pulled up his collar and quickened his steps. The moonlight disappeared when he reached Blake Latherop's store. He focused on the blurred yellow blotches that were the oil lamps on the hotel porch and hurried toward them, bumped headlong into someone coming down the steps and sent both of them tumbling backward.

"Oof!"

"Virginia?" He grabbed her arm and helped her to the porch. "What are you doing out here?"

She pointed to a feeble yellow glow under the snow by the side of the steps. "I thought you might need a lantern."

"*You thought*—are you *daft*, woman! You were going to go out in this weather to bring me a lantern?" He leaned down and snatched it out of the snow to keep from shaking her. He put it down on the porch, stomped his feet, pulled off his gloves and used them to brush away the thick layer of snow clinging to her coat. "Look out there! No lantern would be seen in that thick a snowfall!" He dropped the gloves and shook out the snow trapped in her long curls. "You could have been lost or—"

"There's no need to yell." She stepped back, brushed snow from her skirts. "I can hear you perfectly well. It's like a cave in here. A *snow* cave." She leaned over the railing, stuck out her arms, then immediately pulled them back. Her hands and wrists were piled with snow. She brushed them off, looked at him with a mixture of wonder and fear in her eyes. "I've never seen anything like this. It's like a solid wall of snow. Thank the Lord you got home in time." Her soft voice quavered.

Home. He gritted his teeth, pulled off his hat and slapped it against his pant leg to keep from reaching for her. "We'd better—"

Light streaked through the deluge of snow. *Crack!*

"Oh!" She whirled, threw herself into his arms and buried her face against his chest, trembling.

He pulled her tight against him and cradled her head with his hand, his heart thudding, his pulse pounding.

Flash. *Crack!*

She jerked and pressed closer, tipped her head up and looked into his eyes. "What—"

"It's lightning."

"In a *snowstorm*?" Her eyes widened. "It can't be. Can it?"

Flicker, streak. Boom! The porch shook.

She all but crawled inside his coat. It was too much. He lowered his head, touched her lips with his, then claimed them. She stiffened, then clutched his coat and raised up on her toes. Her soft, warm lips yielded, parted beneath his inviting ones. The kiss sent a shock streaking through him greater than the lightning flashing through the snow. It rocked him to the center of his being, more powerful than the quivering in his chest from the claps of thunder. What had he done?

He set her away from him, cleared his throat. "I'm sorry, Virginia. I lost my head and my manners. I didn't mean to violate our agreement. Please forgive me. I assure you, it won't happen again."

She stared at him for a long moment, then swallowed and nodded. "It was my fault as much as yours, Garret. The storm..." She made a helpless little gesture, opened the door and walked into the hotel with her head held high.

Chapter Thirteen

"Now pull the sheet tight and tuck it beneath the end of the mattress. Fold the corner under like this, then smooth it out..." Virginia made a perfect corner, smiled at the memory of her first attempts at making a bed. "Now you do the same on the other side." She straightened and watched the Chinese woman follow her instructions, amused that she had become the teacher. It was such a short time ago that she had learned how to make a bed from Mrs. Fuller. How thankful she was for the older woman's friendship. "Very good, Liu Yang. Now, do the same with the cover sheet and blanket, but only tuck them in at the foot of the bed."

She moved to the window and opened the shutters. The sunshine had melted the clinging snow, and drops of water slid down the small panes of glass and dripped off the wood that framed them. She blinked at the bright light and looked out at the towering pines. The visible branches were bowed, many of them broken by the weight of the snow that clung to them. The large bottom branches were hidden beneath deep white drifts deposited by that strange thunder snowstorm. It had lasted only a few hours, but it had almost doubled the depth of the snow left by the blizzard.

Thank You, Lord, that Garret reached home just as the thunder snowstorm began. She wrapped her arms around herself, remembering what a close thing it had been. If he'd been caught out—

"What next, mee-sus?"

She turned from the window, pulling her thoughts back to the business at hand. "Put this on the pillow and place it at the head of the bed." She handed Liu Yang a pillow slip, then lifted a quilt from the chair. "And then spread this over the bed."

She glanced at the bedside table. "Do you know how to light an oil lamp?"

"Yes, mee-sus."

"Good." Her thoughts drifted back to the night of the thunder snowstorm. Garret had been furious when she'd told him she'd been going out in the storm to bring him a lantern. Surely that meant he cared for her at least a little.

She closed the shutters, skimmed her gaze over the Chinese woman's work and smiled. "The bed looks fine, Liu Yang. Now I want you to go to the wardrobe in the hall, get the linens you will need and make the bed in room number ten without my instruction. When you finish that, I will show you how to clean the dressing rooms."

She followed the Chinese woman into the hallway,

watched to be sure she chose the right linens, then waited by the door while Liu Yang made the next bed.

Boots thudded on the stairs. Garret came into view, carrying a bucket of coal. Her pulse quickened. She'd seen very little of him since he'd kissed her. Since she'd kissed him back. Warmth spread across her cheeks.

He walked over to her and stopped, looked down at her. "How is Liu Yang doing?"

"Fine." She smiled, grateful for the dim light in the hallway that hid her blush. "She's already learned how to make a bed."

"That's good." He shifted his grip on the pail, frowned. "Have you told her she's not to touch the heating stoves?"

"Yes. That's the first thing I told her." She looked down and smoothed the front of her long skirt to keep from staring at him. "It's good that the trains aren't running today. I have time to teach her the things she needs to know." She smiled and shook her head. "I keep thinking how strange it is that I am teaching her how to make beds and clean the dressing rooms. It was such a short time ago that I learned those things from Mrs. Fuller."

"When you teach, it's not important how long you have known something, but how well."

"That's kind of you, considering I almost burned your hotel down."

He grinned. "Why do you think I told you to tell Liu Yang not to touch the heating stoves?"

"Or stew?"

He chuckled.

Her stomach fluttered. "I don't remember that you

found the burned stew amusing. I was afraid you were going to throw me out."

"Things change."

The look in his eyes stole her breath. Her knees sagged. She groped behind her for the wall. "I—I was so surprised when Liu Yang and Li Min came, I didn't thank you properly for your thoughtfulness."

"No need. The business grew faster than I expected it would. It was obvious that you and Mrs. Fuller would soon be overwhelmed by the amount of work to be done. I don't need you or Mrs. Fuller to make beds or wash dishes. I need her to cook. And I need you to help me with the guests."

He *needed* her. She pressed her hand over a sudden flood of warmth in her chest. Her heart raced beneath her fingers.

"Virginia…" He put down the bucket, stepped closer.

"Bed done, mee-sus."

She drew in air.

He stepped back, picked up the bucket. "Sounds as if you're needed."

"Yes." It came out a whisper. She pushed against the wall until she was sure her legs would support her, then turned and walked into the bedroom.

What was he doing, flirting with her like that! Garret slammed out the door, stomped across the porch and down the steps to the path he'd shoveled across the service road and into the woods. He reached under a tree, dumped the bucket of ashes, threw the bucket up onto his back porch and strode up the road toward the railroad station. He'd lost his sense, that was what! Not to mention his self-control. He'd almost kissed her again! If Liu Yang hadn't called for her...

Fool! He scooped up a handful of snow, pressed it hard and pitched it at the broken branch of a tree. It hit with a satisfying smack. He stooped and made another snowball, drew back his arm.

"Garret!"

He shaded his eyes against the sun and looked up the road. Mitch Todd was walking behind a wooden apparatus about three feet high being pulled by a horse. Snow was flying to the right and left, away from the sides of the device.

He dropped the snowball and broke into a trot, dodged the flying snow and fell into step beside the sawmill owner. "You've got the snowplow finished. And we sure need it."

"That's what I thought." Mitch frowned and shook his head. "I need to make some changes to it. It bucks like a wild stallion, and skips over the snow instead of plowing through it. I think it needs to be heavier in the front."

He studied the snowplow bucking and jumping in front of them. "I think you're right." He ducked beneath the reins Mitch held and leaped onto the bottom boards, then moved to the front. The nose of the plow dug deeper and pushed more snow to the sides. He glanced over his shoulder at the narrow, smooth path cut into the drifts. He wiped moisture from his face and raised his voice. "It's working! But you'll need to make it wider and go deeper!"

Mitch nodded and urged the horse to a faster speed. "We'll go back over the same path again!"

The snowplow lurched. He took a firmer grip on the sides and splayed his legs to brace himself. He hadn't meant to volunteer to be ballast for Mitch, but with the trains not running, there was nothing pressing for him to do at the hotel, and it would keep him from thinking about Virginia. He blew out a breath, blinked snow from his eyes. If she looked at him again with that soft, warm glow in her eyes—

The snowplow pitched. He slammed into the wooden side, righted himself and focused on staying upright.

A train whistle blew. He glanced toward the depot. Must be the Union Pacific workers had shoveled their tracks clear. He'd have a little more than five minutes to get ready for guests. He motioned to Mitch to stop.

"Whoa…"

He hopped off the plow, sank to his knees in the snow. "Let me know how much I owe you for the plow, Mitch."

"When it's right." Mitch shortened his grip on the reins, stepped on the cross boards and clicked his tongue. The horse trotted off.

Garret ran up the steps to the porch, brushed the snow from his pants and jacket and went inside. Movement caught his attention. He looked into the dining room. Virginia was setting the four tables closest to the fireplace. She looked up. Her lips curved and soft laughter, musical as a rippling brook, issued from her. His stomach clenched.

"You look like a *snowman*." She lifted the last dishes

of butter and preserves from the tray to the fourth table. "I heard the train whistle and thought I'd get ready for the rush. Do you want me to take care of the desk while you put on some dry clothes?"

"That won't be necessary. My shirt is dry. I'll just put on my suit coat."

Her smile faded. She nodded and walked toward the kitchen, her dress rustling softly, her long curls swaying with her movements.

He pulled his gaze from her, frowned and hurried to the sitting room, swapped his coats and put on his tie. He hadn't meant to sound so brusque, but things were getting too...*close* between them. Robert's wife had been sweet and warm and loving, until she ran off with another man. He had to maintain his distance from Virginia—stay safe.

He pulled off his hat and ran his fingers through his hair. He never should have accepted her in Millie Rourk's place. He should have sent her on her way and told John Ferndale his intended bride had betrayed him. It was the truth. Ferndale would likely have given him more time. Now he was entangled in an in-name-only marriage with a woman who could be his undoing. If he let her.

He shoved open the door to the lobby and strode to the hearth. The fire chased the chill from his body. Yet the cold in his heart remained. He added a couple logs and poked them into place, turned to dry his pants.

The door opened and four soldiers entered, stomped their boots. A sergeant looked his way. "I know it's not mealtime, but can we get somethin' hot to eat fast? We got fifteen minutes till the train leaves."

"Right this way, gentlemen." He led them to the dining room. "We've got hot coffee, and bread with butter and preserves. Or a doughnut. Or apple pie. It'll cost you seven cents. Five cents for any extras."

"Well, at least the coffee is hot. And anything will be good after helpin' to shovel that pass clear for two days. I'll have pie." The soldier beside him fished coins from his pocket, grabbed a chair and pulled it back from the table. The others chorused agreement and tossed their money into a pile on the table.

Virginia came from the kitchen carrying a coffeepot.

He motioned her to the table. "My wife will serve you, gentlemen."

The soldiers whipped off their hats, stared.

"These men have all ordered pie, Virginia. But they've been helping to shovel out the pass so the trains can run, and would like something hot to eat. If there is soup left from dinner, please bring them each a bowl. And there will be no charge. Put your money away, gentlemen. I appreciate your service in getting the trains moving again."

The front door opened again. He hurried to the doorway, motioned to the soldiers filing into the lobby. "Come in and have a seat, gentlemen." He led them to the prepared tables. "My wife will serve you as quickly as possible."

The bell at the desk rang, and he rushed to the lobby. The conductor and engineer stood there, along with a host of passengers behind them. The conductor smiled.

"Good afternoon, Mr. Stevenson. I've come for that promised dessert, and a good hot cup of coffee to go with it. Jim here came along."

The engineer nodded, scrubbed a hand over his scruffy beard. "I've heard about the good food served here. Been wantin' to come and try some, but never have time." The beard divided to show the engineer's teeth in a smile. "Train followin' me is runnin' late, so I got time today."

"Well, I'm glad you could make it, gentlemen. Please come into the dining room and have a seat. You will be served as quickly as possible." He shifted his gaze to the cluster of passengers. "That goes for any of you, as well. Unless you wish to register for a room."

The people filed into the dining room. The tables filled rapidly. He watched Virginia glide from table to table, greeting the patrons and pouring coffee, then hurrying back and forth to the kitchen for food. She made it look effortless.

Ding! Ding! Ding! "What must one do to get some service in this establishment?"

Garret turned, eyed the older man standing at the desk. There were two expensive leather valises on the floor beside his polished boots. "I'm sorry for the delay, sir." He pasted on a polite smile and strode across the room, took his place of authority behind the desk. "How may I help you?"

"I'd like a room, obviously. The best you have." The man pulled off his gray leather gloves. "I *assume* you wish me to register?"

What he *wished* was to escort the arrogant man out

the door. But he kept the smile in place. "I do." He turned the ledger toward the man and slid the pewter pen and ink holder forward. "The charge will be one and one half dollars per night—in advance. You will share a dressing room with the guests in numbers seven, eight and nine, should they become occupied. The three daily meals are included in the cost, but there will be an additional charge for any extra food ordered, or any other visits to the dining room. Also, for any other items or services requested."

"Rooms seven, eight and nine are not presently occupied?"

"That's correct."

"Excellent! I would like it stay to that way. Put the charges for those rooms on my tab, as well. I shall be staying for three days." The man pulled a gray leather coin purse from his coat pocket and counted out the money, put it on the counter.

"Very good, sir. I have put you in room number nine." He slipped the money into the till, turned to one of the boxes on the wall. "Here is your key. Would you like the keys to the other rooms, also?"

The man waved his hand. "That is not necessary. I only want them to stay vacant."

"Very well. Would you care to visit the dining room for a cup of coffee and a piece of apple pie, before going to your room?"

"I prefer the dining room clear before I visit it. You may send for your man to show me to my room."

"We have only recently opened for business, sir. And help is difficult to come by here in Whisper Creek. I

will show you to your room." He stepped out from behind the desk and picked up the two leather valises.
"This way, sir. Your room is upstairs—" he clenched
his teeth, but couldn't resist adding, "—away from the
patrons of the dining room."

"Well, the rush is over for the day, Mrs. Fuller." Virginia looked up from the dishes she was loading on a
tray and smiled. "The sun has set and the passengers
aren't inclined to walk to the hotel in the dark for supper. Especially the women." She glanced toward the
back door. "I hope Liu Yang and Li Min will get home
safely. Garret told me there are wolves and other animals that might attack because of hunger."

"They will be fine." Garret strode into the kitchen,
walked to the stove and poured himself a cup of coffee. "Ah Cheng is waiting for them at the edge of the
woods. Did they do well today?"

"Yes. Very well. They both learn quickly and work
very hard."

"That's good to know." He looked at Mrs. Fuller.
"Do you share Virginia's opinion?"

His question was so abrupt it felt like a dismissal.
Had she done something to displease him? She looked
down, added cups and saucers to the tray.

The older woman gave her arm a gentle pat. "I do
agree with Virginia, Mr. Stevenson. I haven't washed
a pot or pan all day. And that frees all my time for
cooking."

He nodded, put down his cup. "I came to tell you
there are three new guests for supper. A Mr. and Mrs.

Lowel, and another older man. A very wealthy man, from his appearance and demeanor. It seems odd that a man of his means would decide to stay in Whisper Creek."

"Not when he has come for his daughter."

Father! Virginia swayed, grasped the edge of the table and willed strength into her legs. *Please, Lord, let him be alone. Don't let Emory Gladen be with him.*

She took a breath, turned and faced the man in the doorway. "Good evening, Father."

Chapter Fourteen

Virginia took a deep breath, drifted her fingers over the keys to finish the piece, then closed the cover on the keyboard. She'd put him off as long as she could. The day was over. The guests had gone to their rooms. Except for her father. And Mrs. Fuller. Garret was working in his office. Her stomach sank. Tears stung her eyes. He didn't care enough to even—

"That was lovely, Virginia. I could listen to you play all night. But it's time for me to retire." Mrs. Fuller rose and came to stand beside her. The woman's hand rested on her shoulder for a moment, gave a small pat. "I'll see you in the morning, dear."

She nodded, too choked with gratitude for the older woman's support and friendship to speak. She blinked tears from her eyes and watched Mrs. Fuller walk from the lobby, the long skirt of her worn, dark blue dress swishing softly.

"It's good to hear you play again, Virginia. I've missed it."

"Thank you, Father." She took a steadying breath and rose from the piano seat.

"And it's certainly better than seeing my daughter serving food to strangers in a public dining room." He rose in turn, tugged his suit coat into place. "But that's of no importance now."

"It is to me." She stiffened her spine and lifted her chin. "I enjoy serving the guests. It's not so very different from hosting your social gatherings at home."

"There is no comparison! Don't try my patience, Virginia. Now, come to my room, where we will have privacy to discuss my plans for your return home."

"I prefer to stay here in the lobby. We're quite alone." She moved behind the desk and brushed her hands over the polished wood, drawing strength from the feel of it. She was no longer a helpless daughter dependent on her father for her every need. She was a wife—at least legally. And she now had skills—

"Don't be disrespectful to me, young lady! That's why I've had to come chasing after you in the first place." Her father stepped to the front of the desk, gripped the edge. "I'm your father, and you will do as I say. Now come—"

Garret's office door opened. She glanced that way, caught her breath at the look on his face.

"You are speaking to my wife, sir. And though you are her father, you will do so in a respectful manner, or you will leave my establishment." The muscle along Garret's jaw twitched. "With my help, if necessary."

His voice was quiet, controlled. She stared at him,

shocked by the change. She'd seen Garret angry, but never like this.

"*You* dare to threaten *me*." Her father leaned forward, narrowed his eyes. "I can buy this place tomorrow and set you out in that snow!" He jabbed a finger toward the front windows.

"My hotel is not for sale. And neither is my wife."

Her heart thudded. Garret stood beside her, strong, steady, unmovable. She'd never felt so safe. So—

"She's not your *wife*. Except in name only. And even that will not be for long."

She gasped, jerked her gaze to her father. "How do you know—"

"Millie, of course. She told me *everything* about this ridiculous situation you've gotten yourself into."

Her father lurched back from the desk, yanked at the lapels on his suit coat. Her heart sank. It was a thing he did when he was confident he'd won an argument. She squared her shoulders, tried not to give in to her sudden fear. "Millie wouldn't do that to me. Unless…" Anger constricted her throat. "You *threatened* her with dismissal! And Thomas as well, no doubt."

"That's enough, Virginia. You will pack your things and—"

"Go back to New York and be *coerced* into marrying Emory Gladen? No, Father. It won't work. Not now." She edged closer to Garret, drew strength from his presence. "I'm legally married, if not—if not…otherwise. And you can't force me to marry Emory or anyone else."

"I've no intention of making you marry Gladen. The man has been caught in some scandalous, not to men-

tion cruel, behavior. He is being prosecuted for his acts."
Her father's voice modulated. "But this is all coming as
a shock to you. You're becoming hysterical. It would be
best if we finish this conversation in the morning. I shall
retire now. And I suggest you retire for the evening,
as well. I'll explain my plans for you tomorrow. Good
night." He strode to the stairs and climbed out of sight.

"I see now why you ran away."

She looked at Garret. His jaw muscle was twitching,
his hands clenching and unclenching.

"It will be best if I stay far away from your father."
He turned and walked back into his office.

A horrible emptiness swept through her. She stared
at his office door, longed with all her being for him to
come out and take her in his arms, to hold her and tell
her he loved her. A sob clawed at her throat, pushed upward by the unbearable ache in her heart.

She covered her mouth with her hand, pushed
through the door to their sitting room and ran for her
bedroom.

Garret slammed the front door, pulled on his hat and
started up the road toward the railroad depot. Would
an in-name-only marriage hold up to a challenge in a
court of law? He didn't know. Virginia was young and
innocent—so innocent. And her father, no doubt, had
a handful of smart, successful New York lawyers who
knew how to navigate inside and outside the law in
order to win a case. How could he fight them?

He ground his teeth and increased his pace to put as
much distance between himself and the hotel as quickly

as possible. There were two certain answers for Mr. Winterman's threat to take Virginia home. And if he stayed at the hotel...

A groan ripped from his throat. The way she had *looked* at him. More than anything, he'd wanted to take her in his arms and comfort her—and he couldn't trust himself to do so. She was too vulnerable, and he was so drawn to her that he didn't dare touch her. Not now. Not until he decided once and for all what he wanted— and what he was willing to risk for it. And if he saw her father before he'd cooled down...well, his staying away from the hotel tonight was best for all of them.

The cold air didn't help. He pushed himself to walk faster. There was enough moonlight to identify objects as he neared them, but hopefully, not enough for any- one who happened to look out a window to notice him walking up the road. Thankfully, the depot was only a short distance from town.

He stepped off the road into the deep snow and skirted around the railroad station platform so his foot- steps wouldn't alert Asa Marsh to his presence. The faint moonlight glinted on the metal rails. He crossed the tracks and walked under the water tower to the road that led to Mitch's sawmill and barn, then slowed his steps and looked around to make sure none of Mitch's workers were outside the bunkhouse. How would he ever explain his presence? *I'm spending the night in the barn because I don't trust myself to be in the same house as my wife?* He'd never live *that* down. He crept forward, opened the barn door slightly and squeezed through. The smell of dust and feed and hay greeted him. Low whickers called to him.

He stopped and waited for his eyes to adjust to the deeper darkness. If he remembered right, the stack of hay for bedding was straight ahead, and horse blankets hung over a post rail to the left. He grabbed one, shook it out and carried it to the mound of hay. If he burrowed into the stack, no one would spot him with a casual glance. He brushed the clinging snow from his pant legs and wrapped himself in the horse blanket.

His lips twitched. This would be funny, if he wasn't so pitiful. He owned a hotel with eighteen rooms and his own living quarters, and he was spending the night in a pile of hay! He blew out a breath, pulled hay over the blanket and closed his eyes. He had to decide before morning what he wanted. Should he keep his distance and stay safe? Or should he give in to his emotions, go back to the hotel and ask Virginia to be his true wife? His heart thudded. The way she had returned his kiss…

He shifted his position, pulled his hat down to cover his ears. As painful as it would be to lose her now, if he allowed himself to love her and she deserted him one day…

The thought stabbed like a knife into his heart. The knot in his stomach twisted tighter. Perhaps the best answer for both of them was for her to go home with her father. Virginia deserved a man who could love her wholly, without reservation. He would always be holding part of his heart away from her, watching and waiting…

He opened his eyes and stared into the darkness,

sick at heart and furious for being that way. For the first time since his mother had abandoned him, he wished he still believed in God.

Virginia lifted the damp cloth from her head and waved it through the air to cool it. She refolded it and placed it back over her eyes. She had finally stopped crying and started facing the truth. Garret had challenged her father not because he loved her, but because he was a man, with a man's instincts to protect what was his. And she was his wife, even though a pretend one.

Her mind skipped to the thunder snowstorm, to the way he had held her with such strength yet gentleness. To the way—no! She must stop thinking that his kiss meant he cared for her. He had kissed her for the same reason he had confronted her father—instinct. His kiss had nothing to do with any...*affection* he might have for her. She was nothing more to him than a serving girl in his dining room. It was true enough that he needed her—but only in order to keep his hotel.

The painful truth drove her to her feet. She laid the folded cloth across the glass bowl that held her hairpins and walked over to look out the window. It was dark, with only a sliver of moon showing above the shadowed pines. Tears stung her swollen eyes. She'd come to love the view of the towering trees with the mountains soaring behind them. Would she have to give it up? Would she have to leave Whisper Creek? She had just met the residents at church last Sunday. And she had liked Audrey Latherop and Katherine Warren immediately. She wanted to get to know them. To have the two couples over for a meal and an evening's entertainment.

The tears welled, slipped down her cheeks. She wiped them away and wrapped her arms about herself. She wanted to be married. *Really* married. To Garret. She wanted to have his baby. To have him treat her as if she were fragile and precious, the way Blake Latherop treated Audrey. To have him hold their child with love in his eyes and a proud smile on his face, the way Dr. Warren looked when he held little Howard. She'd never wanted those things before. But she ached to have them now.

What was she to do? The question kept forming in her thoughts, but she knew the answer. Garret had shown her what to do when he'd turned his back, gone into his office and closed the door, leaving her standing outside. He didn't want her in his life—not in any personal way. Certainly not as his true wife. And that meant she couldn't stay.

She wanted to. Her heart longed to. But her pride wouldn't allow it. Not when Garret didn't love her. It was too painful. And it would only grow more so as time went on. It would be better to leave now.

Her stomach clenched, churned. Sobs burst from her throat. She ran to her bed, threw herself facedown and cried out her heartache on her pillow.

She looked terrible. Virginia pinned her hair into a curly mass at the crown of her head, added the flat gray bow and turned from the mirror. She had done all she could to hide the evidence of her sleepless, tear-filled night. A cold cloth had taken away the puffiness around her eyes, but nothing helped the faint lavender circles beneath them. And she had wanted to look her best. She knew it wouldn't happen. But her heart clung stubbornly to the hope that Garret might ask her to stay.

She shook out the top tier of the long skirt on her gray striped dress, straightened the scalloped hem and braced herself to face the day. *Please let it be a busy day, Lord.*

She glanced at the double-door cupboard in the hallway and remembered her struggle to make her bed when she'd first arrived. The sight of the hearth assailed her with memories of Garret bringing her coffee and removing her boots. She'd been afraid of him then. She held her breath to stop the tears stinging the backs of her eyes and walked into the kitchen. "Good morning."

"Good morning, dear." Mrs. Fuller looked up from the bowl she was holding and smiled. "You've put your hair up again."

The first time had been because she wanted to look older for Garret. She swallowed hard and nodded. Must everything have a memory of Garret attached to it? She took her apron off its hook and tied it on, thought about burning his stew. "What's for breakfast this morning?"

"Ham and sausage, pancakes, eggs, fried potatoes, oatmeal and cinnamon rolls."

She put a smile on her face. "And coffee."

Mrs. Fuller smiled and spooned flour into the bowl. "Lots of coffee."

She fought down another rush of tears. She would miss Mrs. Fuller. The older woman had become almost like a mother to her. "Liu Yang, come here, please. I'm going to show you how to prepare the tables for meals." She placed a large tray on the worktable. "We will start with one table with four place settings. Do you know what four is?"

"Yes, mee-sus."

"All right. We will need four large plates, four small plates and four napkins. You'll find them here in the dish cupboard." She pointed to the plates and then the napkins folded and piled in a big basket. "And we also need four glasses and four cups and saucers. And four sets of flatware." She picked them up and carried them to the tray. "Now let's go set the table."

"Yes, mee-sus."

She led the way into the dining room, paused at the sight of Garret building the fire.

He rose. Their gazes met. "Good morning."

Her heart stopped, then beat out an accelerated rhythm. "Good morning. I—I'm showing Liu Yang the correct way to set a table."

He nodded, squatted and poked at the logs. "I won't be long."

"It's no bother." She drew a breath, gathered her scattered thoughts. "Always set these four tables in front of the fireplace first." She selected the things she needed and began. "I'll set this place, Liu Yang, and you set the others the same way. So…center the large plate with the design upright in front of each chair. Next, put the flatware in place—the knife goes on the right with the blade edge toward the plate, then the spoon outside the knife, and the fork goes on the left side of the plate…"

Garret rose and left the room. Tears stung her eyes. Obviously, teaching Liu Yang to serve the tables was necessary. She cleared her throat and continued. "The bread plate is placed above the fork. The glass goes above the tip of the knife…"

Virginia stood outside Garret's office door, her heart breaking. Her prayer had been granted, and she had been busy all day, but that hadn't made it any easier. Every time she saw Garret or stood working beside him at the desk, she could feel him drawing away from her. He didn't want her. She knew it. Deep down inside she knew it. But she couldn't leave until he told her he wanted her to go.

Lord, give me strength. Don't let me cry. Please help me not to cry. Help me to accept the fact that Garret doesn't care for me with dignity and grace. And don't let him guess that I love him, Lord. Please, don't let him guess that I love him.

She took a deep breath, squared her shoulders and knocked.

"Come in."

Help me, Lord! She opened the door and stepped inside.

He rose and stood looking at her, his eyes dark and inscrutable, his face taut.

"I've come to talk with you about the future." She lifted her hand, toyed with the button on her high collar. "I haven't had a chance to apologize for my father threatening you. I am sorry, Garret. It's his way."

He nodded, scrubbed his hand across the back of his

neck. "I've been threatened before, Virginia. And there is no way he can buy this hotel. It's mine. There is no note outstanding for his lawyers to get their hands on. That's not the problem."

"Then what is?"

He jammed his hands in his pockets, blew out a gust of air. "I'm not certain if our in-name-only marriage will withstand a challenge by his lawyers in a court of law. And if it doesn't, Ferndale will own the hotel. There's no way for me to fight that. I signed the contract agreeing to those terms."

"So Father will win."

"In a manner of speaking, yes. He won't have the hotel, but neither will I. And that's what he wants—to punish me for...everything. I can't stop him."

"I can. This is all my doing. I ran away because of Father and Emory Gladen. You had nothing to do with it."

"I made it possible."

"Accidentally, yes." She lowered her hand, smoothed the front of her skirt. "This is my problem and I will fix it."

Something flashed deep in his eyes. He took a long breath. "And how do you propose to do that?"

"I'll tell him if he wants me to go back to New York with him, he must give me his word that he will not challenge our marriage in court. That if he does, I will run away again. And this time I will tell no one where I am going."

If she disappeared... "You would do that?" His stomach sickened at the thought, but it could answer his problem of the five years.

"Can you think of another way?"

He stared at her, a strange expression on his face. One she couldn't understand.

Please let him ask me to stay and be his true wife, Lord. Please let him tell me he loves me. Please—

"Perhaps I will think of a way. Given some time." The words sounded bitter.

"Perhaps." She blinked, swallowed hard and forced a smile. "I'd better go and pack my things now. I'm sure Father can switch his tickets to tonight's train. There is no sense in delaying our departure until tomorrow. Goodbye, Garret, I—I'm so pleased to have met you." She whirled and hurried out into the hallway.

He yanked his hands from his pockets, snatched the Ferndale contract from his drawer, crushed it into a ball and threw it in the fire.

Chapter Fifteen

Virginia sat with her damp, crumpled handkerchief clasped in her hands and stared out the window. Light from the sliver of moon glinted on the deep, shovel-pocked snow beside the tracks. She looked up, watching the train's light slice through the darkness and bounce off the exposed stone wall of the mountain as the engine entered a curve in the high pass.

The car swayed, the relentless rasp of the wheels against the metal rails vibrating through the floorboards beneath her feet. Cold air flowed off the window, chilled her face and neck. She shivered and pulled the collar of her red velvet coat higher. Footsteps approached her seat. She kept her gaze fixed on the window.

"Virginia, I purchased sleeper car privileges for our trip so we will be comfortable. Come to bed."

"I'm not sleepy, Father."

"Then lie down and rest."

"I prefer to sit here."

"Virginia, I insist—"

"Please don't treat me as a child, Father." She turned her head and met his astonished gaze. "I'm not the same person I was when I ran away. I have yielded to your wishes and am returning to New York with you because I love Garret, *not* because I am afraid of you. You can no longer bribe or threaten me with your money." A bitter smile curved her lips. "I have learned I am quite capable of making my own way in this world. And if you do one thing to harm Garret, I will do just that. I will leave your home and you will never see me again."

"You are *threatening* me?"

"It's not a threat, Father. I am merely telling you what will happen if you try to destroy my husband. I need you to believe me, so you will tell your lawyers they are not to try to have my marriage to Garret set aside. I am his *wife*—" she raised her hand when he drew breath to speak "—yes, in name only, but still his wife. I intend to stay married to him."

"Pure foolishness! I'll not have you wasting your life in that—that *excuse* for a town!" Her father caught hold of the lapels on his silk paisley dressing gown and glared down at her. "Now you listen to me, daughter! I shall do exactly as I please, and—"

"And if you do—if you do one thing that causes Garret hurt—I will leave your home forever. It is your choice, Father." She turned back to look out the window.

"I am not going to stand here and catch a chill because of your stubbornness, Virginia. We will continue this conversation in the morning."

She listened to the slap of his slippers against the carpet runner in the aisle fade away, looked down at her reticule and smiled. It held the same coins she'd had when she had run off to escape Emory Gladen. Odd how confident having a few skills made one feel.

Garret shoveled coal into the bucket, straightened and glanced toward the train depot. Where was she now? Was she all right? Was her father still bullying her, or had he stopped now that he'd gotten his way? Though not completely.

He tossed the shovel onto the coal pile, grabbed the bucket and carried it up onto the porch. The image of Virginia standing by the lobby door with her valises at her feet and her chin raised in that way she had was indelibly etched in his mind. He would never forget the way she'd faced her father, laid down her conditions for going back to New York with him, and refused to budge until the man agreed. It had been all he could do to stay in his office by the door, but she'd made him promise...

He shook his head, stomped his feet and went inside. He'd never expected her to take his part that way—to go back to New York to keep him from losing the hotel. Of course, there was always the chance that she really *wanted* to go, and was simply using their pretend marriage as a weapon to make her father stop trying to choose her beaux. And to maintain her hold over him—in case. Though he couldn't figure what that "in case" might be.

The smells of coffee brewing and bread baking floated through the kitchen. His hands tensed on the bucket handle. He swept the room with a quick glance. Mrs. Fuller was stirring something in a bowl, Li Min

was at the worktable chopping potatoes and Liu Yang
was piling dishes on a tray. He wanted to take it from
her. To tell her to stay out of the dining room, that it was
Virginia's place. But it wasn't any longer. She would no
longer charm their guests with her smile or—

"Meester want coffee?"

He took a breath, eased his white-knuckled grip on
the bucket handle and shook his head. "Thank you, Liu
Yang, but I'll have some later—after I've taken care of
the heaters in the dressing rooms. Do you need coal for
your stove, Mrs. Fuller?"

The older woman bent and pulled loaves of baked
bread from the oven. She set the pans at the edge of the
stovetop, lifted one upside down and shook the bread
out. "I'm fine until tomorrow." She placed the golden-
brown loaf on the cooling rack on the top of the cupboard beside the stove and reached for another pan.

He carried the bucket of coal to the water heater and
studied Mrs. Fuller's profile while he shook down the
ashes. Her voice sounded different, as if she were forc-
ing it out. There was a sadness in it that made his chest
tighten. She missed Virginia, too. The difference was,
Mrs. Fuller thought Virginia was only gone for a visit
with her father, and that she was coming back. But why
should she? There was nothing for her here but hard
work and a pretend marriage to a coward too wary of
the future to admit that he had…feelings for her.

His stomach knotted. He finished filling the coal
box on the water heater and strode from the kitchen,
the bucket swinging at his side.

There was no trace of her in their dressing room.
Everything was neat and tidy. And his. He focused on

feeding the coal hopper for the water heater and hurried from the room, paused outside her bedroom door. Had she thought to turn off the heating stove? He sucked in a breath, opened her door and took another punch to his gut. Her quilt, blankets and pillow were in a neatly folded pile at the foot of the bed. The room was cold, the stove draft closed. He glanced at the stovepipe. The damper was open.

This is the damper—I do not touch it.

Memories flared. He'd had to teach her how to work the heating stove. He'd been furious to learn she was helpless at any sort of practical housework. He'd wanted a maid and cook for his hotel. And then Virginia had arrived and turned everything upside down. Now he had two maids and a cook. What he wanted was Virginia. He wanted her quick intelligence, her willingness to learn, her delight when she mastered a new skill. He wanted to see her beautiful eyes sparkling up at him, her soft lips smiling at him. And he wanted to hear her musical laughter. He wanted to have her working alongside him at the desk, soothing and entertaining guests, playing the piano. He wanted his wife!

He slapped the damper closed, stormed out of her bedroom and headed for the first-floor dressing room for guests. Her going home was best for both of them. It would take a couple days, but he would get over her. The hotel work would settle into a routine, and he wouldn't even miss her.

"Come in." Virginia wiped the nib of her pen, stoppered the inkwell and rose from her chair as the door opened. Her maid entered. She took in the woman's red eyes and nose, her lips pressed tightly together, and hurried forward to enfold her in a hug. "Don't cry, Millie. Everything will be fine."

"I—I'm not to be your maid any longer, Miss Virginia. After all these y-years."

"I see. And, I suppose, Thomas is to be dismissed, also?"

"Yes, miss."

"It's Mrs., Millie. Remember, I'm a married woman now." She patted her maid's soft shoulder. "Now stop crying. Father is not going to dismiss you or Thomas. I won't let him."

The maid jerked back, looked at her out of wide eyes. "Beggin' your pardon. *What* did you say, Miss Virginia?"

"I said you have nothing to be concerned about. I will not let Father dismiss you or Thomas."

"But, miss...er, Mrs. Virginia, you can't stop—I mean, your father is... I don't understand."

She nodded, stepped back and tugged her bodice back into place. "I don't blame you for being shocked, Millie. But you will find I am no longer the young woman who ran away. I've changed."

Her maid stared at her, swept her gaze over her simple cotton gown, then looked around the room. Her mouth gaped open. "I've come to—you're already dressed for the day. And you've made your bed!" Millie stepped to the head of the bed, grasped hold of the comforter and pulled it back. "I'll just touch it up a bit, and then..." The maid paused, rubbed her hand across the smooth, taut sheets and blankets. "Why, this is—where did you learn how to make a bed?"

She laughed at Millie's shock and tugged the comforter back in place. "In Whisper Creek, of course. We had the nicest older woman come to stay at the hotel. She sat on the edge of the bed I had tried to make, and the blankets and sheets bunched and tangled around her. She taught me how to make the bed the right way. And how to clean the dressing rooms. She even tried to teach me to cook." Tears stung her eyes. She blinked them away, drew in a breath to control the urge to cry, and forced a smile. "I'm quite hopeless at that, though I have learned enough to help in the kitchen. For the most part, I served in the dining room and helped Garret with the guests." Her voice choked.

Millie's arms drew her close. "I'm sorry you had to go through all of that, Mrs. Virginia. I never thought you would have to do maid's work. I was to do that for a wage."

"I know—but there was a blizzard, and the trains stopped running. And I burned his stew. And Garret had to help shovel Minna out from the avalanche and I had to—to—" She laughed, stepped back and wiped her eyes. "Oh, how I wanted you there, Millie! I was furious at being left in such a situation when I was so *helpless*. But Mrs. Fuller helped me and everything worked out fine. I found out I enjoyed working with Garret. I felt…needed."

She drew a deep breath and glanced at the clock on the wall. "Well, there is still quite a bit of time before Father goes downstairs to breakfast. I have time to fin-

ish my letter before I go down to join him." She smiled
at her maid's gasp. "I no longer breakfast in my room,
Millie. And though Father likes to breakfast alone, that
is going to change. And your duties, as well. I will not
need you in the morning. Tell Martha I said you are to
help her in the kitchen. And tell Thomas he has no reason for concern. He will remain our butler."

"Yes, Miss—Mrs. Virginia." Millie left the room,
still looking stunned.

She smiled and returned to her writing desk,
skimmed the letter she'd started, to order her thoughts.

Dear Mrs. Fuller,
As you know by now, I am at Father's home in
New York City. It was imperative that I return
with him. I am sorry that I did not have the opportunity to tell you farewell, but things happened
very quickly.

I want to thank you, again, for being so gener-
ous with your time and knowledge. I don't know
what I would have done on that first day of the
blizzard if you had not so graciously come to my
aid. I hope you will not think me presumptuous
if I say I have thought of you as my friend since
that time. I truly enjoyed learning from you the
household skills that I needed to be a helpmate
to my husband.

Tears flowed. She rose from the desk and went to
look out her bedroom window, stared at the city street
below. A few inches of snow covered the ground, and

small pockets of packed flakes huddled between the cobblestones. Two men holding what looked to be an animated discussion walked by. A carriage passed. Another followed.

She lifted her gaze to the houses across the street. They stood side by side like soldiers, with one elm tree growing in one yard. She stared at the bare branches, spidery against the gray, overcast sky, and longed for the sight of the snow-covered towering pines with the snow-capped Medicine Bow Mountains behind them. Restlessness took her. Everything was so…closed in. Her chest tightened. She placed her hand at the base of her throat and struggled to breathe.

She whirled from the window, hurried back to her writing desk and took up her pen.

You might be amused to hear that my maid, Millie, is…perhaps *flabbergasted* is the best word to describe her. I was awake and ready for the day with my bed made and this letter started before she came to my room to wake me. She even checked the bed with an eye to setting it right. I wish you could have seen her face when she saw my neat corners and taut sheets and blankets, all thanks to you! Millie cannot believe how much I have changed. Or perhaps grown up would be a better definition. I pray so.

I hope Li Min is sufficient help for you in the kitchen, and that you will oversee Liu Yang until she learns all she needs to know to care for the patrons of the dining room. Mr. Stevenson will be too busy doing his work and caring for the guests to have any time to train her.

My journey back to New York City was long and wearying. It is strange, but in the short time I was in Whisper Creek, I grew so fond of the vast spaces that the city now seems cramped and small. I suppose I will become accustomed to it again.

I shall close now. Thank you again, Mrs. Fuller, for your kindness to me. Please take care of Mr. Stevenson. He sometimes gets so busy with the outside work, he forgets to eat breakfast. I wish I could join you both for a cup of your wonderful coffee and a delicious cinnamon bun.

Your friend,
Virginia

Tears slid down her cheeks. She dropped the pen on the blotter and ran to bury her sobs in her pillow.

Garret strode to the kitchen, filled a cup with coffee and braced himself to talk with Mrs. Fuller. He'd not had to deal directly with the older woman while Virginia—he broke off the thought and set himself to do what had to be done. "Today was quite busy, Mrs. Fuller. Were Li Min and Liu Yang helpful? Were they able to manage all that needed to be done?"

The older woman glanced at him, spooned water into a bowl and tossed the flour mixture with a fork. "They are both very hard workers. And they willingly do whatever I ask of them. Of course, they will be more efficient when they become accustomed to our ways. Some of the foods and customs are very strange to them." She removed the front stove plate, pulled an iron frying pan with melted lard in it forward over the flames.

"That makes sense." He smelled cinnamon. He peered into another bowl sitting on the worktable, sniffed the spices on the sliced apples. When he looked back, Mrs. Fuller was sprinkling flour in a rough circle on the table. She placed a lump of dough in the center, patted it down, then rolled it thin. In a flash she had it cut into circles the size of a saucer. "Do you have a list of any foods you are running out of or want? I'm going to place an order tomorrow."

The woman nodded, spooned some of the apples into the center of each circle. "You'll find it in the pantry on the middle shelf at the end, by the door. Mrs. Stevenson and I write down foods as we use them." She looked up from folding the dough circles over the apples and sealing the edges with a fork. "Will I be discussing the weekly menus with you until Mrs. Stevenson comes home? It helps me to know what foods I will need in what amount."

Until Mrs. Stevenson comes home. Should he tell Mrs. Fuller the truth? No, he wasn't ready to do that yet. He fought back a frown, took a swallow of coffee. "All right. When do you do that?"

"Midweek, after the evening train." She placed one of the small pies on a large spoon and slipped it into the hot grease, then followed it with another and another.

"That gives time for the foods we need to come in before the beginning of the next week."

The next week. And the week after that. And after that... Virginia would not be here. His stomach knotted. He clenched his fingers around his cup and carried it to the sink, rinsed it and set it in the dishpan to keep from throwing it across the room.

"I believe that's all we need to discuss." He scrubbed his hand across the back of his neck and started for the door to the sitting room. "I'll be in my office. If you think of anything else, let me know, Mrs. Fuller, and—" he stopped, stared at Virginia's apron hanging on its hook "—and get rid of that apron! Throw it in with the dirty towels and dishcloths. Ah Cheng will be here to pick up the laundry tomorrow."

He stormed toward the door, stopped and took a deep breath. He had no right to take his frustration out on others. He turned and looked at Mrs. Fuller. She was staring at him with a look in her eyes that made his anger soar. He didn't want her compassion. He didn't want anything from any woman. Still... "I'm sorry, Mrs. Fuller. I didn't mean to be harsh."

She nodded, turned back to her frying. "It's all right, Mr. Stevenson. I miss her, too."

Chapter Sixteen

Virginia stared down at the fried egg on her plate, thought of Garret's "broken eggs" and put down her fork.

Her father cleared his throat, cut into his steak and stabbed the piece with his fork. "Grant makes good sense in his inaugural address. He's calling for a strict accountability by the treasury for every dollar of revenue collected. And for the greatest retrenchment in expenditure in every department of government. I say it's about time!" Her father tapped the newspaper folded beside his plate with the handle of his knife. "And here is something that may interest you, Virginia. Grant is for ratification of the Fifteenth Amendment to the Constitution."

Her stomach churned at the thought of eating. She broke off a bite of bread and smeared it with a dab of butter. "That would make a lot of people happy."

Her father nodded, studied her as he chewed his bite of meat.

She looked down at her plate to avoid his frowning gaze.

"Are you going to eat that, or just sit there and hold it?"

"I beg your pardon?"

He pointed at her hand with the tip of his knife.

"Oh." She placed the bread on her plate and wiped her fingers on her napkin. "If you will excuse me, Father, I will leave you to read your newspaper in peace." She rose and started for the doorway, the silk of her gown's long skirt swishing softly.

"Are you ill, Virginia?"

At heart. She paused, turned to look at him. "Why do you ask, Father?"

"We've been home less than a week, and you've lost so much weight your gowns are hanging on you." He scowled, motioned toward her empty chair. "Sit down and eat your breakfast."

She shook her head. "I've no appetite, Father. And if I eat, I *will* be ill. Excuse me." She lifted her hems and walked from the dining room down the hallway to the spacious entrance hall, ignoring his demands that she return and listen to him.

She skirted around the table in the center of the room, stopped at the bottom of the curving stairs and looked around. Her chest tightened, restricted her breath. She couldn't face another day cloistered in her room. She would suffocate.

She rubbed her chest, glanced at the Windsor bench beside the stairway and moved toward it. Her coat and hat and muff hung beside her father's coat in the nook out of sight beneath the stairs. She grabbed her boots, sat in the chair and tugged them on, the need for fresh air and space compelling her. There was nothing for her to do. Nowhere for her to go. The thought of visiting her old friends made her cringe. The idea of listening to the latest gossip, or talking about shopping and clothing styles and what to wear to the next ball, didn't interest her. The only thing she wanted was to return to Garret and Whisper Creek.

She blinked tears from her eyes and tied on her hat, shrugged into her coat and buttoned it on her way out the door.

She took a deep breath of the cold, fresh air and started down the sidewalk, returning the polite nods of the people out and about on their morning errands. A quick dip of her head shielded her eyes against the sun that reflected off the brass lamps of the carriages that passed by, the passengers huddled inside behind the drawn curtains that held out the weather. The horses' hoofs thudded against the cobblestones. The buggy wheels rumbled. But there were no train whistles.

She glanced at the four-sided clock that stood in the center of the snow-covered circle in the middle of the intersection. It was almost time for the second train of the day to stop at Whisper Creek. Did Liu Yang have the tables ready for the rush of soldiers and passengers who would come for a quick breakfast? Was Li Min giving Mrs. Fuller enough help in the kitchen? Was Garret—

A sob burst from her throat. She stopped and turned toward a storefront to hide her tears from the other pedestrians. *Please help me, Lord. I can't go on feeling as I do. Garret doesn't want me. I must get over—*

A key rattled. The shop door opened. She jerked up her gloved hands and wiped the tears from her cheeks, held her breath to stop her crying.

"Good morning." The well-dressed woman standing in the doorway skimmed her gaze over her. "I see you are looking at my sign. Are you here to apply for the position?"

She glanced down, read the small, discreet sign sitting by the hem of a velvet walking gown worn by a mannequin standing in the window: Shopgirl Wanted. She turned and smiled at the woman. "Yes, I am. I hope I'm not too late."

"Not at all. I only put out the sign yesterday evening." A look of irritation swept across the woman's face. "My girl ran off to marry some man she's only just met. She didn't even have the decency to tell me she was leaving my employ. I found her note on the counter when I closed the shop. But that's not to do with you. Come in." The woman stepped back and opened the door wide.

She lifted her hems and stepped over the threshold, glanced around a small but elegant dress shop. "You have a lovely store. This was a tobacco shop when I left for Wyoming."

"You've been traveling, Miss…"

"Mrs. Garret Stevenson." Her throat tightened. She hurried to change the subject. "Please, call me Virginia."

The woman nodded, fastened a stern look on her.

"And your husband approves of your seeking employment outside of your home?"

The tears threatened to come back. She swallowed hard to gain control. "My husband is in Wyoming. His business is there. I have come back to care for my father. But I find myself with a good deal of time on my hands. I want something to do to fill that time."

"I see." The woman swept her hand toward a cluster of gowns hanging from a wooden rod. "Can you tell me the fabric of each of those gowns?"

She stepped closer and walked down the row. "The first is silk…then faille…moire…satin." She paused to admire the next outfit. It would be perfect for the winter weather at Whisper Creek. "The walking suit is made of delaine…the next is velvet. And this last suit is tweed."

The woman nodded, studied her a moment, then smiled. "I'm Mrs. Lamb. Would caring for your father allow you to tend the shop for me in the mornings, Mrs. Stevenson?"

The train blasted notice of its departure, the whistle accentuating the emptiness inside him. Garret counted the money, tossed it into the till and stepped out from behind the service desk. He'd thought a few days would ease the ache of missing Virginia, but the need to see her, to hear her voice, to *be* with her deepened with every train that came. Part of him kept waiting for her to walk in the door, though he knew that was pure foolishness.

He rubbed his hand over the back of his neck and crossed to the fireplace to tend the fire. The odd thing was, Virginia's leaving had created a closeness between him and Mrs. Fuller, a closeness he didn't want. And it deepened day by day. He found comfort in the woman's presence. There was something in her eyes and voice that soothed some of the stabbing pain he couldn't overcome.

"Garret…"

He jolted from his thoughts, rose to find Blake crossing the lobby toward him. "What I can do for you, Blake?"

His friend shook his head, held out a letter. "I was sorting the mail and found this. I thought I'd bring it to you instead of putting it in the hotel's mail for tomorrow. In case there's some sort of emergency or something."

His heart thudded. He took the letter in his hand, stared down at the name of the sender. *Mrs. Garret Stevenson.* His mouth went dry. He nodded, sucked in air. "Thank you, Blake."

His friend nodded and strode back to the front door. "Your wife and Mrs. Fuller must have become good friends." The door closed on Blake's words.

Mrs. Fuller? He turned the letter over, read the direction. *Mrs. Fuller, Stevenson Hotel, Whisper Creek, Wyoming Territory.* The letter wasn't for him. Virginia had written to Mrs. Fuller!

He clenched his jaw, tossed the letter onto a chair and paced from one end of the lobby to the other, every strike of his boot heels against the floor a declaration of disbelief and anger. Why had she written to Mrs. Fuller? Was there something wrong? Did she have a problem with her father or—

He let out a growl, snatched the letter from the chair and strode to the kitchen. "Blake brought this over for you."

Mrs. Fuller glanced at him, dropped her gaze to his hand. "A letter? For *me*? Who—"

"Virginia."

The older woman's gaze jerked back to his face. He tried to hide his anger, but there was nothing he could do about the muscle twitching along his jawbone.

Mrs. Fuller set down the roller she was using, covered the flattened dough with a towel and wiped her hands on her apron.

He handed her the letter.

"Thank you." She opened it, scanned the writing and looked up at him, her eyes glistening. "She wrote to thank me for teaching her the household skills she needed to learn to be a helpmate to you. And she asks me to please—" her voice broke "—to please take care of you. To remind you to eat breakfast when you have been working outside."

Pressure built in his chest. "That's foolishness. I'm a grown man perfectly able to take care of myself." A shadow darkened Mrs. Fuller's eyes. Sorrow? Regret? What else was in Virginia's letter? He yanked his gaze from the older woman's face and pivoted, grabbed a cup and filled it with coffee. The worry that had been gnawing at him since Virginia went home with her father pushed at him. He leaned against the worktable and took a swallow of the dark, rich brew. "Did Virginia mention her father? Are they getting on well?" *If he hurt her...*

"No. She only wrote about things here at the hotel."
Mrs. Fuller put the letter in her apron pocket, lifted the
front stove plate aside and pulled a frying pan deep with
grease over the hole. "I'm making molasses doughnuts
for tomorrow's breakfast. Would you like one with your
coffee? These will be done in just a minute."

That softness he'd noticed before had crept into her
voice, but for whatever reason, he no longer resented it.
He was getting to know Mrs. Fuller, and to like her—
even if he was still wary. "If you will join me. We need
to go over your menu plan for the coming week."

She cleared her throat and nodded, then lifted a circle of dough, punched her thumb through the center
to make a hole and slid it into the frying pan. The hot
grease foamed up around it. She yanked her hand back
and grabbed another circle.

He poured a second cup of coffee, set the pot back
on the stove and placed the cup on the worktable. Tried
to stop thinking of Virginia.

"Oh!"

He jerked around at the cry of pain. Mrs. Fuller's
sleeve was soaked with hot grease. He grabbed her
hand. She tried to draw it away, but he held it tight and
pulled her toward the sink. "We need to get that grease
cooled!" He turned on the cold water, frigid from the
waterfall, and tugged her forearm beneath the flow. The
grease congealed on the fabric. He reached to fold back
her sleeve. She tried to tug her arm away.

"No, please, you've done enough. I can m-manage..."

Her plea ended in a sob. He turned back her sleeve to
examine the burn, stared at the uneven bump of bones

where none should be, and at the birthmark just below them. His heart lurched, thudded.

What's that, Mama?

It's a bunny, Garry. See, here is his floppy ear. And here is his puffy tail.

He let go of her arm, stepped back and walked away, water dripping off his fingers.

"Garry, *please*! Let me explain…"

He pivoted, his fury clashing with the fear in her eyes. "How do you explain abandoning your child?" His voice was as cold as the water still pouring from the faucet.

"I didn't abandon you. I had to leave. Silas—his drinking had become worse. And the beatings." She took a ragged breath, wiped the tears from her face.

Mrs. Fuller was his mother!

His stomach clenched. His mind reeled. He stared at her while memories of empty, lonely years assailed him. She reached toward him. The flesh above her wrist was flaming red. He tamped down his shock and anger to do what must be done. "That burn needs to be taken care of."

"I'll put a vinegar poultice on it later. I need you to know—"

"I'll listen. But first you need to tend that burn. What do you need?" He stared at her wrist, too unsettled to look at her.

"Vinegar. And a clean cloth to wrap around my wrist."

Anger surged. She wouldn't be able to wrap it her-

self. He'd have to do it. "Go on with your *explanation*."
He strode to the pantry, lifted the top of the box Dr.
Warren had put together for him and pulled out a bandage roll. He grabbed the can of vinegar off the shelf
and stalked to the worktable. She'd turned off the water,
pushed the frying pan to the back of the stove and replaced the front plate. "You were saying?"

"Silas needed money for whiskey, so he decided he
would—" She stopped, pressed her lips together and
reached for the vinegar.

"You can't wrap your arm yourself. Tell me what
to do."

"You don't have to…"

He looked at her.

"Dab some vinegar on the burn, then wrap my wrist
and sprinkle more vinegar on the part of the bandage
over the burn."

He splashed a little vinegar into a cup, stuck his
finger in it and patted it on her arm. "Is that enough?"

Tears welled in her eyes. She nodded, looked away.

"Go on. Silas decided he would…"

"Sell my…services."

He jerked, stared at her lined face, seeing traces of
her beauty when she was young. He thought of his step-
father, clenched his hands.

"I refused, of course, told him I wouldn't do it. He
beat me. And when I still wouldn't agree, he said if I
didn't do as he wanted, he would beat you. And then
he left for town to make his arrangements. He said he
would be back in three days. I was so desperate. I believed him."

Tears flowed down her cheeks. Her eyes beseeched him to believe her. "I never meant to leave you, Garret. You were my life!"

His throat ached. The young boy in him wanted to trust her. She'd made him a birthday cake. It had been sitting on the table when he woke to find her gone. He fought down the memory, put the end of the bandage in place and began to wrap her wrist. "But you did leave me." Eighteen years of bitterness were in his voice.

"Only because I knew you would be safe, and I would be able to move faster on my own. I'd heard of an elderly woman who lived deep in the woods. So when you went to sleep, I left to try to find her, to beg her to give us a place to live in exchange for me working for her. I thought we could hide there until Silas would stop looking for us and we could get away."

"Obviously, you never found this woman in the woods." He tore the end of the bandage strip in two and tied it in place, fought for breath. *He was holding his mother's wrist...* The band of pressure around his chest tightened.

"I never had the chance. Silas decided to wait for dawn to go to town. He came back, found me gone and came after me."

There was remembered fear in her voice. He looked up from sprinkling vinegar on the bandage, saw the horror in her eyes. Words poured from her.

"He caught me at the top of a hill. We fought, and he threw me down the steep slope. He must have slipped when he did. I heard him cry out, and then he was tumbling after me, bouncing from rock to rock. That's when

I got this—" she lifted her twisted arm, then lowered it back down to rest on the worktable "—and a few other injuries. I hit my head on a rock, and I couldn't stay awake."

She took a breath, blew it out. "The old woman found us. Silas was dead. And I was battered and unconscious. She dragged me back to her house and tended to me as best she could. I was very weak, and I—I couldn't see right for a few days. As soon as I was able to walk, I started for home. But by the time I got there, you were gone. I couldn't find you."

Her voice choked. Tears flowed down her cheeks again. "I've been praying and looking for you ever since. I finally decided to come West. And I—I saw your hotel sign. I knew the moment I saw you—"

"Why didn't you tell me?"

She took another breath, straightened her shoulders. "Because of the look in your eyes. I was afraid. That's why I said my name was Mrs. Fuller."

His *mother*. And he'd made her afraid of him. He stared at her, his head and heart aching. He finally knew the truth. A pain knifed through his chest. He'd wasted eighteen years hating a mother who loved him.

He looked at the letter peeking out of his mother's apron pocket. Would he spend the rest of his life regretting letting Virginia go back to New York? It wasn't because of her father that he'd encouraged her to go home. It was because he didn't want to risk falling deeply in love with her.

He cleared the lump from his throat. "I'm sorry that I've made you feel...unwanted or afraid, Mother." He tested the word, smiled. It felt good on his lips. And the warmth of her smile felt good in his heart. "We have a lot to talk about, and a lot of time to make up for." He poured the cold coffee down the sink drain, smiled and picked up the coffeepot. "Shall we start over a hot cup of coffee and a molasses doughnut?"

"What do mean, you've taken employment as a shop-girl!"

Virginia moved to the hearth, turned and held out her cold hands. "I am working mornings at Mrs. Lamb's Dress Shop."

"You'll do no such thing." Her father put down his book and glared at her. "Are you trying to embarrass me in front of my friends, Virginia? Is that your goal?"

"No, Father. I'm trying to fill the empty hours of my days."

"Then go shopping! Visit your friends."

"I have more clothes than I need now. I'm not interested in shopping. And I don't want to visit my friends. Most of them are…are married."

"Then plan a party." He waved his hand toward the window. "The weather will soon change. Hold a spring ball."

"I don't want to plan entertainment, Father. I want to feel…useful." She walked to the front window of their parlor, watched the golden glow of the streetlamps drag across the carriage tops. Did Garret miss her? Was he sorry she had come back to New York?

"It is a ridiculous situation, Virginia."

She turned back to face her father. "I beg your pardon?"

"This in-name-only marriage in which you are involved. It's ludicrous." Her father placed his book on the lamp table and came to stand beside her. "Do you really want to be legally tied to a man who does not care for you? And he doesn't, or he would have fought to keep you from returning to New York."

She stiffened, stung by the truth of his words.

"What if you meet a man who will care deeply for you? And you for him? How will you explain this foolishness to him? And what if it is the other way around? What if this man you are so fond of finds a woman he cares about, one who returns his affection? He is not free to woo her because of this absurd farce." Her father shook his head and walked back to his chair. "The Bible says we are not to be a stumbling block to others, but that is exactly what you and Mr. Stevenson are to one another—stumbling blocks. Think about it, Virginia. And then do something about it and stop this moping about!" He opened his book and began to read again.

He was right. Her heart ached. She had no appetite. She spent her days and nights thinking of Garret and longing to be with him—to be truly married to him. And he didn't care a fig about her. She wasn't a necessary part of his life as long as he had others to do the work at his hotel.

Tears welled, but she refused to let them fall. She took deep breaths to control them, hurried into the entrance hall and climbed the stairs to her room. The soft silk of her long skirt rustled, its hem whispering upon the treads. Garret didn't love her. It was time she faced the truth and removed herself from his life so he could move on. But he would always live in her heart.

She crossed to her dressing room and prepared for bed, mentally composing the letter she would write to him in the morning.

Chapter Seventeen

Virginia twisted her long curls into a loose coil at the crown of her head, secured them with her pearl hair combs and rose from her dressing table. She was ready for work. And she was out of excuses. She had put it off long enough. It was time to write the letter.

Her stomach churned. She ignored the discomfort and crossed to her writing desk, took out stationery and pen.

Dear Garret

No. That was too personal. She wadded up the paper and threw it in the basket beside the desk. She must give him no hint of her feelings for him. She took out another piece of stationery, and began again.

My friend Garret,
I hope this letter finds you well and the hotel prospering.
I am writing you because I have given much

thought to our unique situation since leaving Whisper Creek. I have come to realize that I have become a "stumbling block" to your future. The journey West has become fashionable, and I am sure that one day soon a young woman traveling on the train will enter the hotel and draw your interest. When that happens, you will, of course, want to be free to woo her. It is for that reason I am sending the enclosed letter.

Tears welled into her eyes, clogged her throat. She jerked back so they wouldn't fall and smear the ink, then rose and went to look out of the window until she could gain control. The clock hanging on the wall above her writing desk chimed the hour.

She dried her eyes, took a few deep breaths and hurried back to finish the letter. She wanted to post it on her way to Mrs. Lamb's shop.

My days have been empty of purpose since my arrival in New York. To fill them I have taken employment as a shopgirl in a dress shop. Father is not pleased, but I find the pampered daughter life no longer suits me.

Please give my fond greetings to Mrs. Fuller. With sincere best wishes, your friend,
Virginia

She took another piece of paper from her drawer and quickly wrote out the enclosure.

To whom it may concern:
This letter is to state that I, Virginia Louise Winterman Stevenson, do not in any way oppose the annulment of my marriage to Mr. Garret Stevenson.
Mrs. Garret Stevenson

The tears flowed. She wiped them away, folded the enclosure into the letter and put it in her reticule. It was done. Her ties to Garret and Whisper Creek were severed forever.

She ran from her room and down the stairs, put on her coat and hat, and hurried out the door.

Garret brushed his hair in place, buttoned his shirt and studied his reflection in the mirror. He didn't look any different. But he felt different, lighter. The burden he'd carried for eighteen years was gone. If only Virginia were here to—

He frowned and closed off the thought. He'd spent most of the night thinking about his past and wondering about his future. Something deep inside him had changed since he and his mother had talked. It was as if something tangled and twisted had unraveled and set him free.

Mrs. Fuller was his *mother*. He still couldn't get used to that. He had a lot of changes to make in his thinking. He trimmed his oil lamp and headed for the kitchen, grabbing his work coat on the way.

She was already at work. He frowned, tossed his

coat over a chair back. "Smells good in here. But then it always does."

His mother glanced at him and smiled. "Good morning." She sliced a loaf of bread, cubed the slices and scooped half the pieces into a large baking pan.

"What's that?"

She pulled a pan off the stove, stirred some spices into it, then spooned the mixture over the bread in the pan. "It will be an apple bread pudding when I'm through. Are you ready to have some breakfast? Or are you on your way outdoors?"

"Outdoors. But I want to talk to you first, before Liu Yang and Li Min come." He poured a cup of coffee and watched her toss the rest of the cubed bread in the pan. "How is your wrist this morning?"

"It's better." She dotted the bread cubes with butter, poured a milk concoction over them and sprinkled them with cinnamon. "Thank you again for taking care of it." Her voice thickened. "It—meant a lot to me."

"Well, you won't be burning yourself again. I'm going to the depot this morning to send telegrams posting a notice for a cook in the New York and Philadelphia newspapers."

She straightened from placing the baking dish in the oven and looked at him. "You're unhappy with my cooking?"

"No, of course not. But you're here in the kitchen working when I get up in the morning, and you're here working late at night." He blew on his hot coffee. "I don't want you working that hard. So I'll hire another cook. It should only be a few days until—"

"Please don't do that, Garret."

He stared at her, taken aback by her plea. "I don't understand. I thought you would be pleased."

She smiled and placed her hand on his arm, her touch light and timid. "I *am* pleased that you're concerned for me. But you're my child, and I have missed eighteen years of caring for you and doing for you." She lifted her apron and wiped her eyes. "These past few weeks have given me such pleasure! It was a true blessing when I came here and found you. And an answer to my prayers when your wife asked me to help her during the blizzard. It was a chance to make up a little for all the things I couldn't do for you when we were apart. I like to cook. And I like feeling…needed. Please don't take that away from me."

He put down his cup and straightened, plowed his fingers through his hair. "All right…"

Her smile settled deep in his heart. He took a breath and hugged her close, the tenderness of his mother's touch healing years of hurt.

"I understand you have ignored my wishes and are still working as a shopgirl."

Virginia nodded, glanced at the clock. The trains were so fast. Where was the letter now? Chicago? Omaha? Laramie? Her heart ached to have it back. "Yes, I am. But I don't want to discuss it now, Father—please."

She whirled, the ruffled silk of her long skirt billowing out around her, and rushed from the sitting room.

Tears blurred her vision. She blinked, grasped the banister.

"Virginia, wait…" Her father's hand closed on her shoulder.

She stiffened, tried to stop the tears and steady her voice. "Please let me go, Father."

"Not until you tell me what is wrong."

"What is *wrong*?" She jerked around to face him, shaking beyond her control. "My *life* is wrong! My days are empty—meaningless! I have no use! No purpose! I cry until my head aches. My stomach clenches at the smell of food. And my heart—my heart…" She bit down on her trembling lower lip and buried her face in her hands.

"And your heart is breaking. I can see that now." Her father's arms closed around her. "Forgive me, Virginia. I've made a terrible error. I knew you entered into that pretend marriage to get away from me—to escape my poor choice of Emory Gladen for your husband. I thought your talk of love was mere posturing— strengthening your position against me and my choice of a husband for you in the future." His hands slid to her shoulders, pushed her an arm's length away. "I was wrong, Virginia. I see now that you truly care for Garret Stevenson. And, while I still doubt the wisdom of your in-name-only marriage to him, I believe you should return to Whisper Creek and settle the matter in your own way. And meanwhile, I will be here if you need me."

She stared at him, astounded by his words, stunned by a flash of pain. It was too late.

He reached into his pocket, withdrew his monogrammed handkerchief and held it out to her. "Dry your eyes, daughter. Tomorrow, you will go and resign your shopgirl position, come home and prepare to return—"

She shook her head, took a deep breath. "It's too late. Your remorse comes too late, Father." Laughter and sobs mingled, bubbled from her aching, constricted throat. Her knees gave way and she sank down onto the stairs behind her. "I—I sent a letter telling Garret I would not oppose an a-annulment of our m-marriage."

Her father grasped her arms, gave her a small shake. "Stop it, Virginia. Hysteria will help nothing."

She gulped in air, stared up at him. "Did you not hear me, Father? There's nothing to help!"

"Of course there is." He narrowed his eyes, stared into the distance. "When did you post the letter?"

His brisk, businesslike tone steadied her. "Yesterday morning on my way to the shop."

"Two days then…and you directed it to Garret Stevenson?"

"Yes—"

"And where do the people go to get their mail in that excuse for a town—the railroad station?"

"No, the mail goes to the general store." She watched him turn, stride to the sitting room door and yank on the bell pull. She rose and followed him into the sitting room. "What are you doing, Father?"

"Fixing my mistake." He crossed to the secretary desk in the corner, lowered the writing surface and took out pen and paper.

"But I don't understand, what—"

"You rang, sir."

"One moment, Thomas."

Her father looked at her. "What is the name of the proprietor of the general store?"

"Mr. Blake Latherop." Her heart leaped, reached for a thread of hope. She watched her father scrawl a note on the paper, pull a coin from his pocket and hand both to Thomas.

"Take this to the telegraph office. I want it sent immediately."

"Yes, sir." The butler hurried from the room.

Her father flipped the writing surface closed, clasped his suit coat lapels and gave a nod of satisfaction.

"What did you do, Father? What does that telegram say?"

"It says that you, Virginia, accidentally sent a wrong letter to Garret Stevenson and that you are ordering the postmaster of Whisper Creek, Wyoming, Mr. Blake Latherop, to return that letter to you at this New York address upon receipt. That the letter is *not* to be given to Mr. Stevenson. Now, I suggest you go and pack a valise for your journey back to Whisper Creek. I will have a ticket and money for your trip ready for you in the morning." He rubbed his chin, walked to the window by his chair and looked out. "If you resolve your... situation with Mr. Stevenson and will be staying in Wyoming, write and tell me. I'll have Millie pack the rest of your things into trunks for shipment. If you do not resolve your situation, come home. I'll be waiting."

"Oh, Father..." She ran to him, threw her arms around his neck and squeezed.

He returned her hug, gave her a mock frown. "And

see that you eat a good meal tonight. Or no ticket or money."

"I'll eat, Father. If I'm not too happy and excited." Her smile faded. "But don't buy my ticket for tomorrow. I can't go yet. Mrs. Lamb needs me in the shop in the mornings this week, and I've given her my word." She pushed a strand of hair that had fallen free back into the mass of curls at her crown and met his astonished gaze. "I'll tell her tomorrow that she needs to find a new girl, as I will be returning to Whisper Creek at the end of the week. I can wait, now that I know I'll be returning, and you've sent the telegram so Garret won't be getting the letter."

"Being in Wyoming has changed you, Virginia." Her father studied her a moment, then touched her cheek. "You've grown up."

"I hope so, Father. I want you to be proud of me. And I want—" Her throat tightened, closed off her voice.

"And you want Garret Stevenson to fall in love with you."

She blinked her eyes clear and nodded. "With all of my heart."

"You'll be in room six, Mr. Herzog." Garret handed the well-dressed man the key. "It's the first door on your right at the top of the stairs. And the dressing room you will be using is at the end of the hallway. Dinner begins at twelve o'clock and is served until three o'clock. The dining room is through those doors." He pointed that direction. "Your room is ready, but if there is anything you need, such as an extra blanket, please tell our maid. She will be happy to get it for you. I hope you enjoy your stay."

The man nodded, picked up his bag and climbed the stairs.

The front door opened. Garret looked up from the ledger Mr. Herzog had signed and hurried around the desk. "What can I do for you gentlemen?" He glanced from the engineer to the conductor. "Is there a problem?"

"Not for us." The conductor grinned, took off his hat and stuck it under his arm. "The telegraph line to the east is down again, and we can't move without new orders, so we came to have a good hot dinner. We've heard how good the food is here."

Pride surged through him. It was an odd feeling, being proud of the mother he'd hated for so long. How wrong he'd been! "Right this way, gentlemen." He led them toward the dining room, motioned for Liu Yang to come to the table by a front window. "What happened to the telegraph line?"

"Who knows?" The engineer pulled off his cap and jammed it in his pocket. "Could be some of Red Cloud's warriors decided to cut it. Or could be some buffalo decided to use one of the poles for a scratchin' post. Or half a dozen other things. Whatever it is, it's good news for us. Somethin' sure smells good."

"Excuse me, someone just came in. Enjoy your meal, gentlemen."

He hurried out to the lobby, thinking about Virginia while he ushered a man and his wife to a table. He missed her more every day, couldn't get her out of his mind. And worse yet, his heart—she had taken up residence there and refused to be moved.

He found himself wanting to talk over his problems with her...to share funny little things and big, important things. He wanted to tell her Mrs. Fuller was his mother and watch her face when she heard the news, to see her beautiful eyes shine up at him, to hear her soft exclamation of surprise and joy. He wanted to have his morning coffee with her, and his late night snack. He wanted *her*. His life was empty without her. He'd been a fool to let her go.

"Miss...could I have more coffee, miss?"

The question caught his attention. He scanned the full dining room. Liu Yang was overwhelmed. He rushed to the kitchen, grabbed the coffeepot and hurried back to the man's table. "Here's your coffee, sir. I'm sorry for the delay."

A chair scraped along the floor. He glanced at the clock—ten minutes until supper was over and the dining room closed. He placed the coffeepot on a trivet on the hearth and hurried out to the lobby.

"Good day to you, Mr. Stevenson." The engineer tugged his hat from his pocket and pulled it on his head. "That's the best meal I've had in a long while! I'll be back the next time the line goes down."

The dining room emptied as quickly as it had filled. He picked up a tray Liu Yang had piled with dirty dishes, carried it to the kitchen and set it down on the cupboard by the sink. "The schedule will be off this afternoon, Mother. The telegraph line is down and the trains aren't moving."

His mother looked up from putting the worktable back in order. "What do you want me to do about supper?"

"There's no way to plan—so no cooking. Just give the patrons cold ham and cabbage slaw, bread and butter, some fruit." He looked at the threadbare spot on the arm of her dress, spotted another on the long skirt. "And for now, take off your apron and come with me."

"But the dishes—"

"Li Min will do them. You need to keep that bandage dry." He ushered her through the dining room into the lobby. "Put on your coat and hat while I get mine."

He stepped back into the dining room. "Liu Yang, I'll be at the general store next door. Come and get me if a guest needs something you can't do."

"Yes, meester."

He grabbed his hat and coat from the sitting room, went to his mother's room and knocked.

"I'm ready."

Her coat and hat were more worn than her dress. He led her across the lobby, over the porch to the steps and down to the path that joined the stores, narrowing his eyes at the sunlight glaring on the snow.

"Where are you taking me?"

"To get some new clothes." He grinned at her stunned look, helped her up the porch steps and opened the door of the general store. He blinked at the dimness of the interior after the sunlight and guided her toward the counter. "Good afternoon, Audrey. You're looking well."

"Thank you, Garret. You're very kind." Audrey

placed a hand on her swollen abdomen and gave him a smile that included the older woman at his side. "How may I help you?"

His mother held back, whispered up at him. "Garret, please, this isn't necessary."

He grinned and urged her forward. "I know. This is for my pleasure." He shifted his gaze to the proprietor's wife. "Audrey, this is my mother, Mrs. Fuller. She needs some new dresses and shoes and whatever other, er, items of clothing a woman wears. She's a bit reluctant to spend my money, so I suspect you'll have to do most of the choosing."

"What fun! It's lovely to meet you, Mrs. Fuller. I've heard about your cooking and baking." Audrey smiled at his mother, then shifted her gaze back to him. "And the limit?"

He shook his head. "You'd know the answer to that better than me. So I'll just say however many she needs of whatever she needs, then add a few extra pretty ones just for pleasure. And make sure you include a new coat and hat and boots. How long before you can get an order shipped in?"

"That will depend on the dressmaker. Though they will have the necessary items, such as petticoats that don't need precise sizing, already made and on hand. They'll have skirts and shirtwaists for everyday wear, as well. Those things can be shipped as soon as they receive the order. We usually receive them in two days—when the trains are running." Audrey picked up a paper and pencil and came around the counter. "Mrs. Fuller, if you will join me at that table, we will take your measurements, look through some of my fashion magazines and make out your order. And maybe discuss cooking while we're at it."

He smiled assurance at his mother, who still looked a little stunned and a lot uncomfortable, and went to the back room. "Blake..."

"Over here, Garret. I'm sorting mail while there's a lull in the trains coming into town. You have a letter."

Chapter Eighteen

"Thank you, Blake." Garret took the letter his friend handed him and glanced at the handwriting. *Virginia*. His heart jolted. He folded the letter into his pocket and leaned against his friend's mail sorting table, thankful Blake was busy and wasn't looking at him. "Have you heard anything about when the trains will be running again?"

"No, all Asa said when he brought the mail was that the engineers can't move the trains until they get their new schedules." Blake placed the few letters in the boxes of Whisper Creek residents and removed his sleeve garters. "If they don't get that telegraph fixed soon, you may have a hotel full of guests—the way it was during the blizzard." He glanced toward the women. "Did I hear you say Mrs. Fuller is your mother?"

"Yes, she is." He met his friend's curious gaze, then glanced toward the back of the store. "Have any of the supplies come in?"

Blake shook his head. "I'm afraid not. They're due in on the next train. Does that pose a problem for you?"

"Food could get tight if the stranded passengers all come to the hotel to eat. How is your stock of supplies?"

"I restocked after you bought me out during the blizzard. We should be all right—as long as this delay is a short one."

He nodded, followed Blake over to the counter. "That's good to know. But I've been thinking we need a couple of farms and a ranch in this valley. It's not good having to rely on the trains to supply our food. We're in real trouble when they stop running."

"I agree. John Ferndale needs to change that rule. He could restrict ranchers and farmers by the amount of land he sells them so they wouldn't cause any trouble."

"Exactly. I'm going to talk to him about it before spring." He looked at Blake, weighed the idea that had just come to him and made his proposal. "The hotel is doing well, and I've been thinking about investing in a ranch. Would you be interested?"

Blake rested his palms against the edge of the counter and stared at him. "I hadn't thought about that…" His friend's eyes narrowed, and he nodded. "It sounds good. Of course, I know nothing about ranching or farming. I'll give it some thought and get back to you."

"No hurry. I haven't made up my mind, either—but it seems too good an investment to pass up."

It sounds as if you need to buy a ranch.

Virginia's soft voice echoed through his head. He slipped his hand into his pocket, touched the letter. He was prodded by an urgent need to get back to the hotel and read it. Alone. "I know you've heard the rumor about some cowboys from Texas buying up most of the land in the next valley. If it's true, and we bought the rest of the land, including the gap into Whisper Creek Valley, we'd have a strong bargaining point."

He left Blake pondering his words and moved on to the table where his mother sat looking at magazines with Audrey Latherop. "Mother, I'm going back to the hotel. I don't want to leave Liu Yang alone there for long. No, no, you stay here." He placed his hand on her shoulder when she started to rise. "I don't think Audrey is finished with you yet. I'll be back to get you in an hour. And don't forget the new coat and hat."

He walked to the door, the letter crackling when his sleeve brushed against it. The bell on the door jangled behind him. He hurried across the porch, trotted down the steps and ate up the short distance between the general store and his hotel with his long strides. Why was Virginia writing him? Was the letter a warning that her father was still making plans to destroy him? Or was it something more? Was she coming home?

Home. His chest tightened. For the first time in eighteen years, that word meant something to him. And with Virginia to share it...

He jerked open the door and glanced around the lobby, blew out a long breath. There were no guests in sight. He tugged off his gloves, unbuttoned his coat and hurried to his office and closed the door. He pulled the letter from his pocket and threw his coat in his chair, his heart pounding.

Mrs. Garret Stevenson. The name looked good. He

smiled, slid his finger beneath the fold and broke the seal, unfolded the letter. A piece of paper fell out and landed on the desk. He ignored it and fastened his gaze on the letter. *My friend Garret.* His stomach flopped. Was that how she thought of him—as her friend?

He scowled and read on, skimming over the polite greeting and well wishes. *I have come to realize that I have become a "stumbling block" to your future.* A stumbling block? What did that mean? *I am sure that one day soon a young woman traveling on the train will enter the hotel and draw your interest.*

He stared at the words, a slow burn igniting in his gut. Why would she say *that*? How many times had he told her he was not interested in a romantic relationship with *any* woman! He threw the letter onto his desk, shoved his fingers through his hair and blew out a breath. He'd thought that she cared about him as much as he cared for her—well, certainly more than just as a *friend*, anyway! How could he have been so wrong? Maybe he was misunderstanding her meaning.

He snatched up the letter and read on: *You will, of course, want to be free to woo her. It is for that reason I am sending the enclosed letter.*

Woo her? What letter? That piece of paper. He grabbed it and unfolded it.

To whom it may concern:
This letter is to state that I, Virginia Louise Winterman Stevenson, do not in any way oppose the annulment of my marriage to Mr. Garret Stevenson.
Mrs. Garret Stevenson

A band closed around his chest. His breath shortened. He didn't believe it! She had been so adamant about staying married when she left for New York. This had to be because of her father. The man had convinced her that their marriage meant nothing—unless she had not meant what she said to him. He crushed the paper, thought better of it and smoothed it out, grabbed up her letter and scanned the last paragraph.

She was working as a shopgirl. She wanted him to give fond greetings to his mother.

And there it was again, in the final line:

With sincere best wishes, your friend,
Virginia

Friend. The muscle along his jaw twitched. The burn in his gut flamed into hot coals. It was the betrayal he had expected from the first day. She was joining with her father against him. But she wouldn't get away with it. He grabbed his coat, slammed out of his office and stormed through the lobby and out the door.

"The green watered silk looks beautiful on you, Mrs. Walsh. And the alterations will be finished tomorrow afternoon—before you need it for your party this weekend." Virginia smiled and hung the dress out of sight on the peg just inside the door to the back room. "And before you go, I would be remiss if I did not show you the lovely tatted Irish lace evening gloves Mrs. Lamb just put out for sale yesterday. They're on the counter." She led the older woman away from the path to the door.

"Oh, they are lovely!"

"And this ecru color would be perfect with the gown. Just look at that fine tatting." She handed the gloves to the woman and stepped back. "Mrs. Peters bought a pair in royal blue yesterday."

"Mrs. Ilene Peters?"

"Yes. Do you know Mrs. Peters? She bought the gloves to go with a blue-and-white-striped taffeta gown she purchased."

"Humph. Ilene has no sense of style. She always buys stripes! She thinks they make her look less chubby." The woman handed her the gloves. "I'll take these, my dear. And also that mother-of-pearl hair comb you showed me earlier."

"You have wonderful taste, Mrs. Walsh." She picked up the hair comb and placed it and the gloves on the counter, made note of the purchases in the small, discreet leather book. "Why don't you browse a bit while I wrap these for you? I don't believe you have seen the new hats. They are sitting on the table in the back corner until I have time to put them in the window."

She drew the tissue paper from beneath the counter, placed the gloves on it. She added the hair comb on top and folded the paper over them.

Have you ever wrapped a present? A smile touched her lips. Dear Mrs. Fuller. How wonderful it would be to see her again. She missed her so much.

She tied the package with a silver ribbon and attached one of Mrs. Lamb's cards. "Your package is ready for you, Mrs. Walsh." She smiled as the woman came bustling over to the counter. "Thank you for your patronage. I hope you will come to see us again soon."

"Oh, I shall, my dear—I shall. And I will be waiting for my dress to be delivered tomorrow afternoon!"

Tomorrow. Her heart sang the word. Tomorrow was her last day as a shopgirl. And the next day she would spend packing her things for her journey back to Whisper Creek. Back to Garret. It wouldn't be long now. She picked up the tissue paper and put it back into its place under the counter.

"Good morning, Virginia."

She looked up and smiled. "Good morning, Mrs. Lamb." She walked to the back room and put on her coat, tied her hat in place. "Mrs. Walsh bought the green, watered silk. The paper with the instructions for the alterations is pinned to the sash. I promised her they would be finished tomorrow afternoon, so she could wear the new gown to her party tomorrow night." She buttoned her coat and started for the front door.

"I see several other purchases were made this morning." Mrs. Lamb tapped the book and sighed. "I'm going to miss you when you leave, Mrs. Stevenson. You have a gift for dealing with people."

"Thank you, Mrs. Lamb." She tugged on her gloves and walked out into the flow of pedestrians. Snow began to fall, drifting down to cover the shoveled sidewalk. Small white clumps of flakes clung to her coat and the toes of her boots as she walked. Would it be snowing in Whisper Creek when she arrived? Would Garret be pleased to see her? Would they walk in the snow together?

Her stomach fluttered, tensed. She'd been so caught up in the excitement of returning to him, she'd forgotten he didn't feel the same…regard for her. That he had made no protest to her returning home to New York. Indeed, that he had thought it best.

Perhaps she should write and tell him she was coming. No. She squared her shoulders and lifted her chin. It would be better to just appear—as she had the first time. She couldn't bear it if he told her not to come. And once there—well, once there she would see what would happen.

The snowfall had lost its charm. It was just cold and wet and dreary. She shivered, brushed off her collar and quickened her steps.

The train whistle blasted—blasted again. Twice in quick succession, the signal for departure.

Garret glanced out the window, stared at the train's light piercing the darkness, then looked back at Pastor Karl. "The trains have started running! I didn't expect that. It's been standing so long, I thought they would stay in place until morning." He took a breath, scrubbed his hand over the back of his neck. "I'm sorry to put this on you, Pastor—especially on such short notice—but there's no one else in town I can ask."

"Don't give it another thought, Garret. I'm only too pleased to help." The pastor looked up from the registry ledger and smiled. "What sort of message would I be sending my family and my congregation if I refused to help a friend in need? And it certainly seems as if the

Lord is blessing your plans. That is the first train moving through Whisper Creek today."

He nodded, glanced toward the window again. The beam of light was shining down the valley, fading out of sight. "If the schedule runs as usual, that means a train heading east will be coming through in a little more than an hour. And—"

"And you have told me what I need to know to keep the hotel running until your return. And your mother will be here to help me, should I have a question. Go and pack your things so you will be ready to take that train to New York, Garret. And may the Lord bless you in your efforts to resolve your problem."

"Thank you, Pastor. And if you want to bring Eddie along with you to help carry the guests' bags, I will be happy to pay him two cents for each valise he carries."

"Eddie will be happy to carry the guests' bags for the pleasure of helping a friend, Garret." Pastor Karl grinned. "And, since his spiritual growth is less than mature at this point, for the opportunity to brag about it to his younger sisters. Now, I'll just bank the dining room fire for the night, while you get ready for your trip to New York."

Garret nodded and pushed through the door to the sitting room. He strode down the hallway to his bedroom and pulled a valise from the top shelf in his wardrobe. He didn't need to take much, only his necessaries and a clean shirt or two. He wouldn't be staying long. He couldn't. He had a hotel to run. Virginia either meant what she'd said about staying committed to their in-name-only marriage, or she didn't. The burn in his stomach intensified. He jerked his thoughts back to the business at hand. Two ties should be enough, one gray and one blue.

He carried the valise to the dressing room, filled a small wood box with his toiletries and shaving gear. That should take care of his needs. He closed the lid of the box, latched it and put it in the valise. He was ready.

The heels of his boots thudded against the oval rug in the hallway. He adjusted the heating stove in his bedroom for a slow burn, put on his vest and suit coat and crossed to his office. The crumpled letter and enclosure were on his desk. The muscle along his jaw twitched. He slipped the papers into his vest pocket, unlocked his desk drawer and put some money in his leather wallet. That was all he needed. He carried the valise out to the sitting room and set it on the floor beneath his coat.

The clock chimed. Still forty minutes until the train came—if it was running on the normal schedule. He took a long breath, blew it out and went to the kitchen.

His mother looked up from the dough she was kneading. "My, you look handsome! Are you packed and ready to leave? Do you need any help?" There was a sadness in her voice that tugged at his heart.

"I'm sorry to leave you like this, Mother, but I have to go to New York." He rolled his shoulders to release some of the tension.

"Garret, I don't mean to pry, but I'm concerned. Does this trip have to do with Virginia?" Her gaze searched his face. "Is she ill?" Tears glittered in her eyes.

"No, Mother, she's not ill." He scrubbed his hand over his neck, debated how much to tell her. "I haven't time to tell you the whole story now, but my marriage to Virginia is not a…a normal one. We married for convenience, not love. And our marriage is tied in with my owning the hotel."

He looked away from his mother's steady gaze. "Virginia's father is angry over the situation, and he is determined to annul our marriage. If he does, I will lose the hotel because of a contract I signed with the founder of Whisper Creek. And Mr. Winterman is a very wealthy and powerful man."

"And what has that to do with Virginia?"

"She has agreed with her father to end our marriage."

"That can't be so." His mother turned the dough and kneaded it, turned it again.

"It's so, Mother." The words left a bitter taste in his mouth. "She sent me a letter with an enclosed paper saying she will not oppose the annulment."

"Then perhaps her father forced her to do so." His mother pulled her hands from the dough and fastened her gaze on his. "Listen to me, Garret. I know I haven't any right to speak about your life, but I know how men can force a woman to do things she does not want to do. And I know your wife loves you—whether she did when you were wed or not, she loves you now. And you love her."

He drew breath to protest, but his mother shook her head and smiled.

"Yes, son, you do." She wiped her hand on her apron and placed her palm against the twitching muscle along his jaw. "Forgiveness destroys bitterness, Garret. And love is far more powerful than anger. You go to New York and bring your beautiful bride home."

Chapter Nineteen

Virginia placed the purple gown with the shawl collar in the trunk, tucked her shoes along the edge and closed the top. "You can carry it down and set it by the front door now, Thomas."

The butler lifted the trunk to his shoulder and started for the stairs.

"Mind you don't bump the door frame, Thomas." Millie guided him out the door, then hurried back to help her mistress finish packing. She folded the mahogany-red velvet walking dress into the large leather valise and smoothed out the creases. "That's all of the dresses. What more do you want in the valise? Your nightclothes and slippers?"

"Yes. Oh! And I mustn't forget the paisley shawl I bought for Mrs. Fuller." She hurried to her wardrobe and lifted the tissue paper–wrapped gift off of the top shelf. "And my book…" She pulled a copy of *American Woman's Home* out of the drawer of her nightstand and tucked it in at the end of the valise. "I know Mrs.

Fuller will give me all of the advice I shall ever need about caring for a home, but she might enjoy reading the book. And it might prove useful."

She reached back into the drawer and pulled out a folder, brushed her hand over the top of it and smiled.

It sounds as if you need to buy a ranch.

It's a good idea. If things go as well as I hope with the hotel, I might just do it.

She tucked the folder along the side of the valise where it would be protected and looked around the room. "I believe that's all, Millie. You may go help Martha with supper."

She snapped the valise closed and glanced at the clock. There was still an hour until her train left New York. What could she do until it was time to leave for the station? Her stomach fluttered at the thought. She pressed her hand against it. Obviously, eating supper was not possible. She was far too excited.

She walked to her pier glass, shook out her long, green damask skirt and tucked her Garibaldi shirt deeper under the small waistband. The glint of the gold metal buttons that paraded in a straight line from the blouse's high stand-up collar down the front to meet the skirt gave the outfit a slight military look. She grinned, snapped a salute to her reflection and put on the skirt's matching bolero jacket.

The door knocker echoed through the entrance hall and up the stairwell. She glanced over her shoulder toward her open door and listened for Thomas's footsteps. The door opened and there was the deep murmur of male voices. One of her father's friends stopping in on the way to their club, no doubt.

She turned back to the mirror, checked the loose pile of curls secured at the crown of her head and frowned. With all of the jostling and jolting she would encounter on the long train ride, perhaps she should just let the curls tumble down her back. She reached to pull out her hair combs. Light footsteps running up the stairs stayed her hand. She glanced over her shoulder. What—

Millie burst into view, stopped and grabbed for the door frame, her eyes wide, her face flushed. "Beggin' your pardon, miss, but you're wanted downstairs. He's here!"

She could think of only one man who would so upset Millie. "Emory Gladen? I thought that he—"

"No, Miss Virginia. Him! Your husband!"

"Garret?" The strength drained from her legs. She grabbed for a bedpost. "I don't understand. What is he doing here? Why isn't he in Whisper Creek?" A dozen questions crowded into her mind.

"I don't know, Miss Virginia, but he's not pleased about it. Thomas said your husband and your father are having words."

"Oh no!" She lunged for the door and raced down the steps, stopped short outside the parlor door to compose herself. A deep breath steadied her. *Give me strength, Lord. Please help me!* She squared her shoulders, tugged her jacket into place and walked into the middle of a weighted silence.

"Ah, there you are, Virginia." Her father dipped his

head her direction, then looked toward the fireplace. "You have a visitor."

"Yes, I was told." She turned her head, and there he was—tall, handsome and angry. *Garret.* She moved close to the chair beside the door, rested her hands on its back and held on to keep from collapsing in a heap.

"I am no visitor, sir. I am her *husband*. And I intend to stay her husband in spite of your efforts to annul our marriage."

She jerked her gaze from Garret and looked at her father. "Annul our marriage?"

"Yes. It seems your...husband received your letter—"

"What letter?"

"This one."

She looked at Garret, bit off her gasp. He held the letter and enclosure she had written. "How did you g—"

"I would have been here sooner, but the telegraph line was down a few days ago, and the trains weren't running."

"Oh. *Oh-h-h...*" She darted her gaze to her father. So that's what had happened. His telegram hadn't gone through in time to stop the letter.

"Your husband thinks that I have been up to some skullduggery to dissolve your in-name-only marriage, and that you agree with me. He has been reminding me that though, er...different, your marriage is perfectly legal."

"But—"

"There's no time to discuss our marriage or your betrayal now." Garret stepped close, a muscle in his cheek jumping. "I've come to take you back to Whisper Creek with me. We'll discuss our future on the journey."

Our future. He'd come for her. Her pulse skipped.

"I have a cab waiting outside to take us to the station. Our train leaves in twenty minutes, so there is only time for you to pack the things you will need for the journey." His gaze fastened on hers. "Hurry. Your father can have the rest of your things shipped to you."

The rest of her things. He wanted her to stay. The skipping increased. Her throat tightened. "I—"

"There's no need to wait. Virginia was just leaving for a prolonged visit and is already packed."

Garret's gaze shifted to her father, came back to rest on her. She caught her breath, nodded and pointed toward her trunk, with her valise sitting atop it, beside the front door.

Garret guided Virginia down the aisle, stopped by a seat on the right side of the passenger car. "Do you have a preference, or is this seat all right?"

"It's fine." She edged over to the window and sat. "I like being far enough back in the car that I can see the scenery beyond the engine and tender. The country is so vast, I like watching it pass by when we have left the cities behind."

The tension in his shoulders eased in response to her smile. She seemed to have relaxed since they boarded the train. He set their valises on the floor beneath their seat, placed his hat on top of his and unbuttoned his coat.

The whistle blew. A puff of steam drifted by the

window. The train lurched, rolled ahead, and the station disappeared. Buildings came into view, then vanished. He watched her watching them go by, studied the gentle curve of her brow, the straight, fine line of her nose, admired the soft rose color of her full lips and her small round chin. A tinge of pink washed over her cheekbones. His breath caught. Was her blush because he was looking at her?

"I'd forgotten how beautiful you are." He whispered the words low, for her ears alone. The blush deepened. Her head turned. She glanced up at him through her long lashes.

"Thank you." She straightened the already straight edge of her coat, folded her hands in her lap and turned her gaze back to the window.

He made her nervous. He leaned back in the seat, savoring the knowledge, and watched the lantern-lit buildings outside the window give way to trees and fields bathed in moonlight.

"How is Mrs. Fuller?"

"She's fine." He looked at Virginia, watched her remove her hat and put it in her lap, noted her trembling hands. "Let me get that out of your way." He took her hat and put it on her valise under the seat. "I've learned something about Mrs. Fuller since you've been gone. And something about myself."

"Oh?" She pushed at the curls bunched at the crown of her head. "What is that?"

He shook his head, captured her gaze with his. "I have to tell you something first."

Interest flashed in her eyes. She shifted on the seat to face him. He braced himself for her reaction.

"When I was ten years old, my mother disappeared. I woke the morning of my tenth birthday and found a cake in the middle of the table, but my mother was gone. That was eighteen years ago. I never saw her again."

"Oh, Garret, I'm so *sorry*." Tears welled up in her eyes. "How terrible to not know where your mother is, or—"

"I do know. I found out a few days ago."

She stared at him. The bright blue of her eyes darkened. "How did you find out?"

He blew out a breath, scrubbed his hand over his neck. "I need to move around. Will you come out onto the boarding porch with me?"

"Yes, of course. I would like some fresh air."

He rose, helped her from the seat and guided her to the front of the car. He held her arm, helped her out onto the small porch and stood so he would block most of the wind from her. The shadow of the overhanging roof blocked out the direct moonlight, but he could still see the gold of her curls and blue of her eyes when she looked up at him.

"You were saying?"

"Mrs. Fuller was frying doughnuts. Oil splashed up on her sleeve and burned her. When I went to help her, I saw a birthmark on her arm that I remembered from when I was a young boy."

"When you were— Mrs. Fuller is your *mother*?"

He cleared his throat, caught in the emotion of that moment. "She admitted it then."

She stared at him, her eyes as round as the moon above them. "But I don't understand. If she knew, why didn't she tell you?"

"She said the look in my eyes made her afraid."

"Oh."

His gaze captured and held hers. "Did I make you afraid, Virginia?"

"At first. Until I learned to know you…"

"And then?"

She shook her head, looked away.

"Don't ever be afraid of me, Virginia. Not ever again." He turned and leaned his back against the passenger car, braced his legs and pulled her close to him. "I love you." He lowered his head and claimed her lips, tasted the salt of tears and felt her lips quiver. She went up on her toes, slid her arms around his neck and answered his love.

The metal wheels screeched in protest as they slid against the iron rails. The train shuddered, skidded to a stop. Virginia opened her eyes. She was snuggled in the curve of Garret's arm with her head resting on his shoulder. She'd never felt as happy and safe in her life. She sighed and burrowed closer.

"Are you trying to climb into my pocket?" The low, growled words vibrated through Garret's chest beneath her ear.

"Would you mind?"

"Um-hmm. I'd rather have you in my arms." Garret opened one eye and looked down at her.

She smiled up at him, glanced at the other passengers

and lowered her voice to a whisper. "We've stopped to take on water and fuel. Go back to sleep." She pushed with her free hand against his chest. "Am I making you uncomfortable?"

"Don't move—unless it's closer."

"That's not possible."

He looked at her. Her cheeks flamed. She turned her head to look out the window. The papers in his pocket crackled. She patted them. "Would you take these out of your pocket, please? They're noisy when my head is resting against them."

He nodded, slipped his free hand into his vest pocket and pulled them out. "Why did you write me this letter, Virginia? Did you really want to annul our marriage?"

"Of course not!"

The man in the next seat snorted. She looked at him, waited until he began snoring again, then continued. "When I left to go back to New York with Father, you didn't try to stop me. You said I should go, that it would be best. So I thought you were unhappy with me and would want to be free to—to wed another." She sat upright and wiped the tears from her cheeks. "And I wanted you to be happy. So I sent the letters. And then when Father saw how unhappy I was without you, he said I should go back to Whisper Creek and work things out. But it was too late. I'd already posted the letter."

She sighed, looked out the window. "That's when Father sent a telegram to Blake Latherop, telling him not to deliver the letter to you, but to send it back to me. So I started packing. Of course, we didn't know the telegram never reached Blake Latherop."

"That's why your trunk was packed? You were coming back to Whisper Creek?" He shook his head, grinned. "I don't believe it."

"I can prove it."

"How?"

The train lurched, rolled forward and picked up speed. She lifted her reticule off the seat and reached inside. "Here you are—proof."

He stared at the ticket for one to Whisper Creek, Wyoming, sucked in a deep breath and took hold of her hand. "Come with me. I suddenly need some fresh air."

"Air, sir?" Her eyes sparkled up at him.

He led her down the aisle again, out onto the small platform, pulled her into his arms and kissed her until she was breathless and trembling.

"Will you be my wife, Virginia? My true wife?" His voice was low, husky, his breath warm against her skin. "No more in-name-only marriage, but a true one. Will you love me? And have my babies? And wake up next to me every morning for the rest of our lives?"

"Yes! Oh, yes, Garret. I love you so much." She threw her arms around his neck and returned his kisses.

The train lurched, swept around a curve. Garret turned her around, pulled her back against his chest and raised his hands. "We won't need these anymore." He handed her one of the letters and held the other. Moonlight flickered on their hands as they tore the papers to bits, then opened their fingers and let the wind blow the tiny pieces of their hurtful past away.

The train snaked through the tall grasses of the prairie, a storm its only company. The wind swooped and howled, whipped the tall brown stems of grass into a frenzy. The gloomy, overcast day held a chilly dampness that penetrated the warmest clothes. The heating stove offered little comfort.

She stared out the window at the distant mountains that rose like a formidable wall from the prairie floor—a barrier to keep them from reaching home. Rain splattered against the glass, turned to snow and obstructed her view. She shivered, turned her gaze on Garret.

He pulled her closer against him. "Are you warm enough? Do you want me to ask for a blanket?"

"No, I'm fine. I was wondering if we should send a telegram to Mrs. Fuller, to let her know when we will arrive. But with this weather, that might not be wise."

"I think it's a good idea. I'll send one at the next stop."

"All right. I—" She gasped and brushed at the window with her hand. "Are those buffalo out there?"

He leaned close, peered outside. "Those are buffalo, all right. Let's hope they don't have a sudden itch to scratch and use the next telegraph pole."

"Or decide to bed down on the tracks ahead to wait out the storm. No one could move one of those huge beasts."

"Well, I can think of worse things than to be stranded with you." He grinned at her blush, leaned back against the seat and pulled her close.

The train rolled onward, clattering over the iron rails. The snow hardened to pellets that peppered the windows and rattled on the roof. At the gap in the mountain wall, the train stopped to take on wood and water.

"Let's hope the telegraph is working." Garret pulled on his hat and gloves and hurried outside. He dropped down off the platform and ran to the station through stinging hail driven by the prairie wind.

"Can I help you, mister?"

"I want to send a telegram."

"There's the form. Just write out yer message an' I'll get it on its way."

"Thank you." He picked up the pen, wrote out the message and handed the form to the short, wiry telegrapher.

Mrs. Ruth Fuller
Stevenson Hotel
Whisper Creek, Wyoming Territory

Mother. You are right. Love is far stronger than anger.
 Happier than we ever thought possible.
 Arrive tomorrow late afternoon. If all goes well.
Eager to see you.
Garret and Virginia

"Let's see now…" The man counted the words, scribbled some figures on a pad and looked up at him. "That'll be seventy-eight cents."

Garret handed him the coins. The man limped over to his stool and started clicking the key.

"How do you know if the message goes through?"

"The telegrapher who gets it answers."

"I see." The man was still sitting at the table clicking the key when the train whistle blew. Garret pulled up his collar and ran back to the railway, swung up onto the platform and opened the door. Wind swirled into the car, threw the stinging white pellets against the walls and seats and floor. He stepped inside.

The conductor put his shoulder against the door and shoved it closed, hurried to the heating stove and threw in some chunks of the wood they'd loaded into the wood box.

The train lurched, the couplings clanged and steam hissed by the window. Garret strode down the aisle, swaying side to side as the passenger car rolled down the track. He smiled at Virginia. "Nasty weather out there."

She looked at the hail pinging against the window glass and nodded. "Did the message go through?"

"I can't say. The telegrapher was still sending it when I had to board." He took off his gloves and shoved them in his coat pocket, rubbed his hands together. "There was no place to buy food. We'll have to wait until the next stop."

She nodded and patted the cover spread over her legs. "I asked for a blanket while you were gone. Sit down beside me and get warm. I have something to show you."

"What is it?"

She waited until he was beside her on the seat, then handed him the folder. "Do you remember the first night during the blizzard, when you mentioned how dependent Whisper Creek is on the trains for its food supplies? And you said you were thinking of perhaps investing in a cattle ranch to alleviate that problem?"

"I do." He grinned and opened the folder. "And if I remember correctly, you told me I should buy a ranch."

Her cheeks went pink. "Well, either way, I thought some of these newspaper and magazine articles about ranching might interest you."

"Hmm, trying to turn me into a cowboy, are you?"

She shook her head, her curls bobbing, and gave him a saucy smile. "In case you hadn't noticed, I like you just the way you are."

"I've noticed."

Chapter Twenty

Her husband. In a true marriage. Her stomach fluttered. A tingle chased along her nerves. Virginia put down her fork and looked across the rough plank table at Garret. She could never get enough of looking at him. Of listening to him talk. Or watching him eat, or drink his coffee. He glanced up from his plate and their gazes met. The flutter got stronger. The tingle more intense.

"You're not eating." A frown creased his brow. "The conductor said this is the last place that serves hot food until after the train climbs the steep mountains up ahead."

"I know. I've had enough." She smiled. "I'm saving my appetite for Mrs. Fuller's cooking. I've missed her so much. Oh."

"What is it?"

"I just thought...what am I to call her? 'Mrs. Fuller' seems too formal an address now."

"I'm sure she'd like you to call her Mother. She already loves you like a daughter."

Garret's smile settled in her heart. She blinked a rush of tears from her eyes. "I hope that's true. But I don't want to presume. I'll let her tell me. And meantime, perhaps I could call her Mother Fuller."

The train whistle blew. Garret tossed two coins on the table, stepped close and placed his hand at the small of her back. "Ready?"

She nodded, braced herself for the force of the wind and the sting of the hailstones. He opened the door, put his arm around her shoulders, and together they ran for the train. He lifted her onto the small platform, grabbed the railing and hopped up beside her. He backed her against the end of the passenger car and shielded her from the pelting sleet with his body while he opened the door.

The warmth of the heating stove felt good. She slid into their seat, waited until he unbuttoned his coat and joined her. He slipped his arm around her, and she smiled and lowered her head to rest on his shoulder. His arm tightened. She opened her eyes and smiled up at him. His hand closed over hers, big and warm and strong. She sighed, closed her eyes and listened to the tapping of the hailstones on the roof.

A hard jolt woke her. She stirred and pushed erect to look out the window. They were slowing, coming into Laramie station. "Do you feel better since you rested? You haven't had much sleep on this trip."

She glanced at Garret and smiled. "I've had as much as I wanted." His grin made her heart skip.

The car door opened and the conductor stepped inside. "Next stop, Laramie." He stepped back out the door.

The whistle blew. The train wheels locked, squealed, slid to a stop.

The passengers rose, made their way toward the door.

"Are you hungry? Do you want to get something to eat, Virginia?" Garret stretched his long legs out into the aisle. "We've still a ways to go."

"No, I'm fine." She glanced at the line of people filing out the door. "If you don't mind, I would like to take advantage of the empty dressing room and freshen up before we get home." She smiled at Garret. "My, but that sounds nice...home."

He nodded and rose, stretching his arms and rolling his shoulders. "I'm going to go for a quick walk to get rid of these cramped muscles." He leaned down and kissed her, pulled her close and kissed her again. "You are far too enticing, Mrs. Stevenson." He kissed the tip of her nose and strode out the door.

She pulled her valise from under the seat and hurried to the dressing room. A good brushing would free her long curls to hang down her back. Garret preferred them that way. He'd never said so, but she could tell from the look in his eyes. Oh my, the look in his eyes! She smiled, pulled her flower-scented soap and lotion from her valise and pumped some water into the washbowl.

"What a beautiful day! And it's so warm. After going through that hailstorm on the prairie, I can't believe the sun is shining."

Garret grinned at Virginia. "Whisper Creek is on

her best behavior to welcome you home. Here, let me help you with your coat."

He lifted the coat she had unbuttoned from her shoulders, and draped it with his over the two valises sitting on top of her trunk. "Asa, have these put on Mr. Latherop's delivery cart. I'll get them from him."

"Yes, sir." The stationmaster gave her a smile. "Welcome home, Mrs. Stevenson."

"Thank you, Mr. Marsh." She returned his smile, then couldn't resist adding, "Are there any telegrams for Mr. Stevenson?"

"No, ma'am, but there's one for you." He handed her a telegraph form, bobbed his head and went back to work.

She looked down at the form and smiled. "It's from Father. He says welcome home. He will come and visit us in two weeks." She grinned. "He is coming for a piece of Mrs. Fuller's apple pie." She tucked the form in Garret's vest pocket and patted it. "Your mother's cooking and baking is becoming famous. Oh, I can't wait to see her!"

He took her elbow and helped her down the platform steps, then held her hand. Passengers from the train rushed by, hurried along the snow-spotted dirt road ahead of them and entered the hotel.

Virginia looked at him, worry in her eyes. "Can Liu Yang take care of so many guests?"

"I'm not sure about her, or Pastor Karl." They hurried up onto the porch and opened the door.

"I want a meal for me and my family."

"Me, too. And we only have twenty minutes."

"Do I pay for the room before I go to the dining room to eat?"

Virginia looked at him and laughed. "Welcome home!" She wiggled her fingers in farewell and hurried into the dining room.

He turned his mind to work. "Ladies and gentlemen, if I may have your attention please." He caught a glimpse of Pastor Karl's relieved expression and nodded reassuringly. "Those of you who wish to register for an overnight stay, please form a line at the service desk. And those of you who only wish a meal—"

A hand touched his arm. He glanced sideways. Virginia was standing beside him, wearing a snowy-white apron. He fought down a rush of love that threatened to overwhelm him, and squeezed her hand.

"—please follow my wife."

"Glad you be here, mee-sus."

"Work very much easy."

"Thank you, Liu Yang, Li Min. It's nice to be home."

Virginia closed the door behind the two chattering women and looked around the kitchen. The rush of work had ended, and emotion gripped her. Tears stung her eyes. "It is home." She blinked and cleared the lump from her throat. "And more so because you are here, Mrs. Fuller. I have missed you a great deal."

"Thank you, Virginia. I've missed you, too." The older woman set a bowl of bread dough to proof in the warming oven, put in a second bowl and closed the oven door. "I was so pleased to get your letter."

"I had to explain why I had rushed off without saying farewell. I—I didn't want you to think I didn't care about you." She removed her apron and hung it on its hook. "I had no choice at the time. I did it—"

"To protect your husband from your father."

"You *know*?"

Mrs. Fuller nodded, scraped the flour and clinging bits of dough off the table and into the waste bucket. "I don't know for certain, of course. What I do know is that sometimes women are forced to do things they don't want to do to protect people they love. And I know you love m—Garret."

"You can say son, Mother." Garret strode into the kitchen, walked to the stove and poured a cup of coffee. "I've told Virginia that you are my mother. And about discovering the truth because of your birthmark. I also told her she should call you Mother."

"I—I don't want to presume, Mrs. Fuller. Everything is so new, and—"

"I would like it very much if you called me Mother, dear." The older woman put her hand on her arm and smiled. "You are already a daughter to me in my heart."

"I would like that—Mother." She swallowed back tears, squeezed Mrs. Fuller's hand, then hurried to Garret. She pulled the telegram from his pocket. "I know Garret has not had time to talk with you since our return this afternoon. But this telegram from my father concerns you. He is coming for a visit in two weeks." She smiled and handed her the telegram. "He says he is coming because he wants a piece of your apple pie!"

"That is nonsense. Your father is only teasing you."

"Oh, I don't know about that, Mother." Garret took a

swallow of his coffee and grinned. "There's something powerful about a really good apple pie."

"Well, you may test that theory if you so choose. I made an apple pie to welcome you home. It's in the pie safe. Now, if you two will excuse me, I'm going to take myself off to bed. I have to be up early tomorrow to make cinnamon rolls. Good night, son." She touched Garret's arm, gave him a kiss on the cheek, then came to her and did the same. "Good night, daughter."

Tears stung her eyes. "Good night, Mother." She gave Garret's mother a kiss and a hug, listened to the rustle of her gown and soft tap of her shoes as she left the room.

Silence fell.

Her heart thudded.

Garret put down his cup, reached up and trimmed the oil lamps.

Shyness washed over her. "I—I forgot to give your mother her present. I'll just—"

His hand caught her arm. He pulled her close against him and his lips touched hers. "Tomorrow."

His lips claimed hers, and the word was a promise forever etched into her heart.

Tomorrow…and tomorrow…and tomorrow…

* * * * *

Dear Reader,

I have enjoyed returning to Whisper Creek while writing Garret and Virginia's story. I will miss the growing town and the people who have settled there, but as you may already know, the Love Inspired Historical line is closing. This is, therefore, my last Love Inspired Historical book. I am both sad and excited. I don't know what the future holds for my writing—that is in the Lord's hands. I will follow where He leads.

It has been my great pleasure to write the LIH stories for you. Thank you for your faithfulness in buying and reading them. And I thank you also for the multitude of letters and emails you have sent me over the years. I will miss hearing from you.

I hope you enjoyed Garret and Virginia's story, and I thank you, dear reader, for choosing to read *Mail-Order Bride Switch*. If you care to share your thoughts about this story, I may be reached at dorothyjclark@hotmail.com or www.dorothyclarkbooks.com.

With deepest appreciation,
Dorothy Clark

We hope you enjoyed this story from
Love Inspired® Historical.

Love Inspired® Historical is coming to
an end but be sure to discover more
inspirational stories to warm your heart
from **Love Inspired®** and
Love Inspired® Suspense!

Love Inspired stories show that
faith, forgiveness and hope have the power
to lift spirits and change lives—always.

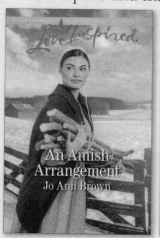
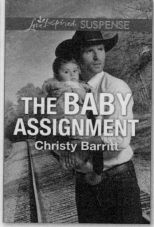

Look for six new romances every month
from **Love Inspired®** and
Love Inspired® Suspense!

HIS SUBSTITUTE MAIL-ORDER BRIDE
Return to Cowboy Creek • by Sherri Shackelford

When the bride train arrives in Cowboy Creek, Russ Halloway is shocked to discover his carefully selected mail-order bride is instead his ex-fiancée's little sister—all grown up. Anna Linford's looking for a fresh start—and to keep her secrets hidden from the one man who, should he discover them, could break her heart.

BABY ON HER DOORSTEP
by Rhonda Gibson

To raise the little girl left on her doorstep, schoolteacher Laura Lee's only option is becoming a temporary live-in nanny for rancher Clint Shepard. The arrangement was supposed to be temporary, but soon the single dad's wishing Laura and her baby can become a permanent part of his family.

ACCIDENTAL SWEETHEART
The Bachelors of Aspen Valley • by Lisa Bingham

Lydia Tomlinson will do anything to keep stranded mail-order brides in the Batchwell Bottoms mining camp—even going up against Pinkerton detective Gideon Gault, who watches over the ladies. But when a gang of outlaws threatens the town, Gideon and Lydia must band together to stop the thieves—and to fight any force that would keep them apart.

LAST CHANCE WIFE
by Janette Foreman

Stranded in Deadwood, Dakota Territory, after a failed mail-order match, Winifred Sattler convinces Ewan Burke to give her a job in the general store attached to his gold mine. Busy trying to keep his fledgling operation open, Ewan has no time for distractions—except he can't stop picturing his life with Winifred by his side...forever.

Get 2 Free Books,
Plus 2 Free Gifts—
just for trying the Reader Service!

*When widowed Anna Linford comes to Cowboy Creek
as a last-minute mail-order bride replacement, she
expects to be rejected. After all, her would-be groom,
Russ Halloway, is the same man who turned down her
sister! But when they learn she's pregnant, a marriage
of convenience could lead to new understanding, and
unexpected love.*

Read on for a sneak preview of
HIS SUBSTITUTE MAIL-ORDER BRIDE,
the heartwarming continuation of the series
RETURN TO COWBOY CREEK.

"I don't want another husband."

Russ grew sober. "You must have loved your husband
very much. I didn't mean to sully his memory by
suggesting you replace him."

"It's not that." Anna's head throbbed. Telling the
truth about her marriage was far too humiliating. "You
wouldn't understand."

"Try me sometime, Anna. You might be surprised."

One of them was going to be surprised, that was for
certain. Philadelphia was miles away, but not far enough.
The truth was bound to catch up with her.

"If you ever change your mind about remarrying,"
Russ said, "promise you'll tell me. I'll steer you away
from the scoundrels."

"I won't change my mind." Unaccountably weary, she perched on the edge of a chair. "I'll be able to repay you for the ticket soon."

"We've gone over this," he said. "You don't have to repay me."

Why did he have to be so kind and accommodating? She hadn't wanted to like him. When she'd taken the letter from Susannah, she'd expected to find the selfish man she'd invented in her head. The man who'd callously tossed her sister aside. His insistent kindness only exacerbated her guilt, and she no longer trusted her own instincts. She'd married the wrong man, and that mistake had cost her dearly. She couldn't afford any more mistakes.

"I don't want to be in your debt," she said.

"All right. Pay your fare. But there's no hurry. Neither of us is going anywhere anytime soon."

She tipped back her head and studied the wrought iron chandelier. She hated disappointing him, but staying in Cowboy Creek was out of the question. Russ wasn't the man she remembered, and she wasn't the naive girl she'd been all those years ago.

Don't miss
HIS SUBSTITUTE MAIL-ORDER BRIDE
by Sherri Shackelford, available May 2018 wherever
Love Inspired® Historical books and ebooks are sold.

www.LoveInspired.com

LIHEXP0418

Looking for inspiration in tales
of hope, faith and heartfelt romance?

Check out **Love Inspired**® and
Love Inspired® **Suspense** books!

New books available every month!

CONNECT WITH US AT:

Harlequin.com/Community

Facebook.com/HarlequinBooks

Twitter.com/HarlequinBooks

Instagram.com/HarlequinBooks

Pinterest.com/HarlequinBooks

ReaderService.com

LIGENRE2018